CW00819535

*Grayson's Challenge* is a work of fiction. Names, characters, places, and incidents are the products of the author's imagination and are used fictitiously. Any resemblance to actual events, locales, or persons, living or dead, is entirely coincidental.

Copyright © 2022 by Tina Folsom

All rights reserved.
Scanguards® is a registered trademark.

Published in the United States

Cover design: Leah Kaye Suttle
Cover photo: istock
Author Photo: © Marti Corn Photography

Printed in the United States of America

# Books by Tina Folsom

Samson's Lovely Mortal (Scanguards Vampires, Book 1)
Amaury's Hellion (Scanguards Vampires, Book 2)
Gabriel's Mate (Scanguards Vampires, Book 3)
Yvette's Haven (Scanguards Vampires, Book 4)
Zane's Redemption (Scanguards Vampires, Book 5)
Quinn's Undying Rose (Scanguards Vampires, Book 6)
Oliver's Hunger (Scanguards Vampires, Book 7)
Thomas's Choice (Scanguards Vampires, Book 8)
Silent Bite (Scanguards Vampires, Book 8 1/2)
Cain's Identity (Scanguards Vampires, Book 9)
Luther's Return (Scanguards Vampires, Book 10)
Blake's Pursuit (Scanguards Vampires, Book 11)
Fateful Reunion (Scanguards Vampires, Book 11 1/2)
John's Yearning (Scanguards Vampires, Book 12)
Ryder's Storm (Scanguards Vampires, Book 13)
Damian's Conquest (Scanguards Vampires, Book 14)
Grayson's Challenge (Scanguards Vampires, Book 15)

Lover Uncloaked (Stealth Guardians, Book 1)
Master Unchained (Stealth Guardians, Book 2)
Warrior Unraveled (Stealth Guardians, Book 3)
Guardian Undone (Stealth Guardians, Book 4)
Immortal Unveiled (Stealth Guardians, Book 5)
Protector Unmatched (Stealth Guardians, Book 6)
Demon Unleashed (Stealth Guardians, Book 7)

Ace on the Run (Code Name Stargate, Book 1)
Fox in plain Sight (Code Name Stargate, Book 2)
Yankee in the Wind (Code Name Stargate, Book 3)
Tiger on the Prowl (Code Name Stargate, Book 4)

A Touch of Greek (Out of Olympus, Book 1)
A Scent of Greek (Out of Olympus, Book 2)
A Taste of Greek (Out of Olympus, Book 3)
A Hush of Greek (Out of Olympus, Book 4)

Venice Vampyr (Novellas 1 – 4)
Teasing (The Hamptons Bachelor Club, Book 1)
Enticing (The Hamptons Bachelor Club, Book 2)
Beguiling (The Hamptons Bachelor Club, Book 3)
Scorching (The Hamptons Bachelor Club, Book 4)
Alluring (The Hamptons Bachelor Club, Book 5)
Sizzling (The Hamptons Bachelor Club, Book 6)

# GRAYSON'S CHALLENGE

**SCANGUARDS VAMPIRES #15**

**SCANGUARDS HYBRIDS #3**

# TINA FOLSOM

# 1

Monique put her last dress on a hanger, before closing her blue travel bag and placing it on the bottom of the closet. The room was large and luxuriously furnished. Her parents, Faye and Cain Montague, had rented this vampire-proof Victorian mansion in Russian Hill, a ritzy neighborhood in San Francisco, because a stay in a hotel wasn't possible for them. As full-blooded vampires they had to stay out of the sun, and this house had been retrofitted with all amenities to ensure a vampire's wellbeing.

As a vampire hybrid, Monique didn't have the same weaknesses as her parents, and she was glad for it. It gave her more freedom, something she craved. Living in her parents' palace just outside of New Orleans came with restrictions: the King's guard, an elite troop of security personnel, was ever present, and she could barely take a step without feeling the shadow of one of the bodyguards on her back. Cain had insisted on three bodyguards accompanying them on their New Year's vacation to San Francisco. However, she had no intention of letting the guards get in the way of her enjoying the city. She was no stranger to ditching her bodyguards, which was something her father constantly kept scolding her about. But at age thirty-one, she wanted to live an independent life, and not the life of a literal princess. She wanted to be normal, or at least as normal as a vampire hybrid could be.

Monique looked out of the big sash window and gazed at the lights of the city. She had a perfect view of Coit Tower, which was illuminated in multiple colors that changed every few seconds. Farther beyond, to the left of it, she could make out Alcatraz Island, the erstwhile maximum-security prison that had been turned into a museum. It too sparkled with bright lights.

At the ringing of her cell phone, Monique walked to the nightstand. When she saw who was calling, a smile curved her lips upward. She clicked to accept the videocall.

"Hey, Zach," she greeted her brother, when she noticed that their brother David was right next to Zach. "Hey, David."

As triplets they'd always been close, and spent as much time as they could in each other's company, even as adults.

"Hey, sis," Zach and David greeted her cheerfully.

"Where are you guys?"

"Still in Gstaad," Zach said. "They've got fresh powder here. You should have come."

"You know how much I hate cold weather," Monique said with a shake of her head. "Besides, I'd rather hang out in a city where I speak the language."

David laughed. "Trust me, half the people here are Americans. In fact, we just got invited to spend New Year's Eve with some hot chicks from New York."

"Yeah, in a remote cabin!" Zach added. "You know what that means." He winked.

She didn't have to be a genius to figure that out. "I'd just be the third wheel."

The video froze, and she heard a crackling noise. "Zach? David? You're breaking up."

"Yeah… connection… There's a storm coming in," David finally said. "We won't be able to ski tomorrow because of it. Just as well that we'll be switching to indoor sports." He exchanged a look with Zach, and both grinned.

She decided not to comment on that remark.

"A storm?" Monique asked instead. "Are you sure you'll be safe? What about avalanches?"

"Don't worry," Zach said quickly. "It's safe. They have an avalanche warning system. It's just a winter storm. We might get snowed in for a couple of days, but it won't be an issue."

"Well, I wouldn't want to chance it. Just as well that I decided to come to San Francisco with Mom and Dad. We have clear weather here, no rain in the forecast. I'm just about to go exploring."

Again, the video pixelated, then froze, and Monique could hear only fragments of a sentence.

"… party at Scanguards …"

"What?" Monique asked. "You guys are breaking up again."

The video finally restarted, and Zach said, "Can you hear us now?"

"Yeah, now I can hear you. What about the Scanguards New Year's Eve party?"

David exchanged a conspiratorial look with Zach.

"What?" Monique asked, impatient now.

"You're probably okay with it, right?" Zach asked then glanced at his brother.

David grunted under his breath. "Leave it be."

She stared at her brothers. "Okay with what?"

"I mean, you probably already guessed why Mom and Dad wanted you to go to San Francisco with them," Zach continued, while David rammed his elbow into his brother's ribs.

"They knew I didn't want to go skiing," she replied, but the hackles on the back of her neck rose. Something was off. "So why wouldn't I come to San Francisco with them?"

"'Cause you're being set up with Grayson," Zach said bluntly.

"Fuck, Zach!" David cursed and glared at his brother.

"What?" For a moment, Monique didn't even know who they were talking about. Then it clicked. "Grayson? Grayson, the arrogant jerk, Woodford?"

Zach made a grimace. "So he's still an ass twenty years later?"

Monique assumed as much. "I haven't seen him since he visited us in New Orleans when I was eleven. You can't possibly think that Mom and Dad would try to set me up with him. That's ludicrous. They know I never liked him."

"Well, I overheard Mom and Dad talking about it a few days before the trip," Zach said and shrugged. "For what it's worth, Mom wasn't keen on the idea, but Dad insisted."

She was pissed. "How could he? Why would he do that? I can find my own boyfriends!" In fact, she was rather good at picking up men whenever she wanted male company.

"I guess Dad doesn't like your taste in boyfriends. No offense, but most of them were doormats," Zach said.

"Hate to agree with Zach," David added, "but you can do better than the guys you've been dating lately."

"You, too?" Monique glared at her siblings. "And you think Grayson is an upgrade from my previous boyfriends? Yeah, right! He was a little prick when he was twelve, and I bet he's gotten worse since then. What the fuck was Dad thinking?"

"I'm sure he meant well," Zach replied.

"He meant well?" she ground out, pressing her lips together tightly. "I'm not gonna date Grayson Woodford even if he's the last man on earth, and the survival of our species depended on it. He's an arrogant fuck!"

David jabbed Zach in the side once more. "See? You shouldn't have told her. Damn it, Zach!" Then he looked back into the camera. "Sis, you could still fly out to Gstaad and join us, though you'll probably miss the New Year's Eve party here. We're nine hours ahead of you."

"I'm glad you told me," Monique said. "At least now I won't be running into an ambush."

"So you're coming to Gstaad?" David asked.

"No, I'm still not interested in freezing my butt off in some remote cabin and feel like the third wheel." She wasn't in the mood to listen to her brothers fuck the women they'd just hooked up with.

"You're gonna have it out with Dad, aren't you?" Zach asked.

"He won't know what hit him. If he thinks he can control me, he's got another think coming."

Both David and Zach grimaced.

"Do me a favor," Zach said, "don't mention I was the one who told you. Or I might have to stay in Switzerland indefinitely."

Monique huffed. "You should have told me before I got on the jet to San Francisco."

"Sorry, sis." Zach looked almost crushed. "Why don't you go out and let off some steam, huh? You'll feel better afterwards."

"That's a brilliant idea," David added. "There are some great bars in San Francisco. The *Black Velvet* is a really classy pick-up joint in the Financial District. I was there two years ago when I visited, and every time I went there, I scored. It's just what you need right now. Trust me."

She let out a breath. "Hmm."

"Promise you'll calm down before confronting Dad," Zach added. "Don't be emotional about it. Just tell him that you can make your own decisions, and that you don't want his interference. I hate to agree with this idiot next to me, but going to a bar and hooking up with somebody is probably the best thing you can do right now."

She hated to admit it, but her brothers were probably right. Having sex with a stranger always helped her see things clearly and get rid of the tension that was coursing through her body.

"All right."

"Okay then," Zach said. "Happy New Year, sis!"

"Yes, Happy New Year," David added. "And I hope you get everything you wish for."

"Happy New Year. I love you both."

Monique disconnected the call. She tossed the cell phone on the bed, still seething.

Why was her father trying to trick her into a relationship with Grayson Woodford, the presumptive heir of the Scanguards fortune? It couldn't be for money or connections, since the Louisiana kingdom was already connected to Scanguards. In January, a new Scanguards branch was going to open in New Orleans, and it would be staffed by select vampires from Louisiana and San Francisco. Who would actually be running the branch hadn't been announced yet, but Monique was hoping that she was on the shortlist of candidates. This position would enable her to finally get out from under her father's thumb, and prove to him and everybody else that she was ready to lead.

But clearly, Cain didn't have enough confidence in her, or why else would he decide that she needed a boyfriend or husband, and in particular one he had chosen?

Getting more annoyed by the minute, Monique opened her closet. Zach and David were right. She needed to let off steam first before she confronted her father and told him what she thought of his plan.

She chose a figure-hugging black cocktail dress that showed off her cleavage but was still understated enough so she wouldn't look out of place in a bar. She opted for simple diamond stud earrings, leaving her bracelets and necklaces in the jewelry box she'd brought. She didn't want to attract the wrong man by flashing expensive jewelry. There was no need for make-up. As a hybrid she was blessed with flawless skin.

When she was ready, she slung a small black handbag over her shoulder, and walked downstairs. Arriving at the foot of the stairs, a shrill sound startled her.

*Cuckoo, cuckoo.*

She looked in the direction of the sound and found a kitschy clock hanging on the wall. She shook her head at it. Some people had no taste. Taking a breath, she crossed the foyer. From the corner of her eye, she saw William, one of the King's guards sitting on a chair in the living room of the large Victorian. He rose and joined her in the foyer.

"William, have you seen my parents?"

"They left earlier to visit with John and Savannah."

Monique remembered that her parents had mentioned that they wanted to get together with John, who'd been Cain's King's guard many years earlier, and had saved his life when Cain's brother Abel had tried to usurp Cain and steal his kingdom and his fiancée, Faye.

"Do you want me to drive you to John's house so you can join them?"

"No, thanks, William. I'm going out to meet friends for a drink."

"I'll come with you," William announced.

"That won't be necessary. I can take care of myself."

"But –"

"I said no," Monique interrupted. "Or would you like me to tell my father that you made sexual advances toward me?"

William glared at her. "That would be a lie."

He was right. "Do you really want to risk my father believing me rather than you?"

He narrowed his eyes. "Is that what you threaten all your bodyguards with so they let you go out without protection?"

She shrugged. "It works. Why change it?" She sailed past him. "Enjoy your free evening, William."

He didn't stop her from leaving. Outside, she hailed a taxi and got in.

"Where to, Miss?"

"The *Black Velvet* in the Financial District. Do you need an address?"

"No, I know it, Miss. No problem."

Monique leaned back in her seat, and the taxi drove down the hill toward North Beach and the Financial District.

# 2

The V lounge at Scanguards HQ was officially closed tonight so it could be decorated for the New Year's Eve party the next night. Grayson looked down at his clipboard where he'd been ticking off task after task. He'd volunteered to be in charge of the event.

"Looks pretty decent so far."

Grayson turned at the sound of his sister's voice and saw Isabelle enter the lounge.

"Decent? It's awesome," Grayson replied. "Wait until you see the lightshow I've got planned."

He pointed to the strings of tiny lightbulbs that were taped to the ceiling in a pattern to mimic the night sky.

"You trying to impress somebody, maybe Dad?"

"Why would I? It's not like he's easily impressed by whatever I do." Though Isabelle was right. Grayson wanted to show his father that he took pride in everything he did, no matter how small the job, even if he'd rather do something more important.

"You wouldn't by any chance be trying to suck up to him so he'll let you lead the new Scanguards branch in New Orleans, would you?"

Was he that transparent? "And you're not interested in the position yourself?" he deflected. "Please! I know how ambitious you are."

Isabelle shrugged. "Nothing wrong with being ambitious."

"Grayson?"

Grayson looked over his shoulder to see Sebastian enter via a back door. The handsome half-Asian guy with short hair and piercing eyes was a vampire hybrid, just like Grayson and Isabelle.

"Hey, Sebastian."

"I connected the wires," Sebastian reported. "It should work now."

Isabelle chuckled. "Sebastian, I see my brother has you doing his work for him again."

"It's called delegating, Isa," Grayson said. "Thanks, Sebastian. Let's try it. Hit the lights."

Sebastian flipped the master light switch on the wall, and the ballroom-sized room went dark. On his cell phone, Grayson tapped on the app that controlled the lightshow he'd designed.

Above their heads, tiny lightbulbs illuminated.

"Wow," Isabelle said on a breath. "Is that the—"

"—the night sky over San Francisco exactly how it will appear at midnight tomorrow night," Grayson said proudly. It had been his idea, even though he'd needed help from several of his colleagues to bring his vision to life.

He pressed the play button, and the lights changed, illuminating various constellations, one after another. He pointed to the ceiling. "That's Orion… and that's the Big Dipper."

"You really went all out for this, didn't you?" Was that praise he heard in Isabelle's voice? She suddenly put her arm around his back. "Well done, bro. I think Dad's gonna love it."

"I couldn't have done it without Sebastian and Adam. They worked their butts off to lay the wires—"

"Aren't you forgetting somebody, bro?" Damian said from behind them.

Grayson looked over his shoulder to see Damian approach them. "I wasn't." He winked. "Damian is gonna supply the music for the light show. Have you finished it?"

"What kind of music?" Isabelle asked and removed her arm from Grayson.

Damian pointed to Grayson's cell. "I just uploaded it to the app. It should have synched by now. Just run it again."

Grayson tapped on the app again to restart the light show. As various different constellations lit up on the ceiling, the theme music of Star Trek came through the loudspeakers in the room. It was even better than Grayson had expected. Damian had outdone himself.

"You even synched the music so that it comes from whichever loudspeaker is closest to the illuminated constellation. Wow, color me impressed!" Grayson said and grinned at Damian.

Damian chuckled. "You're welcome. See you guys later. I'd better run too. I still have to check on a few things at the Mezzanine and try on my tux."

"Thanks, Damian!" Grayson called after him as he left the lounge. He turned to his sister. "That reminds me: could you please pick up my tux from the dry cleaners?"

"Do I look like I'm your maid?"

Grayson smiled at her sweetly. "No, though I saw at the Halloween Party how great you looked in a French Maid outfit."

Not that his sister needed sexy clothes to look ravishing. She'd inherited their mother's beauty, as well as her brain.

"Oh, flattery? That's your angle?"

"It works. At least with most women. I'm told I'm very charming." He smirked.

"So I hear. Unfortunately for you, I'm immune to your charm."

"Well, it was worth a try." Grayson shrugged, not surprised that she didn't want to run errands for him.

"See you later, Grayson," Isabelle said and headed for the door.

The main lights came on again. "Looks like everything is working," Sebastian said.

"Thanks, Sebastian." Grayson looked at his clipboard. "We're pretty much done here for tonight. The food and drinks will be delivered tomorrow during the day. Guess, we can pack up now. How about you and I go out for a drink? I know this bar close to my loft. There are always tons of hot chicks."

"You mean the *Black Velvet*? I think half of Scanguards has been there. Adam's dubbed it the *Sure Thing*."

"The *Sure Thing*? How fitting!"

"Yeah. Wish I could come, but I have to go over to the Mezzanine and help out with the setup for tomorrow night. Sorry."

"No worries, next time," Grayson said and patted him on the shoulder. "But you're coming to the Scanguards party tomorrow night, right? Not the one at the Mezzanine."

"I'll go to both, actually. Probably Scanguards first, and then to the Mezzanine afterwards."

"Why's that?"

"'Cause I really need a little action, and there won't be any available women at the Scanguards party, other than women like your sister."

"She's way out of your league, buddy!"

And it appeared with every year, Isabelle became more selective when it came to relationships, no matter how short they turned out to be. It seemed that she wasn't interested in a relationship. Not that he could blame her. Why get tied down with one person, when there was so much variety to choose from.

"Trust me, I would never date a woman I practically grew up with. It would be like dating my own sister, if I had one."

"Oh, I get it. Where's the mystery in that, right?"

"Totally."

"Well then, thanks for all your help."

"See you tomorrow," Sebastian said and left.

Grayson set the clipboard down on the bar in the middle of the large room, and stepped behind it. Just because the lounge was closed, didn't mean he couldn't pour himself a quick drink. He snatched a clean glass and poured 0-negative blood from one of the taps. He felt famished and downed the glass in one big gulp. But his hunger wasn't stilled yet. He wanted more than just a glass of human blood. He wanted sex.

He'd been so busy preparing for the New Year's Eve party that he hadn't hit the clubs and bars in almost a week. He'd poured all his energy into this event just to please his father and make him realize that he'd changed and was ready to lead. That he wasn't an impulsive kid anymore. That he could be relied upon. But would his father even notice all the work he'd put into this project? He sure hoped so, because Isabelle had guessed correctly: he was after the position to head the new Scanguards branch in New Orleans. It would finally give him the chance to show that he was a born leader, and he would be physically far enough away to escape his father's constant scrutiny.

He knew that Cain, the vampire king of Louisiana, had already arrived in San Francisco, and would attend the Scanguards party. Grayson needed to impress him too, because Cain had a say in the matter as well, because the branch was a joint venture between Cain's kingdom and Scanguards.

Knowing that a lot hinged on tomorrow night's event, Grayson knew that he needed to relax tonight so he could be his confident self at the party. And what better way to relax than to take a woman to his bed tonight to release the tension he was feeling?

The *Black Velvet* it was. Definitely a *sure thing*.

# 3

"I haven't seen you here before. And I come here a lot."

This was the third man in less than an hour who'd uttered the same boring pickup line. Monique ran her eyes over him. At least, this human specimen was rather handsome and had a muscular body to boot. The two men before him had stirred nothing at all in her.

He smiled at her, cute dimples in his cheeks. The bar wasn't busy at all. It surprised her, but maybe it shouldn't have. Clearly, everybody was staying home tonight since tomorrow was New Year's Eve. It appeared that only a few desperate souls had ventured out to try their luck. The pickings were slim, and the later it got, the less choices she had. That was the only reason she smiled at the man now.

"I'm from out of town," Monique said, lending her voice a gentle tone, hiding that she was the predator, not the prey. "I wanted to unwind a little, and this place was recommended to me."

"Oh, it's definitely the right place for unwinding," he said with a wide grin. "I'm Claus."

"Mona. Nice to meet you." She preferred not giving her real name when she was out looking for casual sex.

"What are you drinking, Mona?" he purred and pointed to her glass.

"A Sonoma Zin, from Alexander Valley I believe."

This was her second glass, and while she enjoyed the full-bodied taste of the red wine, it had no effect on her. Vampires and vampire hybrids couldn't get drunk on alcohol. Sometimes it was a blessing, sometimes a curse.

"Another one?" he asked, as he motioned to the bartender and pointed to her glass.

The bartender nodded.

"So what brings you to San Francisco?"

"A family obligation." One she didn't want to talk about right now. The whole reason for coming to this bar was so she could forget about what her family was trying to do. Quickly, she changed the subject. "And you're from San Francisco, Claus?"

"Born and bred. I work in finance."

Ah, yes, she knew the type. With a few words he was trying to tell her that he was a good catch. She wasn't impressed. A man's net worth or background didn't impress her. She wasn't looking for something that lasted longer than a night. Her priorities lay somewhere else. Was he a good kisser? Did he have stamina in bed? Was he a good lover?

"Let's not talk about work. Tell me something more personal."

"What would you like to know?" He leaned closer, and the scent of too much aftershave assaulted her senses.

"What kind of sports do you enjoy?" she asked, employing a husky undertone, trying to get in the mood to flirt with him. Normally it came easy to her, like second nature, but tonight, she wasn't feeling it. Claus didn't excite her.

"Sports?" Claus cleared his throat.

"I love riding."

The answer hadn't come from Claus, but from a man behind her. Monique swiveled on her barstool to look at the interloper. Her mouth went dry. The man who'd spoken wasn't human. His aura identified him as a vampire hybrid. He was dressed in casual black pants and a cream-colored linen shirt with the top two buttons open. His hair was black, and his eyes a mesmerizing green. Her eyes lingered on his neck, where his artery pulsed. Just looking at this man made her fangs itch for a bite.

The stranger stopped only a couple of feet away from her. "And you can do better than him." The hybrid motioned to Claus, barely giving the guy a second glance. "Much better."

Monique inhaled his male scent, drawing it deep into her body. It was pure and unadulterated, only what nature had gifted him with. And by the looks of it, nature had given him plenty. A hot body, a handsome face, and heaps of charm.

"Excuse me," Claus said from behind her. "We were talking… You can't just cut in…"

The sexy hybrid tilted his head to the side and looked past her at the human. "I just did. Beat it."

"How rude!" Claus replied. "I suggest you leave, or I'll have you thrown out."

The hybrid smirked, self-confidence oozing from every pore of his sinful body. "And I suggest you turn around and leave my girlfriend and me in peace, before I toss you out on your ass." Then he met her gaze. "Was he bothering you for long, babe?"

Enjoying the little charade the hybrid was playing, Monique played along. "Not for long, but next time you're late, I won't wait for you."

With a huff, Claus turned around and stomped toward the other end of the bar where he plopped himself on an empty barstool.

Monique turned back to look at the hybrid. "I give you points for originality. Your pickup line is definitely better than that human's. Now the question is, can you back it up with something solid?"

He stepped closer and leaned in. "I never make unsubstantiated claims." He made a gesture toward the other end of the bar. "You weren't really gonna let him ride you, were you? Frankly, that guy would probably not even know what to do with you."

She felt herself get aroused by his suggestive words. "And you do?"

Already now, her heart was beating faster, and she knew he could sense it. His vampire hearing could pick it up standing so close to her.

"As I said, I love riding. And the wilder the filly, the better. I never back down from a challenge."

Monique licked her lower lip. She hadn't expected to meet a vampire tonight, but now that she had, she was glad for it, because his stamina would outdo that of any human, and that's what she needed tonight. A man who took her hard and didn't stop until she was completely sated.

She slid her hand onto his chest, feeling the heat beneath her palm, and the strong heartbeat drumming against her hand.

"I'm only interested in something casual," she warned him. "I hate nothing more than possessive men."

"Casual is all I want." He dipped his mouth to her ear. "Though I have one request."

She pushed against his chest. Just when she'd thought she'd found the right guy for tonight, he had to spoil it by making demands. Men!

"Stay in my bed until sunrise, and I'm yours for anything you want during that time."

Surprised at his request, she raised an eyebrow. "Anything?"

He nodded.

Monique gripped the lapels of his shirt and pulled him closer to her. "Even a bite?"

He pressed his cheek to hers and whispered into her ear, "I can't wait for you to sink your fangs into me."

His voice was raspy now, and she heard the arousal in it. She knew what he was thinking of: the pleasure a vampire's bite caused in the vampire as well as the host. And tonight, he'd be the host. She'd never bitten a hybrid or vampire before. Most of her lovers had been human, and she'd always used mind control on them to make them forget about the bite so that they wouldn't find out what she really was.

"And I can't wait to find out what you taste like," she murmured, and pressed her body to his.

"Then what are we still doing here?"

"Do you have a name?"

"Does it matter?"

"No. But maybe I'd like to call out your name when you make me climax."

"Fair point. How does Gray sound?" He looked into her eyes.

"Just as fake as Mona."

"Then let's get out of here, Mona, before I get 86'd from this bar for life."

# 4

Grayson felt excitement course through his veins. He'd planned on picking up a human woman for some much-needed sex and a quick bite, but the moment he'd laid eyes on the vampire hybrid at the *Black Velvet*, he'd dismissed that plan. Taking the smoking-hot Mona to his bed would be much more satisfying. As a vampire hybrid, she would be able to keep up with his insatiable demands and endless stamina.

Grayson put his arm around her slim waist and led her outside. A light breeze blew through her long dark curls. Her face was like porcelain, her eyes a light green, just like his own. She was tall for a woman, and athletic, with firm, perfectly proportioned breasts. She wore no bra under her figure-hugging black dress, and she didn't need one.

"One more thing," Mona said and turned to him.

A moment later he felt himself being pressed against the wall of the building.

"Name it." Whatever it was, he was confident that it wouldn't be a dealbreaker.

"I hope you're a good kisser."

One side of his mouth rose, and he snaked his arm around her waist once more, and pulled her flush to him. Her lush curves molded to the hard planes of his chest, and farther below, his hard-on was cushioned by her stomach. "Babe, I'm the best."

"Arrogant much?"

"Just stating a fact."

Grayson slid his hand onto her nape and pulled her face to him. Her lips parted, and he noticed the absence of lipstick. He appreciated it, because the taste of lipstick could disguise a woman's natural scent. And Mona's own aroma appealed to him on a primal level. It spoke to the vampire in him, drew him to her just like a moth was drawn to the light.

"You gonna just stare, or are you going to kiss me anytime soon?"

He smirked. "You gonna boss me around all night?"

"If it gets me what I want …"

Grayson captured her mouth and drowned out whatever else she wanted to say. Her lips were firm, yet yielding to his demand. Hungrily, he swept his tongue into her mouth and dueled with its counterpart, enjoying the fierceness with which she stroked her tongue against his. The way she responded to him with barely-leashed passion, made his cock grow even harder. He slid one hand to her ass, grabbing one firm cheek and pressing her to him. She acknowledged his erection with a moan he swallowed into his chest, where it ricocheted against his ribs and made his body vibrate. With male pride, he ground his cock against her groin, while he delved deeper into the sweet cavern of her mouth to explore her.

When he felt Mona's hand on his nape, caressing him there, he moaned and felt a spear of electricity charge through his core and shoot into his cock. With her other hand, she grabbed his butt and jerked him to her. He kept kissing her, and continued to explore her. He swiped his tongue over one of her canines, caressing it softly, until he felt her fangs descend from their sockets and extend to their full length.

"Fuck, yeah," he cursed before he licked first one fang, then the other.

Mona went soft in his arms, her body molding itself to his, her heart pounding, her breaths shuddering. Uncontrolled moans rolled over her lips. She was responding to him caressing her fangs, the most erogenous zone of any vampire or vampire hybrid. To her, it would feel as if he were licking her clit, and he couldn't get enough of it. He wanted her to come apart in his arms, right here where any passerby could see what they were doing.

Holding her head firmly so she couldn't escape the sensual caresses he unleashed on her fangs, he shoved one leg between her thighs. Without inhibition, Mona followed his unspoken invitation and rubbed her pussy on his thigh, riding him like she would ride his cock later. The scent of her arousal drifted to his nostrils, and he filled his lungs with her aroma. Her moans were louder now, more uncontrolled as if she'd forgotten that they were in public.

Another swipe of his tongue over her fangs, and Mona suddenly shuddered in his arms, climaxing.

She gasped, and Grayson released her lips, but tightened his grip around her waist, holding her steady while she tried to bring her breathing under control.

He pressed his face into her hair and inhaled her scent. "So, did I pass the test?"

"Mmm."

"I take that as a *Yes*."

"Smartass," she murmured, but there was no heat behind the insult.

"My loft is only two blocks from here."

Just as well, because that was about his limit of how long he could restrain himself from freeing his rampant cock and plunging into her.

~ ~ ~

Monique still felt a pleasant humming between her legs when Gray ushered her into his top-floor loft in a three-story building on a quiet side street only a stone's throw away from the *Black Velvet*. The moment he closed the door behind them, she shoved him against a wall and kissed him. The way he'd touched and kissed her outside the bar had made her hungry for more. Impatiently, she tugged on his shirt and sent the buttons flying, before reaching for his belt, when he suddenly snatched her wrists.

Surprised, she released his lips. "Chickening out?"

He grinned, and hell, if that expression didn't make him look even sexier. "You've got somewhere to be, babe? 'Cause even if you rush this, you're not leaving my bed till sunrise."

"Worried that you won't keep it up long enough?"

He pulled her hand down to his groin and pressed it on the hard bulge there. Then his green eyes looked at her with an intensity that made her heart flutter. "Does that feel like it's going soft anytime soon?"

She squeezed his hard-on through his pants. "Mind if I take it for a test drive?"

He chuckled, then released her wrist. "You're not the kind of woman who takes orders from anybody, are you?"

He was right about that. "I like to give them. Now strip."

A cocky smile around his lips, Gray shrugged out of his shirt and dropped it to the floor. His eyes still locked with hers, he kicked off his shoes, then opened his belt and his pants and dropped them. He wore tight fitting black boxer briefs, and his erection stretched the fabric to capacity.

Monique ran her eyes over his broad shoulders, his sculpted chest, his flat stomach and narrow hips. He was perfect. And he stood there, his back against the wall, waiting for her to look her fill. She touched his naked skin, loving the soft texture and the warmth, the hardness beneath it, the thin sheen of perspiration covering it. Then she brushed her hands lower until her fingers bumped against the waistband of his boxer briefs.

Gray sucked in an audible breath, and Monique hooked her thumbs underneath it and freed him from it. His magnificent cock sprang free, fully erect and heavy. He was bigger than she'd expected, and more beautiful too. Perfect, as if Michelangelo had sculpted him. Unable to resist the temptation to taste him, she dropped to her knees and brought her face level with his groin.

"Fuck!"

Monique raised her lids to look up at him, and saw his eyes shimmer golden. He was ruled by his vampire side now, and she loved what she saw: a vampire who couldn't control his desire and passion for much longer. Just how she liked it, because driving a man wild turned her on like nothing else could.

"Goddamn it, suck me already!"

She didn't mind following this particular command, because it was what she wanted to do more than anything else. When she licked over the bulbous head and tasted the pre-cum that was leaking from its tip, Monique closed her eyes and drank in the taste and scent of his arousal. Every cell in her body seemed to come alive at once, making her entire body tingle with pleasure.

She closed her lips around his cock, and slid down on him as far as she could, then relaxed her jaw, and took in another inch. Fuck, he was big. And hard. And delicious.

From the corners of her eyes, she saw that he was pressing his palms flat on the wall behind him as if to stop himself from grabbing her head so he could thrust hard and fast. She appreciated that he didn't force her, and at the same time noticed what it cost him: his fingers were turning into sharp claws. The vampire inside him was breaking to the surface. She'd never realized before this moment that she was craving what he was offering: to be desired by a vampire. By a vampire who equaled her in strength and power, in lust and in passion.

She began to move her mouth up and down on him, all the while lubricating his cock with her tongue, while cradling his balls with one hand, and wrapping her other one around his root. Gray moaned in concert with her sucking, and his claws dug into the wall behind him, carving grooves into the drywall. He slowly moved his hips in synch with her movements, and she felt him move faster with every second.

"Fuck!" he hissed and pushed her away so his cock slipped from her mouth.

Eyes blazing red, he grabbed her and pulled her up. His fangs were fully extended, and she'd never seen a sexier sight.

"Take that fucking dress off, or I'll rip it to shreds," he demanded, his voice hoarse, as he motioned to his claws.

Her heart beating excitedly, Monique freed herself of her dress and tossed it to the floor. She stood in front of him in only her black panties and her high heels. His gaze dropped to her breasts, and his chest heaved. Before she could take off her panties, he'd already ripped them off her, and was lifting her into his arms. She kicked off her shoes while he carried her into another room and dropped her onto a soft bed.

Monique felt cool sheets at her back, before Gray covered her with his body, and plunged into her pussy in the same instant. She gasped in surprise. No man had ever thrust into her like this, without touching her first, without making sure that she was wet.

His cock filled her completely, stretched her more than she thought was possible. She let out a breath, the pleasure of feeling him inside her so intense she couldn't think or speak. All she could do was feel how this stranger, this vampire was taking her as if her body belonged to him.

Could he feel it too? Could he feel that her body wanted to surrender to him?

"You feel so good," he murmured as he began to move inside her in a slow and measured tempo. Almost *tenderly*.

No! She didn't want tenderness. She wanted to be fucked, hard and fast. Tenderness was for suckers and hopeless romantics. She was neither.

Monique wrapped her legs around him, forcing him deeper into her. "Fuck me harder!"

"Oh, you don't like it slow?" He shook his head and laughed softly. "Then I'll have to teach you to like it."

"Don't bother. I prefer it hard and fast." She gripped his hips and made him thrust harder into her.

~ ~ ~

Grayson stilled and snatched Mona's hands, prying them from his hips, and pinning them to the mattress on either side of her head. He brought his face within inches of hers.

"I want to get to know your body first, find out what turns you on, before I go all caveman on you." He sucked her upper lip into his mouth and nibbled on it, before releasing it. "Because it'll be even better once I know what your body needs from me."

He moved his hips back slowly, before gently thrusting deeper into Mona's welcoming sheath. Her eyelids fluttered, and her lips parted on a breath, and he repeated the action.

"See? Is that so hard?" he murmured at her lips.

"It's very hard." She freed one hand from his grip and slid it to his nape, making him shudder.

"Mmm," he said. "I like it when you touch me there."

"How about here?" she asked and brushed her finger over his lips, before she rubbed it over his canine.

Instantly, his fangs descended to their full length, the pleasure of her touch so intense, he wanted to spill inside her immediately.

"Babe, you do that again, and I'll come like a green kid."

"Good to know."

But instead of stopping, Mona began licking his fangs. Grayson didn't have the strength to make her stop. Instead, he continued thrusting into her welcoming sheath, his tempo increasing with every second.

She wanted it hard and fast, and now she was getting exactly that, because he couldn't hold back any longer. "You win."

He pounded into her, his cock so hard and relentless that had she been human, he would have hurt her. But the vampire vixen beneath him welcomed his ferocious thrusts, her pelvis lifting each time he plunged into her. When she suddenly released his lips, Grayson gained back a modicum of control, and was grateful for it. But in the next instant, Mona gripped his shoulders and pulled him closer to bring her face to his neck. Instinctively, he tilted his head to the other side to give her better access.

His heart pounded as if it wanted to jump out of his chest, knowing what was coming. When she brushed her fangs over his skin, he shuddered. A moment later, she pierced his skin with the sharp tips and began to suck on his vein.

Fuck!

On the next thrust, he climaxed harder than ever before. But his climax didn't ebb, instead it continued. Wave after wave raced through his body, while Mona drank his blood. He continued thrusting, their combined juices making her pussy slick and hot, until he felt her spasm beneath him. Her interior muscles gripped his cock tightly, squeezing the last drops of semen from him.

He felt her fangs dislodge from his neck, and her tongue lick over the puncture wounds, closing them instantly. Breathing hard, he rolled off her.

"Fuck! That was amazing," he said, his voice hoarse, his heart thundering in his ears.

Next to him, Mona's chest rose and fell rapidly, and she was panting. "Wow."

She turned her face to him. Her eyes were shimmering golden now, a sign that could mean many things: arousal, satisfaction, lust, adoration. He knew his eyes were shimmering in the same color. And he knew the reason for it.

He was under her spell. And he didn't care that it made him vulnerable.

# 5

"How come I've never seen you in the city before?" Grayson asked with Mona still draped over his naked body. "Did you just move here?"

"I'm only here for a week."

"Oh." If he didn't know it any better, he'd say that he felt disappointed, when he knew he shouldn't be. After all, he wasn't looking for something steady, particularly not since he was hoping to land the position as head of Scanguards' New Orleans branch.

"You're here on business then?" he asked.

"No, just pleasure."

"Well, I hope you're enjoying yourself so far." He slid his hand to her delectable ass and caressed her.

"Mmm."

Though that wasn't exactly an affirmative answer, he interpreted it as such.

A soft breath ghosted over his chest, and he felt Mona rubbing her fingers over his nipple.

"How about you use your fangs to do that?" he suggested. He'd enjoyed her biting him more than he wanted to admit. After all, he was normally the dominant partner.

"So you liked my bite?" She lifted her head to look at him. "Do you let all your lovers bite you?"

Was that a veiled question to figure out how many women he'd slept with? "There wouldn't be much point in it, given that all the women I sleep with are human."

He stroked his index finger over her lips, urging her to part them. "Show them to me."

Her eyes instantly began to shimmer golden, and her fangs descended. He caressed one with his finger, and watched how Mona closed her eyes and inhaled deeply.

"And you? Do you bite all your lovers?" he asked.

She opened her eyes, pinning him. "Only the humans. I don't bite vampires. The risk of being tricked…"

She didn't finish her sentence, but Grayson instinctively realized what she meant. An unbreakable blood-bond was established when a couple drank each other's blood during sex. The action had to happen simultaneously, and the bond could only be broken by death.

"You think a vampire might trick you into a blood-bond? Why?"

She shrugged. "My family is rich and influential."

He contemplated her words. He had the same concerns. After all, he was the heir to the Scanguards empire. It was the reason why he hadn't given Mona his real name. Grayson wasn't exactly a common name. And as a vampire hybrid, she would most likely have heard of his family and put two and two together. Or did she already know that he was Grayson Woodford, and all this was a ploy to ensnare him? A very pleasurable ploy. Was it truly a coincidence that they'd met at the *Black Velvet*? Many people knew that he frequented the place, and that it was only a couple of blocks from his loft. Had she planned this because she knew who he was and wanted to land a big fish?

"I get it. If you bite a vampire during sex, and he decided to do the same, you would be bonded." He let out a breath. "So why bite me?"

"Because I'm in a city where nobody knows me, and because you don't strike me as the kind of guy who's interested in anything more than casual sex."

"Now I'm wounded," he said mock-outraged.

She rolled her eyes.

"And now that you've told me that your family is rich and influential, I guess you won't bite me again for fear I'd do the same?"

He could see the wheels in her head spinning.

She hesitated. "We'll see."

She didn't trust him, and he couldn't blame her. They were in the same boat.

"You don't have to sugarcoat it. If you don't want to bite me again, because you don't trust me, just say so. But just to be clear: you're still not leaving my bed until sunrise. 'Cause all that talk about biting is making me horny."

In fact, his cock didn't care if she was trying to ensnare him, and was already rock hard again.

Mona sat up, straddling him, and looked down to where his cock was standing perfectly erect. "I can see that. Maybe I should ride you."

He licked his lower lip. "I think that's an excellent idea."

He put his hands on her hips as she lifted herself on her knees and adjusted her position so the tip of his cock was poised at her pussy. When she bore down on him, all breath rushed from his lungs, and he moaned out loud at the intense feeling of her interior muscles squeezing him like a tight fist.

She rode him hard and fast, her firm breasts bouncing up and down, her long black hair flying, sounds of pleasure rolling over her lips. She looked like a goddess, a goddess of carnal pleasures, of sin, of abandon, of excess. He could get used to a woman like her, a woman who knew what she wanted, a strong woman, somebody who could capture his attention for more than just a night. He realized now that despite his wish to bond with a human woman one day, no human woman could ever be his equal. Maybe he wasn't meant to have a human mate but a preternatural one.

Mona rode him like the devil was chasing her, impaling herself on his cock over and over again. She was an experienced lover, a woman who had no inhibitions, a woman with a perfect body. Her blood smelled sweet, and he was tempted to bite her. But he restrained himself. It was too risky. Sex with Mona would have to do. And the sex with her was amazing.

Her skin was covered in a thin sheen of perspiration, and her entire body seemed to glow. He captured her breasts, and squeezed them, and she leaned over him to give him better access.

"Lick them, baby," she demanded.

Grayson swiped his tongue over the hard nipple and sucked it into his mouth. Mona let out a moan.

"Yes!"

Greeting her enthusiastic praise, he licked and sucked one breast, then switched to the other, while continuing to squeeze both of them. He loved their firm texture, their soft skin, their perfect size. As a vampire she would never have to worry about her boobs sagging when she got older. They would always be this perfect. *She* would always be this perfect.

As he licked and sucked her breasts, he suddenly realized that his fangs had extended, and he was brushing them over her breasts. Mona shuddered visibly, and he did it again and caressed her nipple with his fang.

"Oh God! I'm coming!"

Her pussy spasmed as she climaxed. Her orgasm ignited his own, and he let himself go and spilled his seed into her, his lips still around one nipple, his fangs still extended. When they stopped moving, Grayson released her nipple, and Mona collapsed onto him. He put his arms around her, and held her close to him, loving her weight on his chest, their bodies still connected, his cock still impaling her. Still hard.

He brushed his hand over her hair. "You're so hot, babe. I love the way you let yourself go so completely. I love watching you take what you want."

She shifted in his arms, and his cock slid halfway out of her channel. Not wanting to lose the connection, he adjusted her hips and sank back into her all the way to the hilt.

"Oh," she murmured. "You're still hard."

"Aren't you glad you picked me and not that human in the bar?"

"Mmm, very glad."

With his hands on her hips, he guided her up and down, so he could make small thrusts with his cock. Mona sighed contentedly, her head resting in the crook of his neck.

"Tired?" he asked.

"No."

But he knew it was a lie. He rolled her off his body and spooned her. "Why don't you close your eyes for a few minutes and rest?"

"And what are you gonna do?"

He chuckled and lifted her leg so he could slide his cock between her thighs and plunged into her welcoming sheath from behind. "That."

"Oh." She reached for his hand and pulled it onto her breast.

He moved slowly in and out of her, with gentle, shallow thrusts, with just enough friction so his cock remained in its aroused state.

"So you do like it slow after all, huh?" he whispered into her ear.
"Mmm."

~ ~ ~

Monique stirred, and felt a hot body cradling her from behind.
Immediately, everything that had happened during the night came back to
her. Gray had taken her from behind, his movements tender and slow, and
to her surprise he'd made her come even harder than before. He'd
surprised her with how tender he'd been. None of her vampire lovers had
ever shown such tenderness. Particularly not the good-looking ones: in
general, good-looking men relied too much on their looks to keep a
woman in their bed, rather than expert lovemaking. But Gray was
different—good-looking, and a considerate lover. Not that she would tell
him that. Compliments would make him too cocky.

Sated, she'd fallen asleep in his arms. It was something she didn't do
with her one-night stands. When the sex was over, she normally hightailed
it out of the guy's bed. But it had felt so good to be in Gray's arms that she
hadn't been able to get up. Besides, their deal was that she would stay until
sunrise.

"Good morning, babe," Gray murmured into her ear and followed it
up with sucking her earlobe into his mouth to lick over it with his tongue.
"I'm sorry I fell asleep so quickly. I wish I could make it up to you right
now, but I've got a shitload to do today."

"Maybe tonight then?" The question was out before she could take it
back. Had she just told him that she wanted to see him again? Why would
she do that? She was setting herself up for disappointment.

"I would love to, but I'm in charge of this huge party tonight. It's a
family thing. But—"

"Forget it," she interrupted quickly and sat up. How stupid! "Of
course, you have plans. I shouldn't have asked."

Gray sat up behind her and wrapped his arms around her. He pressed
a kiss to her shoulder blade. "How about you give me your cell phone
number, and the moment I can get away, I'll call you. It might be late
though."

Inside her, a war was raging. Should she give him her number, only to be sitting by the phone all evening hoping he'd call? Or should she cut her losses right now, and tell him that she had a party to go to as well? Making herself too available would give him the upper hand, and she didn't want that kind of power dynamic, not even when it concerned a one-night stand—or a two-night stand.

"Please, babe, I wanna see you again," he begged and planted tender kisses along her neck.

He didn't sound like the kind of man who asked a woman for a phone number only never to call her. *He* was the one begging for the number. That changed things.

"All right," she said, smiling to herself. "Give me your cell phone, and I'll program it in."

Gray jumped out of bed and went to the spot where they'd undressed each other in a hurry. He retrieved his cell phone from his pants pocket and walked back to her. In the light of day, he looked just as sexy and handsome as the night before—and he was sporting a hard-on of massive proportions.

Trying not to stare at his cock so she wouldn't start to drool, she took the cell phone he handed her. He sat down next to her and watched her enter her cell phone number. She pressed the call button, and heard her own phone ring.

"Here you go, now I've got your number too."

"Perfect." He took the cell phone from her. "Five-O-Four? Isn't that New Orleans?"

She looked at him. "Yes, that's where I live."

He smiled broadly. "If that's not a coincidence, then I don't know what is. I just applied for a job in New Orleans."

"Really?" Was he just saying that so that she wouldn't find it strange if he suddenly showed up in New Orleans to continue whatever this was? "Did you get the job?"

"I don't know yet, but I'm definitely on the short list."

"Why leave San Francisco? Don't you like it here?"

"Oh, I do. But here I'll always be my father's son. Everybody compares me to him. It's not easy to step out from the shadow of a successful man."

Oddly enough, she understood exactly what he meant. And the fact that he wanted to make his own success and not rely on his family, made her like him even more. He was definitely a man who deserved a second night.

# 6

Monique had returned to the rental house in Russian Hill, ready for a confrontation with her father, but since everybody was asleep, she'd retreated to her own room and slept too. When the house came alive around sunset, Monique went downstairs, freshly showered and dressed.

*Cuckoo, cuckoo.*

Her heart stopped at the sound. Fuck! Did this stupid clock have a motion sensor, or why was it going off each time she passed it? Annoyed, she headed for the kitchen.

A housekeeper had stocked the refrigerator with human food. Monique would be the only one benefiting from it. Her parents and the three vampire guards only drank human blood. She was hungry and filled her plate with fruit and pastries, and made herself coffee. While as a vampire hybrid she could sustain herself on human blood alone, she enjoyed human food.

"Hey, Monique," her mother said as she entered the kitchen.

Faye looked beautiful and young as always, and when people saw them next to each other, they often assumed they were sisters. Neither Monique nor Faye corrected them.

"Where were you last night?"

"I went out."

"Alone?"

Monique shrugged. "I certainly wasn't gonna take William along. He's a buzzkill."

"I heard that!" William called out from the hallway.

Monique motioned in his direction. "See what I mean? I would never meet anybody if one of the guards was sticking to me like gum on a shoe."

Faye sighed. "It's just your father's way of making sure you're safe. He wasn't pleased when he found out that you snuck out without your guard."

"Oh, is that what William told him? That I snuck out? I didn't know I was a prisoner here."

"Monique, don't talk to your mother like that!"

The sharp words came from Cain, who entered the kitchen and narrowed his eyes at her.

"As for how you got William to let you go out without protection, I'm fully aware of what you threatened him with," Cain added.

Monique raised her voice and looked past him into the hallway. "You had to kiss and tell, William, didn't you?"

"Don't blame William, he's just doing his job."

"Fine! I'm not gonna blame him," Monique said and fisted her hands at her hips. "I blame you. And while I'm at it: I'm not gonna play your little game tonight. If you think you can play matchmaker and force me to go out with Grayson Woodford, then think again."

Cain stared at her, and Faye looked equally stunned. Had they really thought she wouldn't find out?

"Who told you that?"

"It doesn't matter," Monique shot back. "What matters is that you're trying to run my life. I can choose my own boyfriend. And for sure, it's not gonna be Grayson. The guy is an arrogant prick!"

"You don't even know him!"

"I know enough to know that I can't stand the arrogant asshole who thinks the world revolves around him."

"And here I thought the world revolved around you," Cain said, his voice dripping with sarcasm. "I stand corrected."

"I'm not a little pawn for you to push around on your chessboard."

"It's not like that."

"Oh, no? Isn't it enough for you that Scanguards is opening a branch in New Orleans that you'll be involved in? You want family ties too? So the princess becomes the sacrificial lamb."

"Don't be so dramatic. You're blowing this out of proportion."

"Am I? How would you have liked it if your father had decided who you were allowed to love? You would have shoved it up his—"

"Enough!" Faye suddenly interrupted. "You're both hotheads. Calm down."

Monique exhaled sharply through her nostrils, while still glaring at her father.

"Monique," Cain started again. "All we're doing is making an introduction at the New Year's Eve party tonight. Just so you two can get to know each other."

"I'm not interested. I won't be paraded around for a selfish jerk to check out if I'm good enough for him! This is not the 19th century. And I'm not going to that damn party. You can tell Grayson I wouldn't want to date him if he was the last man on earth and the survival of our species depended on it."

"Grayson doesn't know anything about this," Cain said. "If he did, he wouldn't be showing up at the party either."

Monique huffed. "Way to sell it, Dad! He clearly doesn't want me. And you expect me to go to the party so he can reject me in person? Wow, great thinking there, Dad! What a way to boost my self-confidence. Grayson fucking Woodford, the same little jerk who ridiculed me when I was eleven now gets a do-over? So he can embarrass me in front of everybody twenty years later? No, thanks!"

"Ridicule you? What are you talking about?" Faye interjected. "What happened?"

Monique tossed her mother a surprised look. "You don't remember? He and his family were visiting us when he was twelve. We were all playing outside, Zach and David, and Patrick and Grayson. Isabelle was in the house. We went to that small lake just beyond the woods, and Grayson was daring everybody to jump into the water from a rock on its edge. But when it was my turn, I saw an alligator approaching. So I didn't jump. I screamed, warning them to get out of the water. But then the alligator was suddenly gone, maybe because I screamed. And Grayson made fun of me saying I was a coward and a liar."

"Oh, honey," Faye said. "You were just kids. I'm sure he's totally changed."

She doubted that very much. "Oh really? Then maybe you didn't hear what David said about Grayson when he visited San Francisco two years ago. Trust me, he's an even bigger prick now." She lashed a pointed look at Cain. "And that's the guy you want to set me up with? How could you, Dad?"

"Monique, please," Cain said, a little calmer now. "I'm telling you Grayson has grown up to be a very responsible young man, and what you need is a man who's your equal. Not those human men that you lose interest in within a week."

There was a kernel of truth in her father's words. Yes, she needed a man who kept her attention, a man who was as strong and powerful as she was. But there were plenty of vampires and vampire hybrids who fit that bill. And she'd spent an amazing night with one of them. She certainly didn't need Grayson.

"I can find somebody on my own. I don't need your help." And she used the word *help* in a very loose context. "Besides, I'm not desperate. I don't see you setting Zach or David up with somebody. And we're the same age. So they get to make their own choice, but I have to pick a guy you approve of? One you pick out for me? Thanks, but no, thanks!"

"Just come to the damn party tonight," Cain coaxed. "You'd be in the driver's seat, because Grayson doesn't know anything about this."

"Have you not been listening to a single word I just said?" Monique huffed, annoyed. "I don't like Grayson. I won't date him. So stay the fuck out of my love life! And if you can't do that then I'm gonna get out of your life and move away from New Orleans."

When Cain's jaw tightened visibly, Monique pulled in a deep breath and stormed past him into the hallway. Fine, if he couldn't stop meddling, then maybe it was best if she left.

"I'm going out," Monique said to William who was standing in the foyer. "Alone."

# 7

The V lounge looked festive. The women were wearing elegant evening gowns and the men classy tuxedos. Even the few kids in attendance, two-year old Harry and ten-year-old Dean mimicked their parents' elegant clothing. Several waiters were roaming the room, offering alcohol and finger food to the humans, and human blood to the vampires and vampire hybrids.

Grayson looked around making sure everything was perfect. Tonight, after the lightshow at midnight, he would approach Samson and Cain and make sure that they knew he was serious about wanting to run Scanguards' New Orleans branch when it opened in early January.

After the amazing night he'd spent with Mona in his arms, he was determined to pursue her in earnest, which meant it was essential for him to relocate to New Orleans. He wasn't interested in a long-distance relationship, because already he was craving Mona's touch, her fangs in his neck, his cock impaling her. He was surprised at his reaction to her, but he was no idiot: he knew when something felt right. And being with the sexy vampire hybrid who'd sunk her fangs into him felt utterly right.

He'd briefly flirted with the idea of inviting her to the Scanguards party, but had dismissed it just as quickly. He wanted to spend more time with her alone, before he subjected her to his family and friends, and before she found out that he was the heir to the Scanguards empire. He didn't want her to be blinded by who he was, but rather like him for his own sake.

A heavy hand landed on his shoulder, and Grayson turned to look over his shoulder.

"Really nice setup, bro," Cooper said.

"Thanks, Coop! Appreciate it. Did you come alone?"

"No." He motioned to a spot closer to the door, where his parents, Haven and Yvette stood. "I hitched a ride with Mom and Dad. Lydia is coming separately because she'll be singing at the Mezzanine after midnight."

"I suppose that means that Patrick and Damian will be poaching most of my guests after midnight?"

Cooper grinned. "Most of the hybrids will be going to the club later, looking for other entertainment." He winked. "I'm afraid you'll be stuck with the old folks. Or are you coming to the Mezzanine later too?"

"Nope. Got other plans."

"A girl?"

Grayson smirked. "A woman."

"Somebody I know?"

"Definitely not."

"Why didn't you invite her here?"

"Because of guys like you. I'm not gonna have everybody poaching in my territory while I'm still staking my claim."

Cooper grinned. "So she's pretty."

"Gorgeous, actually. And that's all you're gonna get out of me. Off you go." He patted Cooper on the shoulder, and the hybrid walked away.

Grayson's gaze fell on Ryder, who was leading a heavily pregnant Scarlet to a seating area. He bridged the distance between them.

"Hey, Scarlet, Ryder. Didn't know whether you guys would be able to make it or not."

Scarlet sighed heavily as she sat down. "This is our last chance for a night out before the babies come. Didn't wanna miss that."

Ryder put a cushion behind her lower back. "Better?"

Scarlet gave him a loving smile. "Thanks, baby."

"We've got Mom on speed dial," Ryder said. "It could happen any day now."

"Well, at least you won't have far to go if it happens tonight," Grayson replied. After all, the medical center was only a few levels below the V lounge, and Maya, Scanguards' resident physician and Ryder's mother, was among the guests.

"How about I flag down one of the waiters to bring you some food? You hungry, Scarlet?" Grayson asked.

"Famished," she confirmed. "And something to drink. You wouldn't have juice here, would you?"

"Actually, we do. Since Dean and Harry are here tonight, we're stocking a few non-alcoholic options. I'll send a waiter your way."

"Appreciate it," Ryder said.

"Sure thing, bro."

Tonight, everything had to run like clockwork. He needed his father's and Cain's approval so they would entrust him with the running of the new Scanguards branch.

"Grayson."

Grayson pivoted. Theo, the vampire who was manning the bar tonight, waved at him. He quickly approached the bar. "What is it?"

Theo gestured to one of the taps, from which human blood was dispensed. "The B+ seems to be running out. There's just a trickle coming out. But I barely poured any tonight, and the keg was full when I started."

"Fuck!" Grayson cursed. "B+ is Cain's favorite blood type." He'd checked with the palace himself so he could make sure Cain's needs would be met one hundred percent. "Let me check."

Grayson walked behind the bar and ducked down. He opened the cabinet beneath the taps and looked at the clear hoses leading from the taps to a pipe in the floor that led to the kegs in the storage room.

"Hmm."

He checked every hose until he found one that felt loose. It pulled right out of the connecting nut on the pipe. "There it is."

"Found the problem?" Theo asked.

"Yeah, the hose came loose from the connector." Moments later, he'd attached the hose, and rose. "Try it now."

Theo put a clean glass under the B+ tap and pulled. At first there was only air coming out, but a few seconds later, blood was pouring from the tap.

"Thanks, Grayson." Theo handed him the partially filled glass. "Wanna drink it?"

"Sure. Can't let it go to waste." Grayson took the glass and downed it in one big gulp, before handing the glass back to Theo. "See you."

The V lounge was filling up. All vampire employees of Scanguards were invited, and by the looks of it many of them were attending the party. Grayson recognized many of the vampires who were employed as bodyguards: large, intimidating, and gruff-looking guys. Scanguards also employed female bodyguards, Yvette and Roxanne being two of the longest serving female bodyguards. Among the guests Grayson also spotted two witches: Wesley, who was Haven and Katie's brother, and Charles, who was blood-bonded to Roxanne. The two witches worked for Scanguards and ran a laboratory in the building where they cooked up potions and worked on spells. Given what happened in that laboratory, Grayson was surprised the two witches hadn't blown up the building yet.

Grayson let his gaze roam over the crowd and mingled, greeting friends and colleagues, making sure everybody was taken care of. He was about to join his brother, Patrick, who was talking to Gabriel, when Samson's voice drifted to him from his left. He turned his head and saw Samson speaking to Cain, the vampire king of Louisiana. Grayson took a few steps closer and focused on their conversation. The two of them weren't even looking in his direction.

"What did Monique say?" Samson asked.

"She said that she can't stand Grayson, that he's an arrogant prick—her words, not mine—and that she wouldn't date him if he were the last man on earth and the survival of our species depended on it."

Shocked, Grayson let the words sink in. He knew who they were talking about: Cain's daughter.

"So she didn't even want to attend the party? You couldn't talk her into it?"

"She's stubborn."

"Damn it. Now we have to figure out another way to get these two together. I tell you they are perfect for each other."

"Monique doesn't think so. I don't even know who told her that we were trying to set her up with Grayson. She even threatened to move out if I ever tried to set her up again."

Grayson had heard enough. Samson and Cain were trying to play matchmaker. That was bad enough, because he didn't want to be set up with a spoiled princess. But what took the cake was that said princess was refusing to even meet with him. And she'd called him a prick. He couldn't let that stand.

He marched toward them, and Samson whirled his head to him.

"What the fuck, Dad?" He glared at him and Cain. "How could you?"

"Grayson, calm down," Samson said.

"No, I'm not calming down!" He jabbed his finger into Samson's chest. "You have no right to tell me who to date! And I'm sure not gonna fuck a spoiled, headstrong princess who hates my guts."

"Watch it, Grayson!" Cain snapped. "You're talking about my daughter."

Grayson glared at Cain. "Oh yeah? Then tell your prissy princess that I wouldn't touch her with a barge pole!"

"Damn it, Grayson!" Samson cursed.

By now, the people around them had stopped talking and were watching the confrontation. But Grayson didn't care. He wasn't going to be manipulated by his father or by Cain.

"Stay out of my fucking life! Both of you! I decide who I date, who I fuck, and who I blood-bond with. And it definitely won't be Monique Montague, spoiled princess of Louisiana! And you can shove the job at the New Orleans branch up your asses, 'cause I don't want it anymore. Not if it comes with strings. So fuck you both!"

He turned on his heel.

"Grayson!"

But he didn't listen to his father's voice, instead, he marched through the crowd that was parting, his friends and colleagues staring at him in stunned silence, and left. He slammed the door behind him for good measure, fuming, his heart beating like a jackhammer. Outside, in the empty hallway, he took a deep breath. Then another one. But no amount of air could wipe away the fury that coursed through him. He wanted nothing to do with his father anymore, nor with Cain, and certainly not with Monique. He wasn't a pawn in his father's game anymore. It was time to stop trying to please him, when it was clear that he could never do the right thing in Samson's eyes.

Grayson punched the call button for the elevator and waited, tapping his foot impatiently. So much for all his hard work trying to impress Samson and Cain. If he'd known what the two were planning, he would have never bothered taking over responsibility for the New Year's Eve party.

When the elevator door opened, he jumped in and rode down to the parking level. He left the elevator and caught a glimpse of Orlando sitting in his Hummer, waiting for the garage gate to lift, so he could leave. Apparently, Grayson wasn't the only one leaving the party early. He hurried to his car, an Audi R8 he'd purchased only three months earlier, and got in. Moments later, he shot out of the underground garage and merged into heavy traffic on Mission Street.

He took out his cell phone and opened the call app to find Mona's number. He punched it and let it ring.

"Hey." Her husky voice sank deep into his chest, and made him feel better instantly.

"Babe, I'd like to see you."

"Now?"

"Yes, now."

# 8

Grayson stopped his car outside an Italian restaurant in North Beach, where Mona was already waiting for him. Before he could get out of the car and open the door for her, she had already opened the passenger door and jumped in.

"Hey," he murmured. He leaned over and kissed her. "You look great."

She wore a red cocktail dress and a matching jacket over it. Her dark hair cascaded over her shoulders, and her face was beautiful without the help of make-up, just like the night before.

"I wasn't expecting you to be free this early," she said, while he put the car in drive and merged into traffic. "What happened to your family thing? The party? It's not even midnight yet."

He grimaced. "Long story. But let's just say I stood up to my father, when it was clear that he was manipulating me. I told him to stay out of my life."

Mona sighed and slid her hand onto his thigh, a gesture he welcomed. He put his hand over hers, squeezing it.

"I guess I'm not the only one who has an overbearing father," she said. "He constantly tries to tell me how to live my life."

Grayson cast her a sideways look and smiled at her. "Welcome to my world. Is that why you're in San Francisco over the holidays? To get away from your family?"

She looked out of the window. "Basically. Though it's hard to escape them for long."

He understood all too well. "How about we don't talk about our families anymore tonight and just pretend they don't exist?"

She smiled at him. "I think that's a brilliant idea."

She moved her hand up his thigh, and Grayson sucked in a breath. "If you're trying to check whether I'm already hard, let me save you the trouble. The answer is yes."

A soft chuckle rolled over Mona's lips. "I love a man who gets hard so quickly."

He took his hand from hers and reached over to her. He gripped the seam of her dress and pulled the fabric up, before sliding his hand onto her naked thigh. Slowly, he moved it upwards.

"You wouldn't by any chance be checking if I'm already wet, would you?" she asked coquettishly, but didn't stop him.

"Oh, I know you're already wet. I can smell it. I just wanna get a head start on making you come." He brushed his hand against her panties, then slid his fingers under the damp fabric. When his fingers connected with her sex, Mona sucked in a breath.

He moved his hand lower, and dipped it to her drenched pussy, bathing his fingers in her juices.

"Oh babe, you need it really badly, don't you?"

"I do," she said, her voice breathy, her pelvis tilting up to give him better access.

"Tell me: were you thinking of me after you left this morning?" Grayson asked and slid his wet fingers upward to her clit.

Mona gasped. "What if I was?"

He chuckled and turned onto his street. "Then I would tell you that I was thinking of you too. In fact, when I took a shower earlier, I couldn't help myself and imagined you were there with me."

He turned off the street, and the garage door opened in front of him. He drove inside, while he continued to caress Mona's sex.

"Did you masturbate?" she asked.

He brought the car to a stop, while the garage door closed behind them, and killed the engine. Then he released the seatbelt and leaned over to the passenger side.

"I did. It felt good, but not as good as being with you in the flesh."

He pressed a button to lower the passenger seat, and Mona gasped when she realized that the seat was leaning farther back, bringing her body almost horizontal.

"What—"

Grayson pushed her dress up to her waist and shoved her panties down to her knees. Then he lowered his head to her sex and licked over her drenched folds.

"Gray! Oh!"

"Mmm."

She tasted good. Tangy, flowery, like morning dew on a meadow. Her clit was already swollen, responding to his caresses, and more juices seeped from her channel. He used one hand to pull back the little hood over her clit for better access, and licked over the exposed organ. Mona moaned loudly. Then he thrust his middle finger into her tight pussy, her muscles instantly clenching around him. She tilted her pelvis up to rub herself harder on his tongue and take his finger deeper into her.

Fuck, how he loved a woman who offered herself without restraints, who gave herself so freely to a man, trusting him to take care of her. And he wanted to take care of her, pleasure her. He was drawn to her. He'd been with many women before, but never with a woman like Mona. She was strong, but not afraid to surrender to him, just like he wanted to surrender to her. He'd never felt like this before, never wanted to give control to a woman for fear that it made him look weak. But he realized now that opening up to another person wasn't weakness, but a sign of self-confidence, of strength.

As he finger-fucked her in a slow but steady rhythm, he continued to lick her clit, her ragged breathing indicating that she was close to her climax. He doubled his efforts and adjusted his tempo to her movements.

"Oh, yes! So good."

He welcomed her praise, feeling pride spread in his chest. By the time this night was over, he would make sure that she never craved another man's touch but his.

Fuck! That thought struck him like a bolt of lightning. Had he gone completely crazy? Was he pussy-whipped already? But no matter how much he tried to push away the thought that he wanted this woman for more than just a few nights, he couldn't banish it from his mind. He knew virtually nothing about her, but their chemistry was off the charts. Was it just the sex that made him want her more than any woman before her? Or was it more? Did she too feel that they were kindred spirits?

Mona writhed beneath him, her hand now at his nape, caressing him. "Oh, yes, please, yes."

All of a sudden, she stiffened and cried out on a breathy moan. Grayson felt the waves of her orgasm bounce against his lips and her interior muscles squeeze his finger. He stopped thrusting into her, allowing her to ride out her climax, before he released her and sat up.

He looked into her passion-clouded eyes, and she pulled his face to her.

"I've never had a lover like you," she murmured and sank her lips onto his.

When she severed the kiss, he smiled. "I hope that's a good thing."

"Fishing for compliments?"

"You climaxing is compliment enough."

~ ~ ~

Monique still hadn't come down from her high when Gray led her into his loft. She freed herself from her jacket and tossed it on a chair. The heavy door fell shut behind him, and a moment later, he was already on her, pressing her back against the wall, and kissing her with a ferocity she could get used to.

She hadn't expected him to go down on her in the car. But when it had happened, she'd let herself go and enjoyed his mouth on her, letting go of all the tension that had built up during her confrontation with her father. Gray was helping her forget about what had happened, and made her think only of the pleasure they could give each other.

She loved the way he sandwiched her between the wall and his hard body, grinding his erection against her like a promise. As a vampire hybrid, he was more virile than any man in his prime, and she realized now why her relationships with human men never worked: they couldn't satisfy her unquenchable needs. Some of her previous lovers had called her a nymphomaniac, but they never knew that what made her so hungry for sex was the vampire inside her. But Gray understood her, because he was the same, driven by his primal need for blood and sex.

Impatiently, she tugged at his clothes, pushing the tuxedo jacket off his shoulders and getting to work on the buttons of his starched shirt, while he found the zipper of her dress and pulled it down. When she felt cool air blow against her naked breasts, she realized that he was stripping her of her dress. It pooled around her feet. Just as quickly, she helped him rid himself of his pants and boxer briefs. He was still wearing his shirt, when he ripped her panties off her, hooked his arms underneath her thighs and lifted her up, her back pressed against the wall.

On her next breath she felt the bulbous head of his cock at her pussy, before he plunged into her as if he wanted to impale her. He was different tonight, wilder, untamed, unbridled. She welcomed this side of him and urged him on to claim her body with his. Never before had she enjoyed being in a position where she was at a man's mercy, unable to move. Yet she loved the feeling of Gray fucking her hard and fast, taking her as if she were his to do with as he pleased. And in that moment, she was his, and that knowledge shocked her to the core. She'd always believed that she would never give in to a man's demands, yet here she was, allowing this stranger to take her as if she were his to command.

A violent shudder went through her body, and she realized that it was caused by his cock spasming inside her and warm semen flooding her tight channel. Yet despite his orgasm, he kept plunging hard and deep, his breaths uneven, his skin perspiring. When she met his eyes, she saw them shimmer golden, and she noticed his fangs peek out from between his parted lips. They were fully extended, and the sexiest thing she'd ever seen. Instinctively, she tilted her head to the side, brushing strands of hair away from her neck.

She noticed his gaze shoot to where she felt her vein pulse in a rapid tempo and recognized the hunger in it.

"Yes," she murmured.

She wanted this. Wanted to feel his fangs break her skin and sink deep into her.

"Fuck!" he hissed, before he dipped his face to her neck, licked over her vein, and drove his fangs into her.

A bolt akin to an electrical charge shot through her body, threatening to incinerate her from the inside. She felt his heartbeat echo her own as waves of pleasure crashed over her, drowning her in sheer bliss, making the rest of the world and all her problems vanish. In that moment, only the two of them existed.

She'd known that being bitten by a vampire was pleasurable, but she'd had no idea that it could be more pleasurable than being the one who did the biting.

~ ~ ~

Grayson carried Mona into his bedroom and placed her on the bed, both of them naked now. Her blood was coursing through his veins, and he could still taste her on his tongue. He'd never tasted anything more tempting than her blood, and was glad that she hadn't stopped him when he'd extended his fangs to drink from her. In fact, she'd invited him, teased him by offering her neck to him.

He pulled her into his arms, her body partially draped over his.

"You were wilder than yesterday," she murmured, her sweet breath ghosting over his skin, making him shudder with pleasure.

"You like it when I'm wild?"

"Mmm." With her index finger, she painted small circles around his nipple. "I liked your bite."

He put two fingers under her chin to tilt her head up so he could look into her eyes. "I loved biting you. Your taste is... out of this world amazing." There was no other way to describe it. Though he loved human blood and would always have to drink human blood, Mona's was on a different level altogether.

"You made me come really hard when you bit me," she admitted.

Her eyes shimmered golden, the green color in them gone. And though he knew she was satisfied, he also knew that this wouldn't be the last time tonight that they would make love. They both needed this to drown out the problems with their families and the stresses of their lives.

Grayson slanted his lips over hers and gave her a featherlight kiss. "I hope you're not planning on sleeping tonight."

She smiled. "Not if I can help it. But if I do fall asleep, just wake me."

"How would you like me to do that?" He ran his hand down to her ass, caressing her tenderly.

"I'm sure you can think of something."

She wrapped her hand around his cock and tugged on it. His semi-erect shaft pumped full with blood in a matter of three seconds.

"Mmm, that's perfect." He enjoyed her soft palm caressing him and closed his eyes for a moment. "Tell me about yourself, Mona. What do you want from life?"

She suddenly stopped moving her hand up and down his erection, and he added, "Keep going, babe. I can multi-task."

She let out a soft laugh. "You sure about that?"

Suddenly, she increased her tempo, and he put his hand over hers to slow her down. "Temptress. Now talk to me. What do you want out of life?"

"Independence," she said while her hand returned to the leisurely rhythm of earlier.

"From your family?"

"Yes. I want to make my own decisions, chart my own course. I don't want to be judged by anybody just because they think I should be a certain way because of who my father is. It's hard to do that in a place where everybody knows you and your family."

"To them you'll always be the little girl they saw grow up, not the woman you're now," Grayson said.

"Is it like that for you too? Is that why you applied for a job far away from here?"

He knew the job in New Orleans was dead in the water. After the blow out he'd had with Samson and Cain, he had no chance in hell of getting the position. But he didn't want to admit that to her. If what he had with Mona turned into something serious, they could go wherever they wanted, far away from their families.

"Yes, everybody sees me as a spoiled younger version of my father. And my father treats me more harshly than any of his employees. I have to work doubly hard to prove to him that I'm leadership material. It's frustrating, because all I ever wanted was to be like him. And now, it looks like I'll never be able to meet his high standards. I might as well start all over again somewhere else."

Maybe that was the solution to his problems: to make a clean cut from Scanguards, away from his father's influence.

"Sometimes that's what we need to do to show them that we're not mere copies of them," Mona said. "It's just that my brothers don't seem to have the same issues with my dad as I do. He treats them differently. They get away with murder, and they're by no means perfect, but he expects perfection from me. And I can't be perfect. Nobody is."

He pulled her face to him. "You're pretty darn close to perfect. In fact, I haven't found a flaw on you yet. And I'd be happy to tell your dad that he has the perfect daughter and should cut you some slack."

"I can fight my own battles." Her voice was suddenly sharp, and her hand on his cock stilled.

"I didn't say you can't. You are a strong woman, and I love strong women," he said softly and put his hand over hers and moved it up and down his cock. "I just wanted you to know that I'm on your side."

"Gray?"

"Yes?"

"Make love to me."

# 9

Grayson stirred. The sun had just risen and awakened him. He couldn't have slept more than a couple of hours, the vixen in his bed demanding he fuck her over and over again. He'd complied with her wishes every time. Mona was still sleeping, but he felt sweaty and needed a cooling shower. Quietly, he snuck out of bed and walked to the bathroom. He closed the door behind him and caught his reflection in the mirror, recognizing how relaxed and happy he looked. As a vampire hybrid he had a reflection, a full-blooded vampire didn't.

He turned on the shower and stepped into the over-sized shower stall and allowed the cool water to run down his body, caressing him where Mona had caressed him earlier. He could still feel her hands and her mouth on him, exploring every inch of his body. At the thought, he turned hard again. He soaped up and cleaned himself, washed his hair, and rinsed, before stepping out on the bathmat to dry off. Quickly, he brushed his teeth, then finger-combed his hair.

A towel wrapped around his lower body, he walked back into the bedroom. Mona lifted her head and opened her eyes.

"I didn't mean to wake you," he said and sat down on the edge of the bed.

"Hey," she murmured softly and pulled him closer.

He smiled at her. "You hungry? I have bottled blood in the fridge."

"Actually, I'm rather starved for human food."

"I can get us some pastries from a place around the corner," Grayson offered.

"I can come with you."

"Why don't you stay here? No need to get dressed when we both know that I'm gonna rip those clothes off you again anyway."

She chuckled softly. "You're very sure of yourself."

He pressed a kiss to her lips. "That's because I can read the signs. You're in the mood for more." He directed his gaze to her nipples that had turned into hard little pebbles. Gently, he cupped one breast and squeezed it, before he slid his hand down her torso and underneath the sheet until he reached her sex.

"Just as I thought." He dipped his finger into her wet sheath and heard her gasp, before withdrawing it. "I won't be long, babe."

He dressed quickly in jeans and a casual shirt, then looked for his wallet and keys. He found both in his tuxedo pants. When he pulled them out, his cell phone fell out too. He snatched it and glanced at the display. Four missed calls from Isabelle. The cell was set to silent, that's why he hadn't heard it ring.

Odd, Isabelle wasn't one to make multiple calls when he didn't call her back right away. Was she doing Samson's bidding? Or was she in trouble? For a few seconds, he contemplated what to do. He knew he'd never forgive himself if he didn't call her back when she needed his help.

"Something wrong?" Mona said from the bed.

"I've got four missed calls from my sister. But no voicemail." He sighed. "She might be in trouble."

"Call her back."

He nodded and clicked on Isabelle's number. It rang once, before she picked up.

"You've gotta come. Now."

Alarmed by her panicked tone, his heart skipped a beat. "What's wrong, Isa?"

"Dad's been kidnapped, and Mom is injured, and—"

"Oh my God. I'm coming home now."

"I'm in Russian Hill. I'll text you the address. Come quickly. I need you."

"I'll be there in a few minutes."

He disconnected the call and shoved his phone into his pocket, shock coursing through his entire body. Instantly, he was assaulted with guilt. He'd hurled hurtful words at his father, and now he was gone.

"What's going on?" Mona asked, her eyes wide.

"Family emergency. I've gotta go. Now."

She lifted her legs out of bed.

"You can stay here, help yourself to whatever's in the fridge. Just pull the door shut when you leave. I'll call you later when I know more."

She nodded. "Okay. I hope everything will be all right."

He didn't reply, instead he rushed to the door and opened it. A ping sounded on his cell phone, indicating that Isabelle had sent him the address where she wanted him to meet her. At the same time, he heard another cell phone ringing. But it wasn't his. It was Mona's.

Grayson slammed the door shut behind him and rushed to the garage. Moments later, he was in his Audi and shot out of the garage onto the street. There was little traffic. Most people had only just returned from New Year's Eve parties and were now in their beds, sleeping.

During the short drive to Russian Hill, a hundred thoughts bounced around in his mind. How badly injured was his mother? Who'd taken his father? And why? He wanted to scream, to punch somebody, to turn back time. He doubted himself now. If he'd stayed at the party and not left like a spoiled irresponsible jerk, maybe the kidnapping would have never happened. What if it was his fault? And even worse, what if his father died, what if he never came back, and he could never take back the words he'd hurled at him in anger? What if he never got the chance to apologize?

That thought expelled all air from his lungs, choking him. Fuck!

He kicked the gas pedal down, and the car shot over the next speed bump. A few seconds more, and he reached his destination. He realized instantly where he was. This was one of the vampire-proof houses out-of-town vampires rented during their stay in San Francisco. He was familiar with this one, because he'd been the one suggesting it to Cain because of its great location and luxurious interior befitting a king and his family.

Grayson double-parked his R8 in front of the impressive property. He didn't care who he blocked. When he jumped out of the car, he noticed that Isabelle's baby-blue Thunderbird was parked a few cars farther down the street. He charged to the front door. It was ajar, and he pushed it open quickly and entered the small enclosed foyer, already pulling the door closed behind him, before opening the second door that led into a much larger foyer.

There, chaos greeted him. Broken and turned over furniture and lamps were strewn around the floor. In several places the drywall was damaged, and glass from framed paintings littered the ground. He could see and smell traces of blood, vampire blood and human blood. And he saw something else, something that turned the blood in his veins to ice: thin gray ash on the wooden floors, the remains of one or more vampires.

"Isa?" Grayson called out.

"In here!"

He followed his sister's voice and marched into a large living room. Isabelle sat on the edge of the sofa, where their mother, Delilah, lay unconscious. She was bleeding from a head wound, and one eye was swollen shut. With one hand, Isabelle held her mouth open, while she fed Delilah blood from her wrist. On the carpet, a few yards away from them lay Faye, Cain's blood-bonded mate. She, too was unconscious. Maya, Scanguards' resident vampire physician, was kneeling next to her, working on setting an IV, while a vampire Grayson didn't know was helping her.

Grayson approached his mother and sister. "What happened?"

Isabelle looked over her shoulder. "Thank God you're here. A horde of vampires attacked them and kidnapped Dad and Cain. They killed two of the bodyguards." She pointed to the vampire assisting Maya. "William is the only guard who survived."

Grayson turned toward William, and ran his eyes over him. He now saw that he was injured too. Blood was gushing from a nasty-looking stomach wound.

"William, I'm Grayson. You need human blood."

Maya looked over her shoulder. "I told him to drink some, but he insists on helping with Faye."

"I'll get the blood," Grayson said quickly, dashed into the kitchen, and returned with several bottles of blood a moment later. He handed one to William. "Drink, now! That's an order!"

When William began to gulp down the liquid, Grayson looked back at Isabelle. "How is Mom doing?"

"They knocked her out, but she'll heal," Isabelle said confidently.

"Good." He looked back at Faye. "What happened to her? I don't see any wounds."

"Not sure," Maya said, while she held up a bag of human blood so the IV could deliver it into Faye's vein. "I'm hoping the transfusion will reverse whatever knocked her out."

"William," Grayson said, "did you see what happened to her?"

"I'm not certain, but I think they injected her with something."

Grayson exchanged a look with Maya.

"Where's their daughter? Monique? Did she see anything?" Grayson asked, looking at William.

"She wasn't here. I called her."

Grayson nodded. "Okay. How many attackers were there?"

"About a dozen, all vampires," William said.

"Oh my God! Mom! Mom!"

At the female voice, Grayson looked over his shoulder. In the door to the living room stood a woman he knew all too well, a woman he'd left in his bed only minutes earlier. It was clear to him immediately that her name wasn't Mona. Utter disbelief paralyzed him. He'd slept with Monique Montague, the woman Samson and Cain had tried to set him up with.

"Monique!" William called out in relief.

When she took a few steps into the living room, approaching Faye, Monique's gaze suddenly connected with Grayson's. She gasped.

"You," she murmured almost breathlessly.

Perhaps proper introductions were in order now. "I'm Grayson, Samson's son."

# 10

"I'm Grayson, Samson's son."

The words ricocheted in Monique's brain and took several seconds to register. No, this wasn't possible. She'd had sex with the very man her father had chosen for her? The man he wanted her to date? Had Grayson known about this and played along? Or rather, tricked her, when it had become clear that she wouldn't go to the New Year's Eve party to meet him? Had she played right into their hands?

She shook off the thoughts. It didn't matter right now. She could deal with all this later. Right now, only two things mattered: taking care of her mother, and rescuing her father from his kidnappers.

She nodded at Grayson, acknowledging his greeting. "What happened here? Who did this? What's happening with Mom? William? Where are the other King's guards?"

"Dead," William said in a flat tone. "We tried to protect your parents, but we were outnumbered. There were a dozen of them attacking us just as we returned from the party." He motioned to Delilah, who lay on the couch, unconscious and bloodied, while a young hybrid female fed her blood from her wrist.

"Samson and Delilah came with us. They wanted to stay for a while and talk, but then a dozen vampires stormed in and attacked us. We fought. Cain managed to kill one of them, and Samson would have killed one of his attackers too, but when two of them attacked Delilah, Samson tried to defend her, and they overpowered him."

Monique kneeled down to her mother. "What did they do to Mom? Why is she unconscious?" She looked at the vampire female administering an IV and recognized her. She'd met Maya, Scanguards' resident physician, several times over the years. "Maya?"

"I'm not sure why she's out. I can see no obvious injuries."

Grayson stepped closer. "Maya, do you think they could have injected her with dead man's blood? That could have knocked her out, don't you think?"

"You might be right," Maya said. "If that's the case, the transfusion with human blood will purge the effects of the poison from her body. But I've never had a case like that. I have no idea how long it'll take."

Monique nodded. "Please save her." Then she looked straight at Grayson. "And your mother? Will she be all right?"

He looked past her, then nodded and looked into her eyes. "She will be. My sister is giving her blood. She'll heal."

He looked back at William, who was pressing his hand to his stomach wound. "Do you know how they transported Samson and Cain away? By car? Van? We need to find out where they took 'em."

"I glimpsed a black van, but I didn't get a license plate or anything else," William said with regret. "And there might have been more than one van. I can't be sure. There were too many people to fit in just one."

"We need to find the van," Monique said, her pulse racing. If she were in New Orleans, she would know exactly what to do now. But this was San Francisco. "Do you have a contact at the police, Grayson?"

"I'm on it." He pulled out his cell phone and punched in a number. "I'll speak to the police chief directly. I've got his cell number."

"William, how long ago did they leave here with Cain and Samson?" Monique asked.

"Just before sunrise." He looked at a large clock over the fireplace. "About an hour and fifteen minutes ago."

"Fuck!" Monique cursed. "They could be anywhere by now."

"Donnelly?" Grayson said into his cell phone. "It's Grayson Woodford. Listen, Dad and the vampire king of Louisiana were kidnapped an hour and fifteen minutes ago. We need roadblocks. We're looking for a black van." He paused. "Let me hand you over to one of the guards who saw the van. He'll give you all the details. And we need the feed of all traffic cams in the city. Yeah… I'll get Thomas and Eddie on it. Just send us the feeds. Thanks." He handed his phone to William.

While William spoke to the police chief, Grayson addressed Maya. "Who's aware of what's happened?"

"Gabriel knows. He's alerting everybody and calling them back to HQ," Maya replied.

"Good. Isa, you're in charge of security for Mom and Faye. Arrange transport for them to take them to our house in Nob Hill. It has more security features than this rental. I'll be heading the rescue efforts," Grayson said firmly.

"Get in line," Monique snapped. There was no way she would allow him to steamroll her. "My father was kidnapped too. And I'm not gonna just sit back and twiddle my thumbs while you go all *Mission Impossible.*"

"You can stay at our house with your mother. William will go there too. Isabelle will arrange five additional bodyguards to protect all of you," Grayson insisted.

Monique glared at him, fuming already. She fisted her hands at her waist. "I'm not some damsel in distress. I'm a vampire hybrid and just as smart if not smarter than you, and if you think you can sideline me, then think again."

"I'm only making sure you're safe. If somebody targeted your father, then you might be in danger too."

"And you're not? Your father was kidnapped too. So what if he was the target, and my father just got in the way? By the same logic, wouldn't you and Isabelle then be in danger?" She let out a grunt.

Grayson huffed and took a couple of steps toward her. "I can take care of myself!"

Arrogant bastard! "So can I!"

"Is there something going on I should know about?" Isabelle suddenly asked, staring at them.

"No!" Monique and Grayson said in unison.

Well, at least they were on the same page when it came to one thing: hiding the fact that they knew each other intimately. But that was the only thing they agreed on.

"Could have fooled me, 'cause you guys bicker like an old married couple," Isabelle said and licked over her wrist to close the puncture wound.

"Here's your phone back," William finally said and handed the cell back to Grayson. "The police chief said they'll put out an APB for any dark vans, and set up road blocks."

"Good." He pocketed his cell phone.

"We can't just let the police handle it. They're not equipped to deal with this," Monique said, addressing Grayson. If this had happened in New Orleans, she would already be calling all bodyguards, tech support people, and spread the word among confidential informants. "We need to do something."

"We are," Grayson insisted, when his cell phone rang. He answered it. "Orlando?" There was a brief pause, then he said, "Thanks."

He gestured to his sister. "Isa, Orlando is in a black-out van outside. Can you open the garage for him? I'll watch over Mom in the meantime."

"Sure thing," Isabelle responded and left the room.

Monique walked closer to Grayson and lowered her voice. "So what exactly is your plan? Do you even have one?"

He met her gaze without flinching. "Trust me, I've handled kidnappings before. I don't need anybody telling me what to do."

"Nor do I."

"Oh, I got that. I've heard enough about you to know that you're bossy and stubborn."

"Well, it didn't bother you last night that I'm bossy," she hissed under her breath.

Only, last night things had been different. *He*'d been different. He'd been a man who excited her, who turned her on. Now he was Grayson Woodford, the spoiled heir of Scanguards. And the guy who'd humiliated her when she was eleven. And he was about to steamroll her, when she had just as much at stake as he. Both their fathers were in danger.

"We'll talk about last night later. This is not the right place for it. But trust me when I tell you that I'll do everything in my power to bring both our fathers back alive. Even if it's the last thing I do."

"And you think I wouldn't?" She glared at him, outraged.

"I didn't say that."

"Then what did you say? Huh? That I'm not capable because I'm a woman? Spit it out!"

# 11

Grayson took a deep breath to force himself to remain calm and not raise his voice. Why the hell were they even arguing? How had that happened so fast? Only an hour ago they'd been perfectly in synch. They'd been affectionate toward each other. He had to remind himself of how it had felt being with Monique. The memory of their lovemaking finally tamped down his anger and made him look at their situation from a different viewpoint.

They were in the same boat: they had overbearing fathers, and now their fathers had been kidnapped. He suddenly understood what she felt, and why she was lashing out at him. In fact, she wasn't angry at him, she was angry at herself, just like he was angry at himself for how he'd spoken to his father.

"Monique, babe, I know—"

He couldn't finish his sentence, because Orlando and Isabelle entered the room. Orlando was a full-blooded vampire who'd started working for Scanguards only a little over a year ago. He wasn't the talkative kind, and his brawny physique made him look intimidating. But Grayson knew that Samson trusted him, even though his father hadn't disclosed to anybody how he knew Orlando, or where he came from. And Orlando never volunteered information about himself.

"Grayson," Orlando said, "what do you need?"

"Orlando, thanks for coming so quickly."

"I was in the area."

"Please assist Isabelle with transferring my mother and Faye to our house. William will be coming with you too."

"So will I," Maya interrupted. "I need to monitor Faye and your mom for a while."

Grayson nodded. "Good. Orlando, get four additional bodyguards stationed at home. William is injured, make sure he's got time to heal."

"I'm almost healed," William claimed.

"Make the calls, Orlando," Grayson ordered. "And can somebody pack up Faye's personal effects and clothes?" He looked at Monique and softened his voice so it didn't sound like a barked command. "Would you please do that, Monique?"

To his surprise, she nodded without a protest.

"And go ahead and pack your own things too. You can't stay here on your own."

She hesitated, but then she said, "Fine."

Suddenly a soft moan came from the sofa. Grayson's gaze shot to it, and he saw his mother stir.

"Mom!" With two large steps he was at her side and sitting on the edge of the sofa.

"Oh, Grayson, Isabelle," she pressed out, tears welling up in her eyes. "They have your dad, they have Samson."

She tried to sit up, and Grayson pulled her into his arms. "I know, Mom. But we'll get him back. Him and Cain. I promise you. I won't rest until he's back in your arms." He pressed a kiss to the top of her head.

"How are you feeling, Mom?" Isabelle asked and crouched down next to the sofa.

Delilah touched her head at the spot where blood was crusting over a wound. "Better, I think. Did one of you give me blood?"

Isabelle nodded. "Yes, I gave you mine."

Delilah stroked her hand over Isabelle's cheek. "Thank you, Isa." Then she sniffled.

"Mom, can you tell us anything about the vampires that attacked you?" Grayson asked. "Anything that might help us figure out where they took Dad and Cain?"

"I'm not sure. It all happened so fast. They must have been lying in wait outside the house, and they just stormed in when we went inside. There were at least ten of them."

"Did you see them leave?"

"They knocked me down. But I heard one of them saying something about the vans. They had more than one."

Grayson squeezed her hand. He had to ask the next question, even though he didn't want to. "Have you been able to communicate with Dad since he was taken?"

Every blood-bonded couple had the ability to communicate telepathically.

She hesitated and touched her temple, then nodded. "Yes, for a moment. When they dragged him outside, he sent me a psychic message. He said he could see at least five dark vans, maybe six, and that they looked like the black-out vans Scanguards uses. But then he was gone. As if they knocked him out cold."

A tear ran down her cheek, and Grayson knew he couldn't ask her whether she sensed if Samson was still alive. She was in enough pain. "That information helps. Five or six black-out vans can't just disappear. We'll find them."

"Yes, we have to," Delilah said. "I can't lose him."

"I'll bring him back to you, Mom." Not just for her, but also for himself.

She nodded. Then her gaze strayed past him to where Faye lay on the floor. Maya was still holding the IV-bag up to infuse Faye with more blood.

"How is Faye?"

Maya turned to meet Delilah's gaze. "I don't know yet. How are you feeling? Do you need more blood?"

Delilah shook her head. "I think I'm good. Just worried about Samson and Cain." She sniffled. "The attackers staked two of Cain's guards right in front of me. Their families… we have to let them know."

Even with her own worries, Delilah still thought about others. "We will, Mom." Grayson looked at William. "You know their families?"

William nodded. "I do. I'll handle it."

"Thank you," Grayson said. He pulled his cell phone from his pocket. "I'll fill Thomas and Eddie in about what to look for on the traffic cam footage."

He punched in Thomas's number, when he saw Monique enter the living room again. She dropped two travel bags at the door. She'd changed from her red cocktail dress into a pair of tight-fitting jeans and an equally tight cream-colored sweater that accentuated her slim figure and athletic build. Her long hair looked damp, evidence that she'd taken a quick shower. Despite everything that was happening, he couldn't help but let his eyes roam over her body. Even knowing her true identity couldn't diminish his desire for her. He was irrevocably in lust with Monique.

~ ~ ~

Monique noticed Grayson look at her, his expression unreadable. But instead of studying him to try to understand what was going on between them, she tore her gaze from him. She couldn't worry about him and their relationship right now, if it could even be called a relationship. Other things were more important: her mother's wellbeing and her father's rescue. She had to devote all her energy to these two issues.

Monique approached her mother, who still lay on the floor, and crouched down, when she noticed that Faye was stirring.

"Looks like she's coming 'round," Maya said.

"Mom? Mom? Can you hear me?" Monique asked and leaned over her, her hand on her mother's shoulder.

Faye's eyelids fluttered. It took another moment, before she opened her eyes.

"Thank God," Monique murmured.

"Cain. They took him," Faye pressed out and sat up.

"Slowly," Maya cautioned and pointed to the IV that was still attached to Faye's arm. "How're you feeling?"

"As if somebody had poured acid into my veins."

Monique shuddered at the thought. "Do you remember what happened?"

At the question, Faye looked to the sofa, where Delilah sat, looking much better. "Delilah, are you okay?"

Delilah nodded. "I'm fine."

With a sigh of relief, Faye turned her gaze back to Monique. "Oh, sweetheart, I'm so glad you weren't with us when it happened, or they might have taken you too."

Monique didn't agree with her mother's sentiment. Had she been with them, she would have been able to fight the attackers, and maybe Cain and Samson wouldn't have been kidnapped. She put her arms around her mother and squeezed her for a moment, before releasing her.

"William said there were about a dozen vampires attacking you when you got back," Monique said, hoping her mother could provide more details to the story.

"Yeah, they ambushed us. There were just too many. And when they killed Steven and Brock, I knew we had no chance." Faye's eyes teared up, and a pink tear rolled down her cheek. "Oh God, their families will be devastated." She sniffled. "I don't know why they didn't kill me or Delilah, or why they didn't kidnap us too. They certainly had the opportunity."

Monique noticed that Grayson had finished his telephone call and sat down next to Delilah and put his arm around her shoulders, comforting her.

"They must have been targeting Dad and Samson," Monique mused.

"I think so too," Grayson added, his gaze wandering from Delilah to Faye. "Why else would they leave you alive?"

"Mom, did you recognize any of the men?" Monique asked.

Faye shook her head. "Sorry. I didn't."

"I didn't either," Delilah added. "And I know a lot of the vampires living in San Francisco."

"If we had mugshots, would you be able to recognize any of the attackers?" Monique asked.

"I think so, yes," Delilah said.

Faye nodded. "I saw several of them clearly. I'm sure I can identify them if I saw them again."

Monique exchanged a look with Grayson. "Doesn't Scanguards have a database of known vampires?"

"We do," Grayson confirmed instantly. "Good idea. I'll set it up so they can go through the database and look at all the photos. Maybe we'll get a hit or two."

"Faye," Delilah suddenly said, "are you able to communicate with Cain via your telepathic bond? I can't get through to Samson anymore."

"I haven't even thought of it yet," Faye said, then closed her eyes and concentrated. A few tense seconds passed, but then Faye shook her head. "I can't feel him. He's either too far away, or... or they knocked him out like they knocked me out."

"Given your symptoms I think it was dead man's blood they injected you with," Maya said. "It acts like a poison. They could have used the same on Cain and Samson."

"I'll keep trying to get through to him," Faye promised.

Monique motioned to Grayson. "How extensive is Scanguards' database?"

"It lists most of the vampires living on the West Coast, plus some that are associated with our New York office, but it's by no means an exhaustive list."

"Hmm. So what, about ten thousand vampires?"

Grayson nodded. "More or less. Were there any female vampires among the attackers?" He looked at William, then Faye and Delilah.

All three shook their heads.

"Then we can whittle down the list to about half."

Monique thought about it for a moment. What were the chances that the attackers were from the West Coast? What if they'd come from Louisiana? "I think the palace has a database of all past and present employees and clan members. William?"

"You're right," William agreed. "I'll call and have them set up a link for us."

"That's good," Grayson added, looking at Monique appreciatively. "And while we're at it, I'll talk to Luther to get us access to the prison records."

"The prison records?" Monique asked wondering if she'd heard correctly.

"Yes, an attack like this takes planning and experience. I'm sure at least one of the attackers is an ex-VCON. If he did time in one of the vampire prisons in the U.S., we'll find him."

Monique nodded. She liked the way Grayson was thinking.

"Oh my God," Faye suddenly said, "David and Zach! Have you spoken to them?"

Damn! She'd forgotten about her brothers. "I'll call them right now."

"Tell them to fly directly to San Francisco," Faye demanded. "I need them here, so I don't have to worry about them too."

"I'll take care of it, Mom," Monique promised.

"Excuse me," Orlando interrupted, "everything is ready for the transport to the Woodford residence. We're leaving now."

Monique helped her mother up and walked toward the hallway with her, while Grayson assisted Delilah.

"Monique, which one is your bag?" Grayson asked.

"The blue one, why?"

"'Cause you're riding with me."

# 12

Grayson placed Monique's travel bag in the trunk of his car, and got in on the driver's side. Monique was already sitting on the passenger seat, her cell phone glued to her ear.

"Call me," she said in an urgent tone and disconnected the call.

Grayson started the engine. "Did you reach your brothers?"

"No. It goes straight to voicemail. I was afraid that would happen. David and Zach went to a remote cabin in Switzerland, and were expecting a winter storm. It's probably knocked out the cell towers."

"We'll keep trying." Grayson merged into traffic.

There was a pause that stretched for almost a minute. Now was the time to talk in private, but he had no idea how to start the conversation. It turned out that he didn't have to.

"Did you know what our fathers were trying to do?" Monique asked, her voice clipped.

"No. I found out at the Scanguards New Year's Eve party. Guess you figured it out earlier, since you didn't even show up to the party."

She huffed. "Would you have shown up, if you'd found out earlier?"

He decided not to answer that loaded question. Instead, he said, "You must have had a really bad opinion of me. According to Cain you said that you wouldn't date me if I was the last man on earth and the survival of our species depended on us." Did she still think that? Or had what had happened between them changed her opinion of him?

She shrugged and looked out the window. "Like you had a better opinion of me, or why else did you flee the party you were in charge of well before midnight?"

"Fair point." He cleared his throat. "So, uhm, since you got to know me without knowing my name, and we got on really well, can I assume that your opinion of me has improved?"

Monique grunted rather unladylike. "Don't assume anything. For all I know, you set up our *chance* meeting." She made air quotes around the word *chance*.

"Why the fuck would I do that?" He cast her a sideways look. "How would I even have known where to find you? Maybe it's the other way around. Or why would you show up at *my* watering hole? Everybody at Scanguards knows that the *Black Velvet* is where I go several times a week. And of all the bars in San Francisco, you walk into the *Black Velvet*. If that's not an odd coincidence, then I don't know what is."

"David recommended the place."

"Your brother?"

"Yes, he said he went there two years ago when he visited San Francisco."

Grayson sighed, realizing what had happened. "Did he also tell you who took him there?"

"No."

"I did. *I* introduced him to that place. He knew it was my local hangout. He knew that sooner or later you would run into me there."

"I'm gonna shove a stake up his ass! Fucking bastard!" Monique cursed. "And I thought he was on my side! That lying, conniving little prick! Wait until he gets here. I'm gonna—"

"Monique," Grayson interrupted. "Does that mean you regret the last two nights?" He stopped at a red light and looked at her. "Do you regret having made love to me?"

She inhaled, her eyes widening, her chest lifting. Her lips parted, but she didn't say anything. Did she really have to think about whether she regretted having slept with him?

"Damn it, Monique, that should be a simple Yes or No answer."

"It's complicated," she finally said and looked away. "Now that I know who you are, I'm not sure who the person I slept with really is. It was all more clear-cut when I didn't know your name."

"It shouldn't be complicated. I'm still the same person. I wasn't pretending to be anybody else the last two nights. When I was with you, I was myself. Maybe even more so because I didn't have to live up to anybody's expectations of what Grayson Woodford should be like."

~ ~ ~

Monique looked into Grayson's eyes and contemplated his words. Didn't she have the same motives for hiding her identity, because she didn't want to be seen as just a spoiled princess, but a woman with normal wants and needs? A woman who wanted a man to love her for herself, not for the trappings of her heritage.

"Would you have slept with me if I'd told you my real name in that bar?" she challenged.

When he didn't answer immediately, she scoffed. "See, it's not as clear-cut for you either. You were prejudiced against me too, and didn't want anything to do with me either. Don't deny it!"

"But that's changed!" he claimed.

Behind them, somebody honked, and Grayson stepped on the gas and crossed the intersection.

"Why? Because we had sex? It changes nothing."

"It changes everything."

"How so? We're still in the same boat. Our families set us up. And neither of us wants to be told who to date. Particularly not by their parents. You can't possibly be happy about the situation we're in."

They'd just reached the entrance to an underground garage. The gate opened, and Grayson drove in.

"And what situation is that?" Grayson asked bluntly.

"Having to hide from everybody that we had sex."

Grayson glared at her, obviously not liking her remark, and pulled into a parking spot. He switched off the engine.

"Why would you want to hide it? Are you ashamed of being with me?"

She opened the car door and got out without answering his question. She didn't have an answer for him, at least not one that she could articulate. Inside her, different sides were warring with each other. On one hand, she'd enjoyed being in Grayson's arms and wanted more of the same, on the other, she was afraid that their power dynamics would change, and suddenly, she would be the weaker partner. Could somebody with Grayson's reputation ever see her as an equal partner? Wouldn't they constantly fight about who would have the upper hand?

She marched to the elevators and punched the call button. Grayson was at her side a moment later.

"I asked you a question, Monique."

"I heard you. I can't deal with this right now." She needed time to figure out how to proceed with Grayson. Had he still been Gray, the stranger from the bar, the decision would have been easy. But Grayson Woodford came with baggage. "I need to concentrate on rescuing our fathers. Everything else has to take a back seat."

The elevator opened, and she stepped inside. Grayson followed her, swiped an access card and pressed the button for the top floor. When the doors closed, he turned back to her.

"If that's how you want to play it, fine. But this conversation isn't over. Not by a long shot." He pinned her with his eyes. "Because I'm not ready to give up what was between us the last two nights. We're good together. You can't pretend that we're not."

At the intense gaze he lashed at her, a shiver ran down her spine, and she was glad that she wore a warm sweater that hid the goosebumps on her skin. Yes, they'd been good together in bed, but that was no guarantee that they were good for each other outside the bedroom.

# 13

Upon arrival on the top floor, Grayson headed for Thomas and Eddie's office, his mind still on his conversation with Monique, who walked next to him in silence. For the first time in his life, he wished he wasn't Grayson Woodford, heir to the Scanguards empire. He wished he was just a regular vampire hybrid Monique found attractive. But he was who he was. He couldn't change that. All he could do was change Monique's opinion of him, so she would see the man beneath the façade, the man she'd made love to.

The door to Thomas and Eddie's office stood open. Thomas and Eddie were sitting at their desks, staring into multiple computer monitors. Both wore casual clothes, attesting to the fact that they'd already returned home after the party, when they'd received the news about the kidnapping.

"Hey," Grayson said, then pointed to Monique. "This is Monique, Cain's daughter. Monique, meet Thomas and Eddie. Our IT geniuses."

"Hey, guys."

"Hey," Thomas said. "Sorry about Cain and Samson." He motioned to Eddie. "We're already poring over the surveillance footage."

"Anything yet?" Grayson asked eagerly.

Eddie turned his head to look at them. "There were indeed five vans. Identical down to the license plates."

"You're serious?" Grayson stared at the two full-blooded vampires.

"Eddie's right," Thomas confirmed. "All five vans had the same license plates. Somebody went through a lot of trouble to make it almost impossible for anybody to trace the getaway vehicles."

"Stolen plates?" Grayson asked.

"No, totally made up," Thomas replied.

"So where are they now?" Monique asked. "Have they left the city?"

"We're not sure yet," Eddie said in Thomas's stead and pointed to a large monitor showing various different videos. "These are all roads and bridges leading out of San Francisco. We went back as far as the point at which the vans left Russian Hill, and from what we could see, they didn't pass any of these points. And by now, the police have put roadblocks at all roads leading out of the city."

"So you think they're still in the city?" Monique asked.

"Looks that way," Thomas said.

"So, they're trapped?" Grayson asked.

"If you wanna call it that. They had plenty of time to leave the city, but they didn't. Makes me wonder why."

Grayson wondered about that too. Why stay in the city where they were at a disadvantage?

Thomas sighed. "But we need a lot more manpower to go through all traffic cams in the city to trace all five vans, since we don't know with which one they transported Cain and Samson."

"Call in more staff," Grayson ordered.

"They're already on their way," Thomas confirmed. "We might also need security footage from businesses and hotels the vans might have driven past. So, there'll be a lot of legwork involved, since we can't hack into everything."

"But you'll find them," Monique said firmly.

Before Thomas could answer, Grayson took her arm and squeezed it. "Thomas and Eddie are the best. And their IT team knows what they're doing. Right, guys?"

"We'll do everything in our power," Eddie said with a look at Thomas, who nodded in agreement.

"Thank you," Monique said.

"What about the vampire database?" Grayson looked at Thomas. "Did you already send the data over to the house?"

Thomas nodded. "I spoke to Isabelle already and gave her access to the database. She's already accessed it, and Faye, Delilah, and Faye's bodyguard are going through the photos." He pointed to one of the monitors on his desk. "If they recognize anyone, Isabelle will mark the file, and it'll ping me instantly, so we can distribute the picture and see if we know the suspect's whereabouts."

"I appreciate it," Grayson said.

"You can count on us," Thomas replied.

He knew that. Thomas was one of Samson's oldest friends, and they'd been through a lot together. Everybody at Scanguards respected Samson, and they would do everything they could to get him back.

"Grayson?"

Grayson turned at Gabriel's voice coming from the open door. Gabriel's gaze swept to Monique.

"Let's talk, my office," he suggested. "Monique, you too."

They followed him into his office, where Gabriel closed the door. His hair was tied back in a low ponytail, and his scar that stretched from his eye to his chin seemed to throb.

"Any news?" Grayson asked.

Gabriel shook his head. "Your mothers are at the Woodford residence, and we have five bodyguards protecting them. William should be healed soon too, and I just got a hold of Patrick. He'll swing by your house first to check in with Delilah, and then he'll come back to HQ."

Grayson nodded. "Good. We need every hybrid we can get. The full-blooded vampires have limited mobility until tonight. We need to call every hybrid to come to HQ."

"I figured you'd say that. I've already sent an alert to their cell phones."

"Thanks."

"Something else," Gabriel started, then looked straight at Monique. "Given that the attack was at the rental house, I believe that your father was the primary target. If somebody wanted to kidnap Samson, there would have been easier locations where to do that."

Monique took a breath. "You think it was one of my father's enemies."

"Makes sense," Grayson interjected. "Do you know anybody who'd fit that bill?"

Monique shook her head. "Dad didn't exactly involve me in the day-to-day running of the kingdom. Maybe David or Zach know more. But they're skiing in Switzerland. I still haven't been able to reach them."

"Try them again now," Grayson suggested.

Monique pulled out her cell phone and tapped on a contact. The call went straight to voicemail. She disconnected it, and made a second call, this one to Zach. It too went to voicemail.

"Either they're still out of cell tower range, or something happened to them."

Grayson looked into Monique's eyes and saw the worry there. "Let's see if Thomas and Eddie can ping their last-known location."

"Okay."

"Give the numbers to Thomas, and he'll take care of it," Grayson said.

Monique left the office. When the door closed behind her, Grayson turned back to Gabriel.

"I didn't want to say this in front of Monique," Grayson said, "but if Cain was the target, then David and Zach might be in danger too."

"I figured that too. Same goes for Monique. She should stay at your parents' house, so they can all be protected together. Her mother needs her now."

Grayson scoffed. "Yeah, good luck telling her that. I already tried that, and she shot me down. She wants to be involved in the rescue efforts. And frankly, I don't blame her."

Gabriel raised his eyebrows.

"I'll make sure she won't leave my side."

And not just so that whoever kidnapped their fathers wouldn't get a chance to hurt Monique.

"Fine. But we need to do something about her brothers. They don't even know yet what happened. And it bothers me that we can't get a hold of them."

"Me too."

"We might have to send a jet from the New York office to bring them home, once we figure out where exactly they are."

"That'll take too long. For all we know, they're under attack too."

"Then what?"

"I have an idea," Grayson said. He pulled out his cell phone, and selected a number. It rang once, then the call was answered. "Wesley?"

# 14

Monique's entire body coiled with anxiety, though she tried her best not to show outwardly how worried she was. She didn't want Grayson to think she was weak, or he'd insist on her staying with her mother at the Woodford mansion in Nob Hill. What if her brothers weren't simply out of cell phone range? What if something had happened to them? She wasn't stupid. She knew that if Cain had been the attackers' primary target, the rest of her family might be in danger too. However, that didn't explain why they hadn't abducted Faye too.

"We'll be there in a moment," Grayson said to her from the driver's seat of his sportscar.

She nodded, her heart still thundering in her ears, the tension in her body mounting. "And you think they can find them?"

"Yes, trust me."

A moment later, they pulled into the driveway of an Edwardian home on a little hillside. She followed Grayson up the steps that led to the entrance door. Before they reached it, a good-looking man with dark hair opened the door. She recognized his aura as that of a preternatural creature—a witch.

"I'm Wes," he greeted her and ushered them in. "Hey, Grayson. Come in."

Inside, they walked into the open-plan living/dining room, where a gorgeous redhead was strapping weapons to her belt. She too was a preternatural creature.

"You're the Stealth Guardian," Monique said.

"Yes, I'm Virginia. You must be Cain's daughter. I'm sorry about what you're going through right now." She gave her a kind smile, then looked at Grayson. "Hey, I'll be ready in a few minutes."

"Good, Cooper is on his way," Grayson said.

"Cooper? Why?" Virginia asked.

"He'll be going with you."

"I'll be accompanying Virginia," Wesley interrupted. "There's no need for Cooper to go with her."

"Sorry, Wes, but we need you here," Grayson protested. "You and Charles need to cook up some potions and spells for when we have to face the kidnappers."

"No fucking way!" Wesley barked. "You want me to let my wife face God-knows-what-kind-of-enemies alone? Fuck no!"

"That's why she'll have Cooper with her. He's one of our best hybrids. He's strong, and he's smart."

Virginia sighed. "Besides, I can take care of myself."

Wes grunted in displeasure and glared at Virginia. "I hate it when you do that!"

"Babe," Virginia cooed and put her hand on Wesley's shoulder. "You know this is a milk run for me, right?"

"I'm not saying you can't handle it," Wes said, his voice a little softer now. "I just worry when you're not here."

Virginia pressed a soft kiss to his lips. "I'll make it up to you when I'm back."

Wesley rolled his eyes. "You're manipulating me."

"I know." She chuckled. "And were the roles reversed, you'd do the same."

"Touché."

Virginia looked at Monique. "Thomas sent me the last known pings from David's and Zach's cell phones. They came from somewhere outside of Gstaad. He confirmed that a cell tower is out due to a storm that went through the area yesterday. Do you have any other information about what they were intending to do there?"

"When I talked to them the day before New Year's Eve, they said that they'd met a couple of women from New York who invited them to a remote cabin."

"Did they say whether the women were vampires or humans?"

"They didn't mention it."

"Okay, it shouldn't be too difficult to figure out who these women are and where that cabin is located. Gstaad isn't that big. We'll start at the Gstaad Palace, where your brothers were staying before leaving for the cabin. I'll get Pearce to check all lodgings in Gstaad for two American women from New York."

"Who's Pearce?" Monique asked.

"He's a Stealth Guardian like myself. He works out of the Baltimore compound. I figured Thomas and his team are busy enough here, and I didn't want to divert their resources to do something our own people can do."

"I appreciate it, Virginia," Monique said.

"Of course." Virginia shoved a dagger into her boot. "I still need photos of your brothers, so I can be sure that they are who they say they are."

Monique pulled her cell phone from her pocket and unlocked it. "Airdrop?"

"Works for me," Virginia said and took her cell phone from her pocket and swiped it.

There was a soft ping a moment later, and Virginia said, "Got 'em."

"How long will it take for you to get to Switzerland?" Monique asked curiously. She'd heard of the Stealth Guardians' portals that allowed them to teleport to countless places around the world, but had never been in one, or even seen one.

"A few seconds," Virginia replied. "We're lucky, there's a portal in a church in Gstaad, so that'll be the easy part. But it can take hours or even longer for us to get to whatever cabin David and Zach are stuck in, depending on the weather and the road conditions."

"I understand. And you'll be able to transport them all back in the portal? They won't get lost somewhere on the way?"

"As long as they're all holding on to me, I'll get them back here safe and sound."

The doorbell rang.

"Guess that's Cooper," Wesley said and walked into the hallway to let him in.

"Don't worry, Monique," Grayson said, putting a hand on her arm. "I've traveled in those portals before, and while your brothers might suffer from a bit of vertigo, it's quite safe for a vampire."

She appreciated his reassuring words and nodded silently.

"Hey guys," a young vampire hybrid with ultra-short dark hair and a muscled physique greeted them. He wore khakis and a flannel shirt and boots. His jacket was a thin windbreaker.

"You'll need a winter jacket," Grayson said pointing at him. "It's freezing cold in Switzerland."

"Oh," Cooper said, surprise on his face. "Guess I didn't get the whole message. I was only told to show up at Virginia's for a trip through the portal. And to come armed." He patted his windbreaker. "Small caliber semi-automatic with silver bullets, a stake, and a silver knife."

"I'll get you one of my jackets," Wes said quickly and opened a closet in the hallway.

"I'll brief you on the way," Virginia said to the hybrid. "Let's get going. It's already late afternoon in Switzerland. Sun's probably setting any moment. I wanna get there in time to get a lay of the land."

Wesley handed Cooper a thick jacket.

"Thanks, buddy," Cooper said and put it on, then zipped up.

Virginia slipped into a thick parka with a hoodie and shoved gloves into her pockets. "Let's go."

"Where is the portal?" Monique asked.

"In the basement," Wesley said and followed his wife down the stairs. "We built it about nine years ago when the Stealth Guardians recovered the *source dagger*. It's made it possible for new portals to be created."

"The *source dagger*?" Monique asked as she followed the others down into the basement.

"Yeah," Wes explained. "It's an old dagger forged in the Dark Days, and the only tool that can create a portal for Stealth Guardians to teleport. Before the source dagger was recovered, Stealth Guardians had to rely on the few portals that connected their compounds." He pointed to a plain brick wall. "This is it."

Despite the light on the ceiling illuminating the dingy space, Monique couldn't see anything that looked even remotely like a teleportation device. All she could see was a symbol etched in the stone. It looked like a dagger.

Before she could ask where the portal was, Virginia placed her palm on the symbol, and beneath it, the stone began to glow. All of a sudden, the stone wall was gone. Behind it was a small dark cave. Monique stared at it in disbelief.

"It's quite something, isn't it?" Grayson said next to her.

"Be careful, babe," Wesley said to Virginia and pulled her into his arms.

"I'm always careful." They kissed for a brief moment.

Virginia was about to step into the portal, when Monique remembered something. "Wait."

She looked over her shoulder.

"My brothers don't know you. They have to be sure they can trust you. Take your cell phone and record me."

Virginia nodded. "Good idea." She pulled out her cell phone and pointed it at Monique. "Go ahead."

"David, Zach, you can trust Virginia and Cooper with your life. They will bring you back home. I love you."

"All right," Virginia said and shoved her cell phone back into her pocket.

Cooper stepped into the portal with her, and Monique noticed that Virginia grabbed the young hybrid's hand.

A moment later, Monique was staring at a brick wall again. "Wow."

"I got used to it," Wes said with a smile. Then he cast his gaze at Grayson. "So, what's the plan?"

"Call Charles, and have him meet you in your lab. Since you can't scry for a vampire, you can't help us find where they're holding Cain and Samson. But we'll need whatever weapons you can come up with that work on vampires—spells, potions, anything that might help us knock them out before they see us coming."

"Okay, we can do that."

"So you and Charles, you're both witches?" Monique asked as they walked upstairs again.

"Yes, and we're both very accomplished," Wes claimed.

"So there's no scrying for vampires?" Monique said. "Are you familiar with voodoo?"

"I know some voodoo magic, but that's not my strong side."

"I've heard there's a location spell that voodoo practitioners can perform," Monique said, remembering something an acquaintance in New Orleans had mentioned once. "But I don't have any details."

"Do you remember who told you that?" Grayson asked, interested.

"It was an older woman who took care of the drycleaning of the guards' uniforms. I should be able to find her contact info."

"It's worth a shot," Grayson said. "Right, Wes?"

"Sure. If I can talk to her about what's needed for the spell, we can try it out." Then he looked back at Grayson. "So, I'm assuming that neither Delilah nor Faye have been communicating with their mates via their telepathic bond?"

"No, they haven't been able to. We're assuming that they're unconscious. They knocked Faye out with what we believe was dead man's blood."

"That's bad mojo. It acts like a poison in a vampire's body. Same can be accomplished with silver nitrate. Though if you wanna keep somebody alive, you would use dead man's blood rather than silver nitrate," Wesley said.

"Why is that?"

"Because dead man's blood won't kill you. It's perfect for prolonged torture without the risk of silver nitrate, which will eventually kill the subject. So, if the kidnappers want to prevent Cain and Samson from communicating with their mates, they would use dead man's blood. It knocks the person out, and makes them weak. Not sure how high the dosage has to be to prevent them from using their telepathic bond, but I assume the kidnappers would inject them regularly, maybe even use an IV to administer it. Though, of course, when it comes to Samson, it's even easier. Pump him full with any human blood other than Delilah's, and he'll be in the same state as if they gave him dead man's blood. With the difference that he would eventually die."

"Hmm. I know."

"Well, I'll speak to Charles about any possible location spells, and if you, Monique, speak to that voodoo practitioner, put her in touch with me."

"Thanks for your help, Wes," Monique said, casting him a grateful smile.

# 15

"What was it like to teleport?" Monique asked.

They were back in Grayson's car, heading to Scanguards' headquarters in the Mission. Traffic was still light since most people had the day off, and many stores were closed.

"A little disorienting. The first time I traveled through one of the portals, it felt as if I was in a dryer being thrown around like a wet sock. But I got used to it. I spent a couple of years with the Stealth Guardian compound in Baltimore."

"Doing what?"

"Helping out. Learning from them. Killing demons. I wasn't the only one. Ryder was there too. He's Maya and Gabriel's son. Scanguards made a deal with the Stealth Guardians. In exchange for them helping us out, Ryder and I worked with them, helping where our skills were useful."

"The Stealth Guardians, is it true they can make themselves invisible and walk through walls?"

Grayson smiled. "Yep, it's true, and not only that. They can also make others invisible either by touch or with their minds. It's a pretty handy skill. And you don't feel anything."

"What do you mean?"

"They've made me and Ryder invisible countless times, and I could still see myself, and I didn't feel any different. If they hadn't told me that I was invisible, I wouldn't have known."

"And did you also walk through walls with them?"

He shook his head. "No. That's something only the Stealth Guardians can do."

"I can see now why you want them as your allies. They can approach an enemy without being seen, and get into locked spaces."

"And they're good people. They're sworn to protect humans, just like Scanguards."

He still looked back at his time with the Stealth Guardians in Baltimore with fondness. He'd learned so much from them, and fighting demons had been a highlight in his time training as a warrior. He'd made friends with the men in Baltimore, and with their women too. He had nothing but respect for them, and knew he could count on them if he needed their help. That's why he hadn't hesitated to ask Virginia for this big favor.

"Virginia is a great warrior," he said and glanced at Monique. "She'll find your brothers."

"Thank you for doing this for me."

He didn't know how to respond to her words of gratitude. It turned out he didn't need to. His cell phone rang. He pressed the accept button on his steering wheel.

"Yeah?"

"Hey Grayson, it's Luther."

"Hey, Luther."

"About your request to get access to the prison records, I've run into a problem."

"What problem?"

"The new council president says he can't just allow any civilian access to the prison's database."

"Doesn't he know that my father was kidnapped?" Grayson snapped, outraged.

"He knows. But apparently, he and Samson don't see eye to eye."

"Fuck!" Grayson cursed. They needed access to those records, because the chances that an ex-VCON was involved in the kidnapping were high. The attackers weren't amateurs. They were hardened criminals who'd come prepared. "Then we have no choice but to hack into their system. Thomas can—"

"Not happening," Luther interrupted. "It would take Thomas days to hack into it. The last security update made sure of that."

"Fuck, fuck, fuck!" Grayson cursed again. "And you? Don't you have access?"

Luther sighed. "My access is limited, and I can only see that part of the database that covers the VCONs housed at the Grass Valley facility. And even for that, I'll have to physically be at Grass Valley. I mean, I'll do it, no problem, but that only gets us part of the data. For all we know, the attackers weren't local. They could be from New Orleans, particularly if Cain was the main target."

"Luther?" Monique said.

"Who's that?"

"This is Monique, Cain's daughter," she said.

"Hey, sorry I don't have any better news."

"Not your fault. So that new council president, is that Bill Wheeler?"

"Yeah, that's him. Why?"

"I know his wife. She's originally from New Orleans. She owes me a favor. I'll talk to her."

"Good luck," Luther said. "Talk later."

"Later," Grayson said and disconnected the call. He cast Monique a sideways glance. "You have friends in high places?"

"Occasionally, it's useful to be a princess." She unlocked her cell phone and navigated to a number, then put the phone to her ear.

"Clarice? It's Monique," Monique said and let out a sob.

Grayson whipped his head in her direction, surprised to see Monique crying.

"I don't know whether you heard, but my dad was kidnapped this morning, and Mom is badly injured. We're not sure she's gonna make it."

That was a blatant lie, because he'd seen with his own eyes that Faye had looked fine after Maya had given her human blood, but Monique continued undeterred.

"I'm so scared. I don't know what to do… yes… I know… so terrible." She let out another sob. "But there were witnesses to the kidnapping, and we know that the attackers were vampires, most likely ex-VCONs, you know, vampire convicts. If only we could get all their mugshots, so we can find them and save my father, but I'm told that civilians like myself can't access the database. I would never ask, but…" There was a pause, during which Monique listened. "Yes, oh would you really? I don't know how to thank you. You're the sweetest person in the world, Clarice." Another sob, and Monique said, "Thank you."

She disconnected the call, then looked at him with a smirk. "She'll send the data via a secured link to my cell."

Her voice was totally normal again, and there were no tears. She'd been acting. And boy, her sobs had looked and sounded real.

"You… uhm…" He shook his head.

"Oh, the tears?" She made a dismissive hand movement. "I can turn them on whenever I need them."

"Good to know. And Clarice, is she really gonna get us the data?"

"She's a total softy, sucker for a sob story. And her mate can't say no to her." Monique winked. "She's very persuasive."

"She'll withhold sex and blood until he gives in, won't she?" Grayson guessed.

"Whatever works."

"And they say that women are the weaker sex."

"We are when we need to be."

"Uh, huh."

Despite having seen Monique's manipulation skills in action, he couldn't help but admire her. She was ruthless when she wanted something and used dirty tricks until she got it. He was glad that they were on the same side, because he didn't want an adversary like Monique: smart, strong, and cunning.

"We need to go to your parents' house," Monique demanded. "When I get the link, we can download the data onto a computer there so your mom and mine can go through the photos."

"No problem."

He made an illegal U-turn at the next intersection and headed for Nob Hill.

"We should be there in about twenty minutes."

He reached for her hand and squeezed it. To his surprise, she didn't withdraw it, and instead, held on to it. There was nothing sexual about the touch. It was a gesture between two friends who showed their support for each other during a difficult time. There was no need for words. They were both thinking about the same thing: how to rescue their fathers.

# 16

The Woodford residence was guarded like a fortress. Two human bodyguards were standing sentry outside the home. Grayson knew both of them. They let him and Monique pass with a short greeting. In the foyer, they ran into Patrick.

"Hey," Patrick said, patting him on the shoulder. "Any news yet?"

Grayson shook his head. "Nothing. How's Mom?"

His brother shrugged. "Physically she's fine. But she's an emotional wreck." His gaze strayed to Monique. "You must be Monique. Faye mentioned that you weren't home when the attack happened."

"Yeah. You're Patrick, right? How's my mother doing?"

"Putting on a brave face." He motioned to the end of the hallway. "They are in the study looking through Scanguards' database. I'm on my way to HQ. Thomas needs more people to go through traffic cams and security footage."

"We'll see you there shortly," Grayson said. "Monique managed to get us access to the prison database. We're just here to set it up for them to look at."

Just before they'd parked outside the house, Monique's cell phone had pinged with a message from Clarice. She had indeed been able to convince her husband to grant them access to the database of all VCONs in North America.

Patrick left, and Monique let her gaze roam. "So this is where you grew up."

"Yes. Though when we were little, the house was half the size. But later, my father bought the house next to ours and combined the two homes and turned it into one. It's about 6000 square feet in total."

"But you decided to move out nevertheless?"

"After I came back from my stint at the Stealth Guardian compound in Baltimore, I just never moved back in. I wanted to have my own place. And the loft suits me."

"Hey, guys!"

Grayson turned at the sound of Isabelle's voice. She descended from the stairs. "Hey, Isa."

She forced a smile, and he noticed the strain she was under. He took a step toward her and embraced her. For a moment, nobody said anything, then Isabelle peeled herself out of his arms and sighed.

"Thanks, Grayson." She smiled at Monique and reached for her. "Hi, Monique, sorry we didn't get a chance to properly say hello earlier." She put her arms around Monique. "Have you spoken to your brothers yet?"

"No. I can't get through to them." Monique motioned to him. "Grayson arranged for a Stealth Guardian to travel to Switzerland to look for them."

Isabelle cast him a quizzical look.

"Virginia," Grayson said. "She took Cooper with her."

"That's good," Isabelle said. "Virginia is one of the best warriors. She can kick anybody's ass. And Cooper is great."

"I hope they'll find them soon," Monique said. "I haven't told Mom yet that I can't get a hold of them. I don't want her to worry even more."

"If she asks, just tell her they're on their way back," Isabelle suggested. "Sometimes a little white lie is kinder than the truth."

"You may be right." Monique forced a smile.

"Where are all the other guards?" Grayson asked.

"Orlando is in the study with Mom, Faye, and William. William is healing. He'll be at his full strength in a few hours. One of the vampire guards, Conrad, is upstairs in your old room, where he has a view of the street, and Robbie is in the master bedroom overlooking the backyard. When the sun sets, vampire guards will replace the two human guards out front."

"Good. Orlando and the two vampire guards upstairs should be relieved at sunset too so they can rest," Grayson suggested.

"Not gonna happen."

Grayson looked to the kitchen door, from which Orlando suddenly emerged. "What's not gonna happen?"

He approached. "I'm not leaving my post. I'm staying here until Samson is back." The massive vampire folded his arms over his chest and squared his stance.

"That can take days," Grayson said in a low voice, not wanting the sound to carry all the way to the study. "You need rest just like everybody else."

"I won't leave, and there's nothing you or anybody else can do or say." Orlando narrowed his eyes.

Annoyed at the giant's stubbornness, Grayson grunted. "I said—"

"Let me propose a compromise," Isabelle interrupted.

To his surprise, Orlando's expression softened, when he looked at Isabelle. The tension in his jaw seemed to subside.

"You can stay at the house, if you agree to sleep in one of the guestrooms—"

"I don't need to sleep!" Orlando protested.

"—for at least six hours," Isabelle continued undeterred. "And while you rest, we'll have an additional bodyguard stationed at the house."

Orlando grunted into his non-existent beard. "Hmm."

Grayson had to suppress a smirk. Apparently, Isabelle knew exactly how to put a vampire double her size in his place.

"Deal or no deal?"

Another grunt from Orlando, but then he nodded. "Fine." He turned on his heel and marched to the end of the hallway. There, he opened the door to the study and disappeared.

"Stubborn idiot." Isabelle shook her head. "He's bossing everybody around here as if he owned the place. I really don't know why Dad hired him in the first place. He's got no manners."

Grayson chuckled. "Well, looks like you've got him under control."

"And manners aren't necessary," Monique added, "when you're as big and strong as that guy. It's not like anybody is gonna pick a fight with him for being ill-mannered."

"Isn't that the truth," Isabelle replied.

"Isa, can we set up an extra computer in the dining room, so we can download the prison data?" Grayson asked.

"Let me grab my computer," Isabelle said and walked upstairs.

When she was gone, Grayson turned to Monique and bridged the distance between them with two steps. "How are you holding up?"

"I'm fine."

He shook his head. "No, how're you really doing?" He put his fingers under her chin and tipped it up.

"The truth?" she asked, her voice low. She met his eyes. "I'm scared shitless that I'll lose my father and will never be able to take back what I said to him the last time I saw him."

"I feel the same way." He pressed his forehead to hers. "We'll get them back."

Or die trying.

# 17

*Gstaad, Switzerland*

It was dark by the time Virginia and Cooper reached the Gstaad Palace, which looked like a small castle with turrets rather than a five-star hotel. Just like the rest of the town, it was brightly lit and still decked out with Christmas decorations. This was the hotel where David and Zach Montague had been staying until the morning of New Year's Eve.

Cooper unzipped his thick jacket as he and Virginia entered the hotel lobby. Outside, it had been colder than he'd ever experienced, but inside the hotel it felt balmy. Traveling from San Francisco to Gstaad via the portal in Virginia's home had taken only a few seconds, though it had felt much longer. He'd felt nauseous, but no way in hell would he admit that to anybody. If Grayson and Ryder had used the portals repeatedly while working with the Stealth Guardians in Baltimore, and hadn't complained about the disorienting weightless feeling, then he wouldn't complain either.

"How can people live in such a climate?" Cooper asked with a sideways glance at Virginia.

"Spoken like a true Californian." She smirked.

"Let's do this," Cooper said with a nod at Virginia as he approached the rustic reception, while Virginia headed for the restrooms.

Behind the front desk, three staff members were working, two were young women, one an older man.

"Hi, ma'am," he said with a broad smile, addressing the pretty woman with the dark pixie haircut.

She smiled back at him. "Checking in?"

"No, I'm afraid I'm supposed to meet up with my two friends, who were staying at your hotel, but I'm two days late because of the storm…" He sighed. "Thing is, we were supposed to go to a cabin together, but I don't know where that cabin is, and how to get there. And there's no cell phone coverage, so I can't get a hold of them."

"Oh, yes, the storm knocked out our cell tower for a while, but it's back already."

He grimaced. "Still can't reach them. I wonder if you have any idea where they were heading?"

"You said they were guests here?"

He nodded.

"Names?"

"David and Zach Montague."

"Oh, I think I remember them. Americans, right?"

"Yes, from New Orleans."

She typed something on her keyboard, and Cooper inhaled deeply. He picked up Virginia's scent close by. It now was strongest near the receptionist. Virginia had made herself invisible and stepped behind the woman to look over her shoulder into the monitor.

"Hmm. All I can see is that they checked out early in the morning of New Year's Eve."

"Did they mention where they were going?"

"I'm afraid I wasn't on duty, when they checked out."

Cooper glanced at the two other staff members. "Maybe one of your colleagues checked them out?"

She looked at the screen and shook her head. "Franz checked them out. I'm afraid he's off duty today."

"Thanks for trying."

He walked away and waited near a corridor leading to the restrooms. It took a few minutes until Virginia came out of the ladies' room and joined him.

"I got her password, and used a computer in the office behind the front desk. She's right, they checked out the morning of New Year's Eve. I found a charge for a car service for the day of departure that the concierge arranged for them."

"Excellent. And the two women from New York that invited them to that cabin? Any trace of them?"

"No. I checked every female who checked out on New Year's Eve. There weren't many. None were Americans in the right age range."

"Let's check with the car service. They should have a record of where David and Zach were dropped off."

They'd just crossed the street, when Virginia's cell phone rang.

She looked at the display. "It's Pearce." She answered it. "Hey, Pearce. You've got good news for me?"

Standing close to Virginia, Cooper's sensitive vampire hearing picked up Pearce's voice.

"I have no records of two women from New York having checked into any hotels or bed-and-breakfasts in Gstaad."

Virginia's forehead furrowed. "Then where else would they have been staying?"

"Probably some private lodgings. I did find that two American women in their twenties flew into Bern. But they weren't from New York, they came from Alabama, though they changed planes at JFK."

Cooper exchanged a surprised look with Virginia. "Hey Pearce, it's Cooper. Were those the only American women who fit the age profile?"

"I'm afraid so. So, unless the two women who invited David and Zach to a cabin have been in Switzerland for more than just a couple of weeks, it has to be those two: Sharleen Harlow and Barbie Franklin."

"Thanks, Pearce."

"Pearce," Virginia added. "Do me a favor: run their credit cards and find out where they used them last. And check their backgrounds."

"Give me a few minutes. I'll call you right back."

Virginia shoved her cell phone back into her pocket. "If those are the women David and Zach met, then why would they lie about where they were from? And how would they even pull it off? David and Zach would recognize their accents easily."

"Lots of people are good at pulling off different accents. Actors do it all the time," Cooper said, shrugging.

He met Virginia's gaze. "You're right. Actors learn it so they can slip into different roles."

"You don't think—?" He didn't finish his sentence.

"That's exactly what I think."

"Fuck! If they were hired to lure them somewhere remote, David and Zach would have been unprepared for an attack... We could already be too late."

"We'd better find out where the car service dropped them off," Virginia said.

It didn't take long to access the records of the car service the hotel used. Cooper had to admit that Virginia's ability to make herself invisible was handy. A few moments after getting an address, they were sitting in a stolen four-wheel drive heading south.

It was pitch-black on the street that was still covered in snow. Luckily, the car they'd stolen was equipped with chains, and the gas tank was full. The headlights penetrated the darkness, but it started snowing again, and it was hard to see where the road ended and the wilderness began.

Cooper was driving, thankful for his superior vampire vision. He drove fast.

Virginia's phone rang. She set it to speaker mode. "Pearce? What have you got for us?"

"The two American women are adult actresses."

"Adult what?"

"Porn stars," Pearce replied, the sound cutting out for a moment. "...their agent and pretended I wanted to hire them. I was told they're currently on a job abroad."

"Oh fuck!" Cooper cursed. "You think they were hired to lure David and Zach to catch them off guard?"

There was some crackling in the line, then Pearce's voice was back. "...assume that. Be care—" Pearce cut out completely.

"Pearce? You there?" Virginia asked. "Pearce?" She looked at her cell phone. "I just lost the signal."

"Fuck!"

"Cooper, step on it. There should be a fork in the road in about two miles."

"Okay, almost there. Left or right?"

"Right."

The turnoff came too quickly, and Cooper had to turn the steering wheel hard to the right to make it. The back of the car spun out, but he managed to keep control of the car.

"In another three miles there should be a turnoff to the left."

There were no streetlights anywhere. Cooper could only rely on the headlights of the car capturing any street signs, but the falling snow reflected the headlights back at him, making it look like the road before him moved toward him.

"I hate snow," he ground out.

"Yeah, right now I do too," Virginia confessed. Then she suddenly pointed to the left. "There."

Cooper stepped on the brake. He focused on the small street sign, but couldn't read what was written on it. Snow covered most of the writing. He took the turnoff. There was a sharp incline, but the chains on the wheels made it possible to follow the road until it suddenly ended.

"That must be it," Virginia said.

In front of them was a cabin. From its chimney, white smoke rose into the dark night sky. Cooper shut off the car's engine and jumped out. The snow crunched under his boots. Virginia was already a few steps ahead of him, and he caught up with her. He noticed that Virginia had already pulled her dagger, and he now reached for his gun too. It was loaded with small-caliber silver bullets.

There was light coming from a window, but the curtains were drawn, preventing them from looking inside. Cooper exchanged a look with Virginia, and silently, they walked to the front door. When they reached it, he realized immediately that it wasn't closed all the way.

His heart began to thunder. Nobody would leave a door ajar in this weather, wasting the precious heat supplied by the woodfire. This wasn't good. Not good at all.

Cooper pushed the door open another couple of inches so he could peer inside. He saw an overturned lamp, a broken wine bottle, and glass chards on the floor. Flickering light illuminated the wooden floor in the room, reflecting in a pool of blood. Shock coursed through his body, and his fangs instantly lengthened. He moved the door another inch, allowing him to see more, when he saw gray ash covering a dark carpet. In the corner of his eye, he perceived a movement, and ripped the door open fully, his gun pointed at the person charging at him.

Fuck!

# 18

"The waiting is driving me crazy," Monique said.

She and Grayson were back at Scanguards' HQ. Monique had left a message for Delphine, the voodoo practitioner in New Orleans, but hadn't received a call back yet.

William had confirmed that he'd contacted the palace in New Orleans and given them instructions to send the database of former and current employees as well as clan members to Faye's email address, so the three of them could look through the photos to see if their attackers were among them.

Three of the kidnappers' vans had been found abandoned in the city, and several teams had inspected the vans to see if the kidnappers had left anything incriminating behind. However, no clues as to the whereabouts of Samson and Cain had been found.

With every hour that passed, Monique was becoming more anxious. It felt like nothing was moving forward. No progress was being made. The sun had set just a short while earlier.

"There's nothing we can do right now," Grayson said with a sigh. "Thomas's teams are combing through the footage."

"We can help with that," Monique insisted and looked at Thomas and Eddie, who were both staring into their monitors, just like two dozen other employees who were in the computer lab on one of the lower floors.

"You should rest," Thomas said.

"Maybe we can help with something else?" Monique asked.

Grayson took her hands into his. "Everybody is doing what they do best. Your mother and mine are still looking through the database, hoping they'll recognize somebody. We can't help them with that. We'd be better off resting for a few hours, so that we're ready once we have a location."

"I just feel so useless right now." And she hated feeling like that. She needed to do something, to contribute to the rescue efforts, but nothing had panned out so far. "I wish we'd at least have news of my brothers. Why is it taking so long?"

"You said yourself that they went to a remote cabin. It'll take Virginia and Cooper a while to find that cabin, and to get there. Don't forget that they arrived there just as the sun set in Switzerland. Depending on the weather situation there…"

"I know that," she said. "I'm just worried. Why has Virginia not called us yet?"

"Let me try her." Grayson pulled his cell phone from his pocket and scrolled through his contacts. He hit the number, then put the phone to his ear. A moment later, he shook his head and put the phone away. "Goes straight to voicemail. She's probably out of cell tower range in the mountains. That could be good news. Maybe she and Cooper have already reached the cabin."

Monique forced herself to nod. "I hope you're right."

"Come, let's get out of here."

Grayson took her arm and ushered her to the door. "Thomas, call me the minute you've got something actionable."

"Will do," Thomas replied without taking his eyes off the monitor.

A few minutes later, they shot out of the underground garage in Grayson's sportscar. Monique remained silent, her mind spinning, her worries about her brothers and her father intensifying. Every possible what-if scenario played out in her mind. When the car finally slowed, and Grayson drove into a garage, she realized that he hadn't driven them to the Woodford residence. Instead, they'd arrived at his loft in the Financial District.

"I thought we were going to your parents' home."

"Neither of us would be able to relax there. Besides, your mother doesn't know that we haven't reached your brothers yet. The moment she looks at you, she would know. And I don't think she needs any more worries."

Monique nodded. "You're right."

She didn't want to face her mother, because she couldn't be strong for her right now, when she was close to breaking down herself.

"Come," Grayson said.

They got out of the car, and Grayson took her travel bag out of the trunk. Moments later, they were inside his loft, and the door shut behind them. Silence greeted them, and Monique took a deep breath.

She followed Grayson into the open-plan kitchen, where he opened the refrigerator and took out two bottles of blood. He handed her one.

"Here, you need your strength." He twisted the cap open and started drinking.

Monique opened her bottle, and did the same. When the viscous red liquid coated her tongue and throat, she felt her cells awaken with new energy. Her entire body seemed to revitalize. Her senses sharpened, and her mind became clearer.

She emptied the bottle and set it on the kitchen counter. "Thank you. I needed that."

Grayson set his empty bottle down next to hers and took her hand. "Come."

She allowed him to lead her to the large sectional sofa in the living area. He sat down and pulled her on his lap, so she straddled him.

"What are you doing?" Monique asked, but didn't try to get up. She liked being close to him.

"I want to hold you," he murmured and pulled her to his chest.

She put her arms around him and pressed her cheek to his. The embrace felt comforting and made some of the tension in her body seep from her.

"Do you believe that we'll find your dad and mine soon?"

"Yes," he murmured. "Our best people are working on this. We will find them, I promise you. And then we both get to apologize to them."

Monique pulled back and looked at his face. "You too? What did you say to your father?"

"I told him to stay out of my life, or he would regret it." He gave a light shake of his head. "Now I'm the one who's regretting it. It was a stupid fight. I was out of line. And for what? Because I didn't even want to meet with you, just because the idea was my father's." He sucked in a breath. "When in reality, Dad really does know what's good for me." He pinned her with his eyes. "*You* are good for me."

"We barely know each other," she said though his words made her feel warm inside. But she didn't want to read too much into her relationship with Grayson. She couldn't trust her own feelings right now, not with the rollercoaster that she was on.

"Then we'll have to make an effort to get to know each other better." He lifted his hand and stroked his knuckles over her cheek. "Don't you agree?"

His gaze lowered, and she realized that he was looking at her lips. She inhaled, taking in his masculine scent, and the fact that they needed to rest was suddenly forgotten. She was drawn to Grayson like a bee to the sweet nectar of a flower. Maybe their fathers had been right after all to try to bring them together. It couldn't hurt to get to know Grayson better. Nobody had to know.

"But we won't tell anybody about what's happening between us," she conceded. In case this didn't work out, she didn't want to have to answer anybody's questions.

"Just you and I. Nobody needs to know about this." Grayson put his hand on her nape and drew her closer to his face, until their lips were almost touching. "I've never been with a woman like you."

"Like how?"

"Strong, demanding, bossy."

"You think I'm bossy?"

"Oh, hell, yeah. And I love it."

He slanted his lips over hers, not demanding but coaxing her to part them, waiting for her to invite him in. He gave her control over what was going to happen. And she needed that right now, needed to be in control of something, because everything else in her life was spinning out of control.

Monique licked over the seam of Grayson's lips and felt them part.

"Oh, babe," he murmured, before she delved into his mouth to explore him.

~ ~ ~

Grayson welcomed Monique's tongue lapping against his, his heart beating rapidly at the sensual contact. Monique was in charge, taking from him what she needed right now, and he couldn't have been happier about it. Or more turned on. He'd always been the dominant partner during sex, thinking that it was what every woman expected from him. But right now, it felt liberating to follow Monique's lead.

Her hands were in his hair, her fingers massaging his scalp, making him shiver with pleasure. He slid one hand onto her lower back, pulling her closer to his body. She rocked her pelvis against him, and at the contact, a bolt of electricity charged through his cock, making him moan out his pleasure.

"You're hard," she murmured at his lips, her hot breath ghosting over his face.

"Your fault," he managed to reply, before she intensified the kiss, and silenced him.

Fuck, this woman could kiss, and she wasn't even licking his fangs, yet his arousal was already spiking. If she continued in the same manner, he would come without even undressing. Knowing he had to stop her, he ripped his mouth from hers.

Her eyes shimmering golden, she looked at him. "Something wrong?"

"You're making me come, babe," he murmured. "And I'd prefer being inside you when that happens."

She smiled mischievously. "I thought you had more self-control."

"So did I." With both hands on her ass now, he pulled her pelvis to his and rubbed his hard-on against her. "But it looks like I'm fresh out of self-control."

"Then maybe we should get undressed."

"That's a good idea." He smirked and grabbed the seam of her tight sweater. He pulled it over her head and tossed it on the couch. She wore not a stitch beneath it. "You're not wearing a bra."

"How very observant of you."

He dipped his head to her cleavage. "Yeah, Scanguards trained me well." He sank his lips onto one breast and licked over her nipple.

"Did they teach you that at Scanguards too?" Her voice was soft, teasing, her arousal evident in its cadence.

He let go of her nipple. "No. Private lessons." He captured her other nipple and drew it into his mouth. It turned hard instantly, and a soft moan came from Monique.

"You must have had a good tutor."

"Mmm."

While he continued to lavish her breasts with caresses, Monique began to free him from his shirt. He shrugged out of it, then pulled her closer again, their chests touching now. The skin-on-skin contact sent his heartbeat into the stratosphere, and pumped more blood into his cock.

When he felt her hands on his waistband, opening the button, he rose with her in his arms, and put her on her feet. Quickly, he rid himself of the remainder of his clothes, while Monique slipped out of hers. The moment they were both naked, Grayson let himself fall back on the sofa and pulled Monique back onto his lap, making her straddle him.

He brushed his lips over hers in a featherlight touch. He wanted tenderness tonight; he wanted gentle and slow. He slipped his hand to her sex, stroking her slowly, her juices coating his fingers.

"I love how soft you are," he whispered at her parted lips, inhaling her breath. "Yet so strong."

Monique raised herself onto her knees, adjusting her position to hover above his cock. "I want to feel you inside me."

"Then take what you want. I'm all yours."

"Good." She pulled his upper lip between hers and bit down gently without breaking his skin.

His cock jerked at the sensual bite, and a gasp escaped him. "Fuck, babe, you're driving me crazy." The lust coursing through his body had him teetering on the edge of a monumental climax, and he wasn't even inside her yet.

"Mmm." She hummed softly, while she lowered herself, taking his cock into her tight and wet sheath, her interior muscles clamping around him like a vice.

He dropped his head back onto the backrest of the couch and let out a long breath. He raked his gaze over Monique's gorgeous body, enjoying the sight of her exquisite breasts as they moved up and down, side to side, while she rode him slowly as if he were a stallion she had to break in. And maybe he was just that, a stallion its new owner needed to tame.

One hand on her hip, the other on her lower back, he pulled her to him until her breasts were right in front of his face. They bounced happily, and he captured one of them and sucked on it.

Monique moaned softly, her head falling back as she gave herself to this moment, the long column of her neck exposed as if in invitation. His fangs lengthened at the tantalizing sight, but he held back. He wanted more of this, more of the slow and sensual lovemaking that they were engaging in now. And if he bit her, it would be over too soon.

He kissed her breasts, kneaded them, licked her silky skin, inhaled her sweet scent. Her breasts fit perfectly into his palms, and her tight sex was a fitting home for his cock. They moved in synch as if they'd been lovers for a long time, as if they knew exactly what the other needed. There was no rush to reach their climax, no need to reach the finish line just yet, because the journey itself was the reward.

Small pearls of perspiration covered Monique's soft skin. As they mixed with his own sweat, they created a unique aroma that drugged him, while all he could think of was making love to this woman for the rest of his life. That thought should scare him and make him want to withdraw, but no such feeling took hold of him. The idea of never touching another woman but Monique didn't frighten him. Instead, it filled him with excitement.

Monique leaned closer, her mouth at his ear. "Your cock is perfect. I love the way you fill me."

"Oh, babe, you can ride my cock anytime you want to." He would never be able to deny her.

"Good, 'cause I need this." Soft moans rolled over her lips, before she added, "Can you do something for me, please?"

"Anything you want."

"Bite me."

Her demand almost made him climax right there and then. "Fuck yeah, babe!"

"But not my neck," she whispered.

"Where?"

She raised her head and drew back, then thrust her breasts toward him.

He realized instantly what she wanted and met her eyes. "Oh, babe..." He captured one breast in his palm and guided the nipple to his mouth. Trembling with excitement, he licked over the hard nipple, then drove his fangs into her firm flesh and began to suck. Monique shuddered, and her pussy spasmed around him, while his own arousal spiked as her blood coated his throat.

Monique cried out in ecstasy. The waves of her orgasm sent visible shudders through her body, pushing him over the edge. His orgasm hit him like a massive ocean wave, drowning him in a sea of bliss and satisfaction.

Everything around him seemed to fade into the distance. All he could feel was Monique. He removed his fangs from her breast and licked over the puncture wounds, before lifting his head to look at her.

Her lashes were fluttering like the wings of a butterfly, her breath uneven, her heartbeat racing. "Grayson, I... that was..." She licked her lips, starting again, "I never thought it could be so good."

He brought his face to hers. "Monique, babe, you're the most amazing woman I've ever been with." And he'd been with many. "I can't get enough of you."

"Then we'll just have to repeat this," she murmured and smiled.

"Good, 'cause I'm in the mood for a lot more." He grabbed her hips and made her move up and down on him, while he thrust upward, his cock still hard despite his climax.

Monique moaned softly and put her hand on his nape, caressing him. "I'm all yours."

Farther below, her hips moved in synch with his, and she held him tightly so he couldn't escape, even if he wanted to—which he didn't.

# 19

A persistent sound pulled her from her slumber. Monique opened her eyes and realized immediately that she'd fallen asleep on the couch with Grayson holding her in his arms. The sound repeated, and she recognized it as the ringtone of her cell phone. She sat up quickly, and Grayson did the same.

"Yours?" he asked.

"Yeah." She grabbed her pants and pulled her cell phone from her pocket, hitting the accept button before she even saw who was calling, afraid that the call would go to voicemail. "Yes?"

"Monique?"

She recognized the familiar voice in a split second. "Zach? Oh my God, are you and David okay?"

Grayson gestured at the phone, and she understood and put the call on speakerphone so he could listen in.

"I was so worried about you two. What happened?"

*In the mountains south of Gstaad, Switzerland – several hours earlier*
The rented house to which Sharleen and Barbie had invited Zach and David Montague for New Year's Eve and New Year's Day was a cozy two-story chalet with a rustic great room and a small kitchen on the first floor, and two bedrooms and a bathroom on the second floor. The log cabin was located about an hour south of Gstaad, tucked away in a forest in the middle of nowhere. The big wood-burning fireplace heated the entire house, and the Christmas decorations inside the home gave it a romantic and festive feel.

Zach was glad that Monique had decided not to join them, because she would definitely have been the third wheel. And having to listen to her two brothers having marathon sex with two girls from New York would have annoyed the hell out of her.

Zach turned to the side, but the space next to him in bed was empty. "Sharleen?"

Nobody replied. Most likely she'd gone downstairs to get something to drink. He sat up in bed, grabbed a pair of shorts and put them on, then left the room barefoot. He walked down the wooden stairs. Despite being scantily clad, he didn't feel cold. The fire was still burning in the fireplace, and as a vampire hybrid, he could tolerate the cold better than a human. A standing lamp was still lit in the great room, and light came from the open kitchen door.

"Sharleen?"

He walked to the door and took a step into the galley-style kitchen. The refrigerator door was open, obstructing his view, but he recognized Sharleen's slim legs peeking out from beneath.

"You're hungry?" he asked and walked closer.

She closed the refrigerator door, a bottle of water in one hand. She wore one of his shirts with only one button fastened. Her ample breasts and hard nipples were barely covered by the white fabric. She tossed him a coquettish smile.

"Just needed a drink. You're wearing me out."

She batted her eyelashes, and he knew she was only teasing him.

"Oh yeah?" He bridged the distance between them with a couple of steps and slid his hands onto her ass. Just like he'd assumed, she wasn't wearing any panties. "Then why are you running around the house half naked, when you know I have a hard time resisting that kind of temptation?"

"My mistake," she purred, and her lips formed into a sexy pout.

He squeezed her ass and yanked her to him. "And what if my brother or Barbie saw you like that? What then?"

"Then maybe I would have asked them to join us... you know... for a *ménage-à-quatre*."

Zach nearly choked on his own saliva. She was up for a foursome?

She chuckled. "Isn't that what you and your brother were hoping for when you took us up on our invitation?"

Was she for real? "Well, let's wake them, shall we? And see if they're game," he suggested, wondering if she would chicken out when push came to shove.

Sharleen moaned softly. "I'd like that." She pulled his head down to her cleavage. "But first, how about a quick one right here?"

He didn't need to be told twice. He spun her around and bent her over, her naked ass pointing at him, her breasts resting on the quartz countertop. He was about to free his cock from his shorts, when he heard a sound from the living room.

"We've got company."

He let go of her and walked to the open kitchen door. "David? You up?" What he saw made him curse. "Fuck!"

A big vampire stood in the living room, a gun in his hand. Behind him, another person entered the chalet.

"Vampire attack!" Zach yelled to warn his brother, already charging at the intruder.

The assailant aimed with his gun, but Zach dove out of the line of fire, snatching a chair in midflight, just as a shot rang out. Sharleen screamed a high-pitched scream. Zach flung the chair in the attacker's direction, while he landed hard on the wooden floor, sliding behind the dining table. The second intruder, whose aura identified him as another vampire, barreled toward him, the light from the fireplace reflecting on the silver knife in his left hand. In his belt, Zach saw a wooden stake.

Zach grabbed another chair and broke it, fashioning a makeshift wooden stake. Both attackers now barreled toward him. He grabbed the standing lamp next to him and tossed it toward the vampire with the gun, barely slowing him down.

He heard steps on the stairs, and hoped for reinforcements, but to his horror, it wasn't his brother descending from the second floor, but Barbie, dressed only in a short nightie. Where the fuck was David?

Zach collided with one of his attackers, and flung him against the wall, while the other guy aimed his gun again. Zach dove in the other direction, snatching a heavy vase and tossing it in the shooter's direction. One of the girls screamed, and another person charged into the chalet. In the corner of his eye, Zach recognized David carrying a stack of firewood, wearing only a pair of jeans and boots. He flung one heavy piece of wood at the vampire with the gun, making the guy whirl around toward David, while firing.

Meanwhile, the attacker with the silver knife was getting to his feet again, and Zach lunged for him, kicking his knee into the asshole's balls, then swiping his neck with his claws, leaving deep gashes, blood splattering on the floor. But the attacker's claws were out now too, as well as his fangs, and he snarled viciously. Zach, all vampire now, grabbed him with his claws, slicing deep into the guy's stomach. The asshole retaliated by swinging his arm holding the knife. It cut deep into Zach's side, the silver burning like acid. But the jerk would have to do better if he wanted him to give up the fight.

Another scream from one of the women reached his ears, but he had no time to look who needed help, because his attacker was lunging at him again. This time, Zach sidestepped him, then jumped behind him and plunged the makeshift stake into the vampire's back, aiming for the heart. For a split second, the vampire froze, then he dissolved into ash.

"David?"

Zach swept his eyes around the room, looking for his brother. He lay with his back on the floor, the large vampire with the gun above him. They were struggling for control of the weapon. And it looked like David was going to lose.

"Shit!"

Zach charged toward them, when he stumbled over something. He glanced down. Sharleen lay lifeless on the floor, blood gushing from her neck. Knowing he couldn't help her anymore, he lunged for the vampire, and slammed the makeshift stake into the bastard's back. At the same time, the gun went off. When the vampire dissolved into ash, Zach fell onto his brother, his hand jerking toward David. He stopped it just as the stake touched David's skin.

Zach rolled off his brother, his heart racing, his breath uneven. "Fuck!"

Next to him, David breathed hard and sat up. "Yeah, what the fuck was that?"

Labored breathing tore their gazes to the stairs. Barbie lay on the landing, holding a hand to her chest. She was bleeding profusely.

David ran to her. "Fuck!" He took her hand and looked at the wound beneath it. "Gunshot wound." He pulled her toward him and looked behind her. "No exit wound."

Zach knew what that meant. "Small-caliber, silver bullet."

"We've gotta get it out," David said, agreeing. "Barbie, just keep calm, we'll take care of you." Then he looked to where Sharleen lay on the floor.

Zach shook his head. It was too late to save Sharleen. She was already dead.

Barbie continued crying. "Nobody... was supposed... to get hurt," she wailed.

Zach snapped his gaze to her. "What?"

David stared at her in utter surprise. "What the fuck, Barbie? What was this about?"

Barbie shrieked, and suddenly collapsed. David caught her before she could hit her head on the stairs.

"She's breathing," he said.

"We can't let her die," Zach said.

"Agreed. She knows something about this attack. I'll give her some blood." David bit into his wrist.

Zach turned away to look at what was left of the two attackers: a whole lot of gray ash, a couple of cell phones, car keys, the gun, the silver knife, and a few coins. Why the fuck had they targeted him and David?

A sound at the door made him spin around. Another vampire! Fuck! He charged toward him, just as the intruder crossed the threshold, gun pointed.

"Zach, no!" a woman screamed, while he tackled the intruding vampire, or rather vampire hybrid. They crashed to the floor together. Zach pressed the silver knife he'd collected from the floor against the vampire hybrid's neck, making his skin sizzle.

"We're from Scanguards!" the woman yelled. "Monique sent us!"

Zach hesitated, and suddenly realized that the vampire hybrid he was fighting with was only defending himself, rather than attacking him.

"Who are you? Talk fast," Zach demanded, glancing up at the woman who stood in the door to the chalet. Her aura identified her as a preternatural creature, but she wasn't a vampire.

"We have a video message from your sister." She lifted her hand. "I'm gonna reach into my pocket to retrieve my cell phone."

He watched her closely as she pulled out her phone, unlocked it and tapped on it. Then she turned the screen so he could see it. It was indeed his sister on the video.

*"David, Zach, you can trust Virginia and Cooper with your life. They will bring you back home. I love you."*

Zach sat back on his haunches and released Cooper. "Fuck!"

"I'm Virginia, a Stealth Guardian. We're allied with Scanguards. And this young man is Cooper Montgomery, Yvette and Haven's son."

"Hey," Cooper said, and sat up.

Zach rose and offered his hand to help him up. "Hey, Cooper, sorry about that. But we just got attacked by two vampires. They killed one of the girls, and the other one is badly injured. Did you know this was gonna happen? Is that why you're here?"

"I think you might want to sit down for this," Cooper said with a serious look.

Fuck! Nothing good ever started with somebody saying to sit down.

*San Francisco – now*

"And the two girls? Were they in on it?" Monique asked after listening to her brothers recounting the attack on them.

Grayson was sitting next to her on the couch, his arm around her back, both of them still only partially dressed.

"After Virginia helped dig the silver bullet from Barbie's chest, and David healed her," Zach explained, "she told us that she and Sharleen were hired for what they thought was a surprise birthday present for David and me. They were supposed to invite us to this chalet, all expenses paid, and were to cater to all our sexual needs. Apparently the two worked as adult film actresses."

"Porn stars?" Grayson said, shaking his head.

"Yep. And we fell for it. Should've known it was too good to be true."

A grunt came through the line. Then David spoke. "I don't believe they knew that the people who hired them actually wanted us dead. That's why they wanted us in a remote area without cell phone reception. Because had we heard that Dad and Samson had been kidnapped, we would have taken every precaution and flown back to the States immediately."

"Did the surviving girl tell you who paid her?" Monique asked.

"I'm having Pearce dig into that," Virginia interrupted. "We should have an answer by the time we're back."

Monique exchanged a look with Grayson. "Good. Thanks, Virginia. David, Zach, I think the fact that you guys got attacked only confirms that the main target was Dad and not Samson. Somebody wants to wipe us out."

Grayson nodded. "Guys, how far away are you from the portal?"

"Virginia?" David asked.

"You can expect us in San Francisco in about forty-five minutes," Virginia said.

"Good. Mom will be happy to know you're all safe," Monique said. "In the meantime, I'll check in with the palace, see what's going on there."

"Good idea. See you soon, sis," David said.

Zach added, "Hang in there."

"Bye, guys."

Monique disconnected the call and let out a sigh of relief. "Thank God, they're safe now."

Grayson squeezed her in reassurance. "You think somebody is trying to usurp your father as the king, and wipe out his successors?"

"Why else would they kidnap Dad and try to kill David and Zach? And who knows, had I been with my parents that night, they might have tried to kill me too."

"I shudder to think that could have happened. Thank God you were with me," Grayson said. "Let's get dressed. We've got things to do."

The doorbell suddenly chimed. Grayson tapped on his phone to see who was at the door downstairs. He glanced at her. "It's John."

# 20

Grayson, now dressed in jeans and a dark shirt, opened the entrance door and let John in. John Grant, a tall vampire with long hair and a Southern accent, had been with Scanguards for over a decade. Before that he'd been the leader of the King's guard at Cain's palace outside of New Orleans, and had saved Cain's life single-handedly after an assassination attempt.

"Hey, John," Grayson greeted him.

"Grayson."

John looked past him, and the surprised glint in his eyes told him that he hadn't expected to see Monique here.

"John, it's so good to see you."

"Monique. Hey, kiddo."

He pulled Monique into a hug, and at the sight, Grayson felt a twinge of something he didn't want to examine further. When John released her, his gaze bounced between Monique and Grayson. Grayson didn't have to be a mind reader to know what John was suspecting.

"I didn't realize…" he started, then shrugged. "Does anybody know?"

Grayson exchanged a look with Monique, who shook her head.

"No. And maybe right now it's better if nobody does," she said softly. "It will just distract everybody…" She didn't finish her sentence, didn't need to, because they all knew what was more important right now.

"What brings you here?" Grayson asked. "Do you have any news?"

"Not news per se," John said evasively. "But, uhm…" He looked at Monique. "I didn't want to add more worries than you already have. That's why I came to speak to Grayson. But since you're here, I suppose I might as well tell you too. I think there's something nefarious going on at the palace."

"What do you mean?" Monique asked.

"I made a few calls. I wanted to figure out whether Cain had received any threats lately, or made any new enemies, so I called a few of the guys I knew from back when I was the leader of Cain's King's guard."

"And what did they say?" Grayson asked eagerly.

"That's just it: they didn't say anything. I couldn't get a hold of them. So I tried a few more of the guards I knew I could trust, men who would never turn against Cain. And not a single one was answering his cell phone."

"You think they've been locked up?" Monique asked.

"Or worse, killed," John replied. "We have to assume as much. Which brings me to my theory."

"You think that somebody is trying to seize the kingdom," Monique interrupted.

John tossed her a surprised look. "How did you—"

"We just found out that Monique's brothers were attacked by two vampires in Switzerland," Grayson explained.

"Fuck!" John cursed.

"They were able to kill their attackers," Monique added. "They're on their way here. One of the Stealth Guardians is bringing them back."

John nodded, a breath of relief rolling over his lips. "Virginia?" he asked with a look at Grayson.

"Yep. I sent her and Cooper to Gstaad when Monique couldn't get a hold of them."

"Good thinking. I don't suppose they got a chance to ask the attackers who'd sent them before they dusted them?"

"Afraid not," Grayson said with regret, "but one of the girls who was hired to lure them to a remote cabin and distract them, is alive. Pearce is working on finding out who paid her and her friend to be honey traps. We should know more soon."

"Damn," John hissed. "This is worse than I thought. This looks like a really well-planned coordinated attack. Somebody spent a lot of time and money to orchestrate this."

Grayson was thinking the same thing. "I can't help but think this is personal. Cain knows the person behind this." He looked at Monique and saw her concerned expression. "And maybe that's a good thing. William, the surviving bodyguard, already asked the palace to send the database of all former and current employees as well as clan members to Faye, so she and my mom can go through it to see if they recognize any of the men who kidnapped Cain and Samson."

Monique nodded and pulled her cell phone from her pocket. "Let me talk to Mom, and ask her and Delilah to make the palace's database their first priority. They can go back to the Scanguards database after they're done."

Grayson nodded. "Good idea."

Monique was already selecting Faye's number, when Grayson's cell phone rang.

He looked at the display and answered it, stepping away from Monique so he could speak to Isabelle without interfering in Monique's conversation with Faye.

"Hey, Isa. What's up?"

"Mom and Faye identified one of the attackers. He's an ex-VCON."

He motioned for John to approach. "That's excellent news."

"I'm sending you his file and photo right now. He was incarcerated at the Grass Valley prison, but he's originally from Louisiana."

Grayson wasn't surprised to hear that, not after the attack on David and Zach. "We'll check him out. And FYI, David and Zach are safe and on their way back from Switzerland. They were attacked but killed the vampires who attacked them. Just keep it to yourself for now. I don't want Faye to worry even more. Monique will talk to her."

"Understood. Talk later," Isabelle said and disconnected the call.

A moment later, his cell phone chimed with a message. Isabelle had sent the file of the ex-VCON. Monique disconnected her call at the same time and looked at him and John.

"Mom said the palace hasn't sent her the database I requested. She's asking William to call them again." Her lips twisted in displeasure. "I don't like it. It's as if they don't want us to look at the database because we might find the kidnappers in it."

John grunted. "It only amplifies my suspicion about a takeover."

Grayson could only echo that sentiment. "Let's see who this guy is." He pointed to his cell phone and looked at Monique. "Your mom and mine identified an ex-VCON from the prison database. He's originally from Louisiana."

Monique sidled up to him, and John stood to his other side as he clicked on the file and opened it.

The photo of a man with short blond hair, light-brown eyes, and a goatee appeared on the screen. He wasn't smiling. Rather, he looked pissed off, maybe because the photo was taken when he was arrested by the vampire council and incarcerated.

"Cheerful looking fellow," Grayson said.

"I know him," John said.

Grayson turned his head to look at him. "You do?"

John nodded slowly, his facial expression more serious now than when he'd entered the loft.

"Who is he?" Monique asked.

"His name is Rufus. I don't remember his last name, but what I do remember is that he was tight with Abel. Very tight."

Shock charged through Grayson. He knew about Abel, about the evil things he'd done in the past.

Monique's chin dropped. "Abel? My uncle?"

"Yes. Rufus was Abel's right hand before Baltimore showed up and became indispensable to him. I never knew what happened to him. But him showing up here, being among the kidnappers who took Cain, can only mean one thing."

"Abel is behind the kidnapping," Grayson guessed. "He's going to finish the job he couldn't complete over three decades ago."

John nodded again. "He's here to seize Cain's kingdom and take revenge on Scanguards, because they helped Cain defeat Abel back then. And he'll hurt Faye for rejecting him."

# 21

Cain groaned. It felt as if battery acid was running through his veins. He was in and out of consciousness, barely aware of his surroundings. The silver shackles around his hands and feet burned into his flesh, leaving angry bleeding sores that, without receiving human blood, had no chance of healing. He tried to push away the pain, willing himself to ignore it. But he was weak from whatever they were injecting him with every couple of hours.

He was held in a dark, musty-smelling place that appeared to be a warehouse of some sort. The walls were concrete. He wasn't alone in the large space. On the opposite wall, Samson was chained in the same fashion, his body convulsing in painful spasms. Their jailors hadn't injected Samson with whatever they were giving Cain. Instead, they were force-feeding him human blood every couple of hours. Cain could smell it, and was hungering for it so he could heal and become strong again. But the blood they were giving Samson did the opposite to his friend. Cain understood why: as a vampire blood-bonded to a human, Samson could only drink his mate's blood. Blood from any other human made him sick, and, if continued long enough, would eventually kill him.

Cain didn't have that particular kind of vulnerability, because his mate was a vampire. He could live on any human's blood. The kidnappers clearly knew that, and therefore gave him something else to keep him subdued. But his senses were too dulled to figure out what it was. Just as his senses were too weak to use the telepathic bond he shared with Faye to communicate with her.

Was Faye alive? He'd seen her collapse to the floor when they'd dragged him out of the house and tossed him in a dark van. He'd fought as hard as he could, but there'd been too many assailants.

"Samson?" Cain called out, his voice hoarse and low.

A grunt came from Samson, but no words rolled over his lips. He was curled up in the fetal position in obvious physical pain. At least he knew that Delilah was still alive. Were she dead, the human blood they were feeding him would make him strong, rather than sick. Only her death would break the bond and release him. At least this knowledge gave Cain hope that the kidnappers hadn't killed Faye either.

The sound of a heavy door opening, its hinges creaking from decades of rust, alerted him to somebody entering. Cain focused his eyes on the door, the action exhausting and painful. There was light behind the person standing in the doorframe now. Like a halo it surrounded the vampire.

"Hello, Cain. Long time no see."

Despite not having heard the voice for over three decades, he recognized it instantly. "Abel."

He stepped into the room, and the light from outside fell on him from a different angle, illuminating his face.

"Yes, brother, it's me. Did you really think you'd never see me again?"

Cain swallowed hard. He'd hoped his evil brother had found a fitting end in the over thirty years since he'd been chased out of Louisiana after a botched coup attempt. Alas, Abel proved to be more resilient.

"What do you want?" he pressed out, the effort of speaking depleting his strength.

"Not feeling so great now, are you?" Abel said in a smug tone. "What you feel running through your veins is dead man's blood. We're giving you just enough so you don't pass out. What would be the point in you being oblivious to what's happening, right?"

A chuckle echoed against the walls.

"They'll find us and kill you," Cain promised.

"Oh really? And who would that be? Your sons maybe?" Abel put a finger to his lips in mock-thought. "Oh, sorry to disappoint you, but your two boys are already dead. Guess going skiing in Switzerland wasn't a good idea after all."

Shock coursed through Cain's body. "You, you…" But his body betrayed him and didn't let him form the words he wanted to hurl at Abel.

"And I see that Monique has turned into a beautiful young woman. I'm a little disappointed that she wasn't with you when my men took you. But don't worry, we'll get her later. And then I'm gonna enjoy fucking her."

Cain screamed, the sound coming out of his throat like that of an animal, a hurt animal. He pulled on the silver chains, but pain seared through his wrists, the stench of burnt skin and hair assaulting him even worse than before.

"Faye should've been mine. She made the wrong choice. And now she's gonna pay for it. I'm gonna hurt both of you. You'll both be watching when I fuck Monique."

Cain tried to block out his brother's hateful words. The King's guard and Scanguards had already been mobilized, he was sure. Together they would find him and Samson and defeat Abel.

"And then I'll ascend to your throne. My men are already preparing the palace for my coronation, getting rid of the people still loyal to you."

Cain's eyes went wide.

"Oh yes." Abel chuckled. "Did you really think the handful of men I brought to San Francisco are the only ones I command? I've got an army to take what should have been mine all along."

Fuck! It was worse than he'd thought. This meant that only Scanguards could help them now. "Let Samson go. He's got nothing to do with this."

Abel marched deeper into the room and approached Samson. "You really think that?" He kicked Samson, wringing grunts of pain from him, then looked over his shoulder back at Cain. "He's got everything to do with this. His men helped defeat me. Now he and his people will pay for it."

He turned his back to Samson. "And he's so easy to subdue. Because he's stupid. He bonds with a human, making himself vulnerable. He's dependent on her for his survival. All I need to do with him is continue feeding him human blood, and he'll die an agonizing death." Abel grinned. "Don't worry, brother, I'll think of something fitting for you too."

"Go to hell," Cain pressed out with his last bit of energy.

"No, that's where you're going."

Abel's cell phone suddenly rang, and he pulled it from his pocket. He answered it, pressing it to his ear. "What is it?"

Cain strained to hear the other side of the conversation, but he was too weak, his senses too dulled.

"How?"

There was a pause, then Abel ordered, "Then burn his fucking place down. Now!"

# 22

The door to Wesley and Virginia's house was opened seconds after Grayson rang the doorbell. Monique flew into her brothers' arms, hugging them tightly. Grayson entered the house behind her, followed by John.

"Hey, sis," Zach and David said.

"I'm so happy to see you guys," Monique replied.

"Hey, John," Zach said, and David greeted him in the same manner, while keeping one arm around Monique's waist. John hugged both of them briefly.

Grayson instantly felt the closeness between John and the triplets. After all, John had seen them grow up; he'd worked at the palace until their late teens. When David had visited San Francisco two years earlier, he'd referred to John as his uncle, even though they weren't related by blood or marriage. Grayson felt the same connection to many members of Scanguards. To him, the hybrids were his cousins, their parents his uncles and aunts.

"Grayson, thanks for sending Virginia and Cooper to get us," David said and patted him on the shoulder.

Grayson nodded, acknowledging his gratitude. "I'm just glad you guys made it. Monique was quite worried about you."

Monique cast him a thankful smile, and looking into her eyes now, he realized that he would do anything never to see worry in them again.

Zach gazed at John and Grayson. "Any news about Dad? And Samson, sorry," he added with an apologetic gesture.

"We still don't have a location," Grayson started. "But we're 99% sure who's behind it: Abel."

Zach and David stared at him in disbelief, then looked at John and Monique for confirmation. When both nodded, their facial expressions serious, the brothers cursed.

"Fuck!"

Behind them, Virginia and Cooper emerged.

"Hey," Grayson said with a nod. "Thanks, Virginia, Cooper. Good work."

"Anytime," Virginia said, then gestured to the cell phone in her hand. "Just got off the phone with Pearce. He was able to trace the money that the two porn actresses received to a shell company. When he dug a little deeper"—which Grayson interpreted as hacking into various systems— "he found that the company belongs to Abel Montague. He said that the setup wasn't very sophisticated. As if Abel didn't even try to hide that it was him behind the shell company."

"Odd," David commented.

"Maybe not," Grayson mused. "He only needed to hide that he's behind all this until he had lured you into a trap. He already has our fathers, so at this point he probably doesn't care that we know it's him."

"Grayson is right," John interjected. "Knowing Abel, he wants us to know he's behind it. He's a sadistic jerk and likes to taunt people. His men could have simply killed Cain and Samson, but he preferred to kidnap them instead. He wants to watch all of you suffer."

"He's gonna pay for that," Monique ground out.

For a brief moment, Grayson locked eyes with her, promising her silently that he would make sure of that.

"So, what's the plan now?" Cooper asked into the short silence.

Grayson tore his gaze from Monique and noticed David look at him with a glint of surprise in his eyes. Had David noticed how he'd looked at Monique? Was it evident that there was something between them?

"John thinks that Abel might have sent some men to New Orleans to take over the palace," Grayson said with a look at John.

"How's that?" Zach asked.

"I called a few of the guards I trust," John explained. "I couldn't get a hold of anyone. I'm worried that those guards that are absolutely loyal to your father are gone. Either locked up or killed."

Zach exchanged a look with his brother. "Let's go there and take them out. You coming with us, John?"

"Of course," John said immediately.

"You need more backup," Grayson said. "I wish Monique and I could go with you, but we just got a lead on one of Abel's men here in San Francisco that we have to follow up on."

He motioned to Virginia and Cooper. "Virginia, you mind going with them? Cooper?"

Both nodded.

"But we need a couple more Stealth Guardians. I can't make four of you invisible on my own and fight if need be. That requires too much energy. I'll make some calls." Virginia pulled out her cell phone and stepped into the living room.

"Thanks," Zach said before turning to Monique. "So how much does Mom know? Have you told her that Abel is behind this?"

Monique nodded. "I called her on the drive over here from Grayson's loft." She stopped abruptly, sucking in a quick breath.

Grayson realized that this piece of news had slipped out accidentally. Zach's and David's gazes immediately landed on him.

"Uhm, yeah, we were strategizing how to proceed," Monique said, her voice trembling for a second.

"Yeah," Grayson helped, knowing that Monique wanted to keep what was between them a secret. "We brainstormed." Well, not even he believed that. Thankfully, her brothers didn't probe further.

"So, Mom knows about Abel?" David asked, bringing the conversation back to the subject at hand.

"She does," Monique said, her voice strong again. "I got the feeling she suspected it deep down."

"Let's call her quickly," David suggested. "Knowing Mom, she'll worry even more if we don't."

Monique pulled her cell phone out and scrolled to Faye's number. She put the call on speaker phone.

"Monique? Are the boys all right?" Faye's voice was laced with both hope and worry.

"Don't worry about us, Mom," David said.

"You know us," Zach added, "we're pretty indestructible."

"Thank God!" Faye replied. "What'll happen now?"

"We'll be going to New Orleans," Zach explained.

"But you can't go alone. Knowing Abel, he probably has a bunch of his men there. You can't defeat them on your own. It's too dangerous. Wait until we've rescued your father and Samson."

"No, Mom, it's gotta be done now," David interjected. "Right now, Abel probably thinks we're dead. His men won't expect us. Besides, we'll go there with the Stealth Guardians. And John and Cooper will be with us. They literally won't see us coming."

A sigh came through the line. "Still, I worry. Abel is cunning and evil."

"Don't worry about us, Mom," Zach said, his tone gentle. "We won't let Abel win."

"I love you, boys."

"Love you, Mom," both Zach and David said and disconnected the call.

David handed the cell phone back to Monique, when the door to the basement opened, and Zoltan and his mate Enya appeared.

Enya was a natural blonde with long tresses she'd braided and pinned in circles around her head. Next to Zoltan, she looked tiny and fragile, but Grayson knew better. Enya was a formidable warrior. Zoltan had once been her archenemy, the ruler of the underworld. But when he'd fallen in love with Enya, his life had changed and his origins been revealed. With Enya's love he'd been able to gain back his birthright. The erstwhile demon had shaken off evil.

"Zoltan, Enya," Grayson greeted them, hugging Enya briefly, then slapping Zoltan on the shoulder. "Great to see you, guys."

"Grayson," Enya said. "Everybody in Baltimore is sending their love. We miss you and Ryder."

"Miss you guys too." Then he motioned to the triplets. "I don't think you know Zach, David, and Monique, do you?"

As they all greeted each other, Grayson caught John's eye. He was just shoving his cell phone back into his pocket.

"Savannah should be here in a moment," John announced.

"Good, then you guys can leave for New Orleans shortly," Grayson said, realizing instantly why John had called his blood-bonded mate.

Monique took a step toward him and John, while Zoltan and Enya continued talking to David and Zach.

"John, you can't take Savannah with you. It's too dangerous for a human." She put her hand on John's forearm.

"Of course not," John assured her quickly. "I just need to feed before leaving. I need to be at my top strength, since we don't know what we're facing in New Orleans and how long we have to stay."

Monique released a sigh of relief, and at the thought of John feeding from his mate, Grayson's gaze was drawn to Monique's neck, then lower to her breasts. Only a few short hours ago, his fangs had been in Monique's breast, lodged deep, her delicious blood filling his mouth and running down his throat.

He forced himself to rip his gaze from her because looking at her for a second longer would give away how he felt about Monique.

He was glad when Zach approached. "Hey, Grayson. You said you've got a lead on one of Abel's men?"

Grayson cleared his throat. "Yeah, John recognized him from a photo in the prison records. Name's Rufus. Thomas just texted me his last known address here in San Francisco. Your sister and I will check it out. Doubt he'll be there, but we might find something in his flat that could give us a clue as to where they're keeping Cain and Samson."

"I hope we'll find them soon," Zach said.

"You and me both."

"We'll be back as soon as we can."

It took a few more minutes until Savannah arrived. When she and John disappeared into a room, so John could feed from his mate in private, Grayson put his hand on Monique's lower back.

"Time for us to go."

"Yeah." She looked at her brothers and the Stealth Guardians. "Stay safe."

# 23

"Do you think my brothers suspect anything?" Monique asked as they sat in Grayson's car and drove along busy Mission Street.

Grayson glanced at her from the side and put his hand on hers, squeezing it. She let it happen, the touch soothing her frayed nerves.

"Would it be such a disaster if they did?"

His voice was coaxing, tender almost, and so very different from how she'd imagined him when she'd found out that her father had tried to set them up. This was a different side of him. But could she trust her gut that the Grayson she was with now was the true Grayson, the man behind the façade?

"I guess not," she said hesitantly. "It's just that I don't want to have to explain to anybody… I mean… after everything…" She couldn't finish her sentence, not sure about anything anymore. What if what she felt right now was an illusion because of the trauma they were going through?

"Babe," he said softly. "You don't have to explain anything to me or to anybody else. I didn't mean to put you on the spot. But I want you to know something…"

She looked at him from the side, her heart pounding all of a sudden.

"The last forty-eight hours with you top every experience I've had in my thirty-two years. And I'm not saying that so you'll sleep with me again." He chuckled. "Though, trust me, I do want to sleep with you again…"

His words made her chuckle involuntarily. "Are you trying to tell me that you enjoyed having sex with me?"

"Having sex?" He shook his head. "Monique, we didn't just have sex. It was more than that. Or are you saying that I'm the only one who felt the connection we had when we made love?"

Her heart beat uncontrollably. He'd felt that too? When he'd made love to her and bitten her, drinking blood directly from her breast, she'd felt a high that couldn't be explained by sex alone. It had been more than that—something more personal, more intimate.

"I could feel you as if I was inside you," Monique murmured. "Even though it was the other way around. I know it sounds crazy."

"Not crazy." Grayson pulled her hand to his lips and kissed her knuckles. "I felt close to you. And I want that again." He took his eyes off the road and met hers.

His eyes were shimmering golden, and the sight made her heart skip a beat. He guided her hand to his thigh and rested it there. Monique felt his muscles twitch under her palm and loved the heat emanating from his body.

"You're so different from what I thought you'd be like."

"I hope that's a good thing." Grayson suddenly stepped on the brakes and brought the car to a stop.

In front of them, a cable car had broken down in the middle of an intersection, and an ambulance and a taxi were blocking the road. In the distance, she heard a siren, but it seemed far away. Monique perused the scene, and noticed what looked like a mangled bicycle stuck underneath the front wheels of the cable car.

"Oh my God," she said putting her hand on the door handle. "I think a bicyclist might be trapped underneath the cable car. We have to help."

She jumped out of the car and heard Grayson kill the engine, while she hurried to the cable car. The few people who'd been riding it, had gotten off and stood around, the cable car operator directing them away from the accident scene. Shock was written on their faces.

The EMTs were crouching down near the front of the cable car, trying to reach underneath it.

Monique felt Grayson's hand on her arm. "The bicyclist is trapped."

"Can we help?" Grayson asked the EMTs.

Both shook their heads. "We need the jaws of life. Fire engine is on its way."

Monique exchanged a pleading look with Grayson, the moans of pain from the trapped victim drifting to her. "He needs our help."

Grayson nodded. "Guys," he said and looked into the EMTs' eyes, pinning them. "You'll let us lift the front of the cable car, and then you'll pull out the bicyclist."

His soothing tone indicated that he was using mind-control on the two humans.

"Here we go." Grayson gave her a sign, and together they gripped the front of the cable car, and used their combined vampire strength to lift the vehicle just a few inches, sufficient for the EMTs to be able to safely pull the bicyclist out from underneath the cable car.

"Got him," one of the EMTs said.

Monique looked at the bicyclist and reassured herself that he was breathing, before she looked at the two EMTs. "You managed to pull him out yourselves. We were never here," she murmured, before she and Grayson turned around and walked back to the car.

The fire engine arrived a moment later, and blocked the street, forcing them to make a detour.

"Thanks for doing that," Monique said, looking at Grayson and taking his hand.

He smiled at her, looking contented. "We should be there soon."

It took another half hour until they finally turned onto the street where, according to Thomas, Abel's accomplice Rufus lived.

"Fuck!" Grayson cursed and stopped the car. He pointed to a building.

"That can't be!" she said, shaking her head. "Don't tell me that's Rufus's flat."

"Shit!" Grayson cursed.

Thick smoke and flames shot out of the building, the blaze spreading from floor to floor of the old Edwardian apartment complex.

"That can't be a coincidence," Monique uttered. "They knew we were coming."

Grayson nodded. "Abel is smarter than I expected. He's having us watched. He knew we were coming, so he destroyed the only lead we had so far."

Shock coursed through Monique. "Grayson! We have to warn my brothers and the others. What if Abel already knows that they survived and are on their way to the palace?"

Turning the car around, Grayson ordered, "Call them! Now!"

Monique dialed John's number. The call went straight to voicemail. "John's not answering." She tried first Zach's number then David's. None of them replied. Her heart clenched in fear. "They're not answering, Grayson. What if they ran right into a trap?"

"Try them again. Keep trying. I'll try to reach Cooper and Virginia."

Panic froze the blood in her veins, her fear of losing her brothers rising with every second.

# 24

*Outside of New Orleans – one hour earlier*

The underground tunnels leading from the woods outside the palace grounds into the palace were only known to a select few: the king and his family, and the leader of the King's guard. They stemmed from the time when the palace had been a plantation, and slaves had worked on the fields.

Zach was familiar with the hidden entries and exits, and together with his brother, David, he led the small contingent through the dark and musty labyrinth. The trip through the Stealth Guardian portal had been disorienting, and he appreciated having firm ground under his feet again.

"Brings back memories. Nothing's changed here," John said as he walked next to Zach.

"Dad, David, and I reinforced the tunnels a bit where it was absolutely necessary, so they won't cave in," Zach said, "but we can't exactly do a major renovation. It would mean exposing the existence and location to outsiders."

And right now, he appreciated that the rest of the palace employees and clan members didn't know where the tunnels were located. It made it possible for them to enter the palace without anybody knowing.

Zoltan sidled up to him, while Virginia, Cooper, and Enya walked behind them. "Once we're inside, what are we gonna do about the fact that the vampires can still smell us even though we're all invisible?"

"We'll have to wing it and hope we're not getting too close to anybody, while we scope out the situation," Zach said with a shrug. "At least we'll have the advantage that we'll be invisible."

"We've got a little more than that," John announced and pulled out a small bottle with a spray nozzle. "Wesley brewed this up for us."

"What is it?" David asked curiously.

"A little potion that will temporarily cloak our odor and make it virtually impossible for any vampire to smell us."

"Cool," David said.

"How long will it last?"

John shrugged. "Not sure. Wesley hasn't actually had any time yet to test it out in a long-term trial."

Zoltan grunted. "So, what you're saying is that it might only give us a few minutes."

"Even a few minutes is an advantage," Zach said. "How is it administered? Do we drink it?"

"No, we spray it on us," John explained.

"Better than nothing," David said.

They continued to walk in silence, until they reached an area where the rough earthen tunnel turned into a wood-framed corridor. There were two doors. One led into the King's chamber, the other into the Queen's, though the room had been converted, because his parents always slept in the same room. Now the Queen's bedroom served as a private library and sitting room for the couple. Zach and his siblings rarely intruded on their parents here, because they knew how much they enjoyed their time alone with each other. Like newlyweds.

That thought made his heart ache. If they couldn't save Cain, it would break Faye's heart, and Zach knew that she would never recover from it.

Arriving at the door to the Queen's chamber, they all stopped. Zach looked through the spy hole into the room. It was empty. He turned around and addressed the group.

"Once we're inside, we'll split up into three groups. Virginia, you'll go with John, he knows the palace as well as David and I. Enya, you'll be going with David and Cooper, Zoltan, you're with me."

Everybody nodded.

"Let me check if the coast is clear beyond this room," Virginia said. "Back in a sec."

"Hold it," John said and lifted the spray bottle.

Virginia waited, while John sprayed her with the fine mist from the bottle which looked more like a fog.

"Thanks." Virginia approached the door then went through it with the left leg first.

Zach watched in fascination as she disappeared completely. He stepped to the spy hole to look into the room and watched Virginia as she gazed around the room, then walked to the door leading into the hallway. Two yards from the door, she vanished before his eyes, having turned invisible, and he had to assume that she was walking through the door to scout out the hallway.

He waited, but didn't see her come back. Had she run into trouble already?

Suddenly, he was pushed back, and almost fell on his ass had his brother not caught him. Virginia was stepping through the door, and bumped into him, suddenly visible again.

Virginia gasped. "Whoa."

"Sorry, didn't see you there," Zach said. This little mishap made him think of something. "Guys, once we're all invisible, does that mean we're gonna be bumping into each other?"

"That's a problem," David added.

"It's not," Enya claimed. "We have different levels of making others invisible, and allowing select people to still see us and each other. Don't worry, we'll make sure everybody in this group can see everybody else."

That was a relief. "All right then." Zach nodded at John. "Hit me with it."

John sprayed Zach, and in turn everybody else, until everybody including John had received some of Wesley's potion. Zach inhaled deeply trying to discern the different smells coming from his companions. To his surprise, he couldn't smell them. It was as if he was alone.

"Pretty cool," David said, also sniffing visibly.

"Let's go," Zach ordered, cast another look through the spy hole, then opened the door to the chamber and entered.

When everybody was inside the room, David closed the door. An ornate piece of art covered the wall, making it virtually impossible to see that a secret door was hidden there. Even the spy hole was cleverly disguised.

"Cloaking now," Virginia said in a whisper and looked at her fellow Stealth Guardians. Both nodded, and she added, "We're all invisible now."

"Good," Zach answered equally quiet, "John, take the guards' quarters, David, the private rooms upstairs, I'll check the offices and outside. And remember, we'll need to figure out first, how many hostiles there are, before we take them out. Understood?"

All nodded.

Virginia and John were the first to leave the room. They headed for the back stairs, while the rest of them walked along the empty corridor toward the main stairs of the building. The palace was a massive mansion with the royal family's quarters on the lower floor, offices, a ballroom, and other public rooms on the ground floor. On the second floor were the quarters of the guards who lived in the palace, and on the third floor were guest rooms as well as rooms the triplets used in order to have a little separation from their parents.

Silently, all wearing soft-soled shoes, they walked up the broad stairs. On the landing, Zach nodded at his brother, and pointed to the left, while he motioned to Zoltan to follow him to the right. As he turned the corner, he stopped abruptly.

In the hallway, a dozen guards stood in formation, armed to the teeth. But that wasn't the worst of it, because Zach and Zoltan were invisible. Or would have been invisible, if it hadn't been for the fine white powder that was coming from a hose hanging from the ceiling, and blowing the particles onto them. The dust stuck to their clothes, skin, and hair, and turned them into a chalk outline of themselves.

"Shit!" Zach cursed.

# 25

Thomas looked up from the computer. "We tried all their phones. They all went dead at the same time."

"Shit!" Grayson cursed.

Next to him, Monique tensed. "Oh my God."

"Since John and Cooper used their Scanguards' phones, I was able to get the exact GPS location. They definitely made it into the palace."

"Abel's men must have been waiting for them," Monique said, her entire body on edge.

"John sent a text message just before the phones went out," Thomas added.

"What did he say?" Grayson said, hoping for a piece of good news.

"I don't know. He didn't send it to us, but to a number I don't recognize. We're working on figuring out who he contacted," Thomas said with a look at Eddie, who was hacking away on his keyboard. "It's an unlisted number."

Amaury appeared in the door to Thomas's office. "Hey, any news of them?"

Thomas shook his head.

"I need to go to New Orleans," Monique said. "Thomas, can you call another Stealth Guardian to take me?"

"Out of the question," Grayson snapped. "You're not going."

"I have to save my brothers!"

"And put yourself in danger? Over my dead body."

Monique glared at him. "You don't get to decide what I do or don't do!"

"I do when it means I'm protecting you!"

"You're just as much of an arrogant asshole as you've always been. How could I have been so stupid to think you've changed?"

"What the fuck do you mean? All I'm doing is trying to stop you from running into a trap."

"Yeah, 'cause you know everything better, don't you? And I'm just a hysterical girl, aren't I? Just like when I was eleven."

Grayson ran a hand through his hair, his mind working overtime. A memory, one he'd pushed back into the dark recesses of his mind, tried to surface, but he couldn't quite grasp it.

"I have no idea what you're talking about."

"Of course, you don't," Monique snapped, glaring at him. "Because all you think about is yourself. You don't care about other people's feelings. No, you'd rather humiliate someone than admit that you're wrong."

"Monique! Damn it, I have no idea what this is about. I thought you and I were on the same page." After all, they'd gotten close and comforted each other only a few hours earlier.

"We were never on the same page." She sucked in a breath. "And you're still the arrogant little prick you were when you were twelve and called me a coward and a liar when I didn't want to jump into alligator-infested waters. You had to humiliate me, because you wanted to be the brave one. And it didn't matter to you that you hurt my feelings. Because all you care about is yourself."

Fuck! The memory of that summer in New Orleans suddenly flashed in front of his eyes. Every single second came back to him now.

"Oh, God," he murmured and looked at Monique with different eyes. He ignored the fact that they weren't alone and that his colleagues were watching them in silence. He had to clear this up with Monique now.

"Monique, I was twelve years old. I… uhm, I…" Fuck, this was hard. "Damn it, Monique! I had a crush on you back then. And your brothers knew it and teased me relentlessly. I was embarrassed. Hell, what twelve-year old wouldn't feel embarrassed about having a crush on a girl who didn't even give him a second glance? So I lashed out. I had to prove to your brothers that I wasn't soft on you. That's why I called you a coward. When really I was the coward, because I couldn't admit to anybody that I liked you."

Monique stared at him, her lips slightly parted.

"But I'm not that kid anymore. And I don't care who knows about it." He glanced at Amaury, Thomas, and Eddie, then back at Monique. "So I might as well tell you how I feel about you. I'm in love with you, Monique. And I'm not gonna hide that fact this time, no matter what anybody says."

"Grayson…" she murmured, the fury visibly seeping from her body.

"And the reason I don't want you to go to New Orleans is because I could never forgive myself if you got hurt. But since we both know that you're not gonna back down, and will go no matter what anybody says, I'll go with you. Whether you like it or not."

It was so silent in the office that a pin could have been heard falling to the floor. It seemed that he wasn't the only one waiting for an answer from Monique. Amaury, Thomas, and Eddie seemed just as curious how she would react to this confession.

~ ~ ~

Monique's heart beat into her throat. She hadn't expected this. Grayson was in love with her? And he'd announced it in front of his colleagues as if he didn't care who knew about it. His confession that he'd had a crush on her twenty years ago, and had acted out of embarrassment was equally unexpected. He was laying himself bare in front of her and his colleagues. It took a strong man to do something like that, to make himself vulnerable. She'd completely misjudged Grayson. He wasn't the spoiled heir of Scanguards right now. He was so much more. He was a man who knew exactly what he wanted, and wasn't afraid of opening himself up to get it.

"Did you mean everything you said?" she murmured.

She stared into his eyes and noticed how his irises began to shimmer golden. It drew her to him. He was Gray again, the stranger she'd made love to.

"Yes, babe. Every single word."

Her feet moved of their own volition as she bridged the distance between them. Standing only a foot away from him, she put her hand onto his chest and felt his rapid heartbeat beneath her palm. Her own heart was beating just as frantically.

"Forgive me, Monique," he whispered. "I never meant to hurt you back then."

At the recollection of what had happened twenty years earlier, she suddenly realized why she'd been so hurt. It was so obvious now, yet all these years she hadn't been able to see it. She too had had a crush. A crush on Grayson. And when he'd hurt her, it had turned into resentment. The rejection had stung, because his opinion of her had mattered. It still mattered. Even more so now.

Monique put her arms around him and hugged him tightly. His arms came around her, and he held her closely. She buried her head in the crook of his neck, inhaling his enticing scent.

"I forgive you," she whispered into his ear.

"Will you trust me now that everything I do, I do because I couldn't live with myself if anything happened to you?"

"I will. I trust you."

She lifted her head and looked into his eyes. His lips parted on a breath, and she brought her lips to his.

Somebody cleared his throat. Suddenly remembering that they weren't alone, Monique pulled out of Grayson's arms and turned. All three vampires suppressed smiles.

Grayson cleared his throat. "Uhm, Amaury, could you do me a favor, and call the Stealth Guardians and see who's available to take us to New Orleans?"

"No problem," Amaury replied and pulled out his cell phone. "But you should take a few people with you as backup. You still have four hours until the sun comes up in Louisiana. Take Blake. He knows the palace."

Monique's gaze fell onto Thomas and Eddie, before she dropped it, unable to look at anybody. She wasn't used to public displays of affection. She'd never felt so naked in her life.

"Don't mind us," Thomas said with a smirk. "We were taking bets how long it would take for Grayson to finally grow up."

Eddie chuckled. "Turns out it took a real princess for that to happen."

"Guys, are you done embarrassing us?" Grayson asked, though he didn't sound upset.

He squeezed her hand, and she cast him a brief glance, and noticed that his eyes were still shimmering golden. Were hers too? She assumed as much, because what she felt inside her was hard to contain. She had feelings for Grayson. Strong feelings.

Amaury finished his call and shoved his phone back into his pocket. "Hamish and Logan will meet you at the 16th Street portal in twenty minutes."

"Thanks, Amaury. Oh, and… uhm, doesn't Wesley know the palace too?" Grayson asked.

Amaury nodded. "Yes, he was part of the team that helped Cain defeat Abel. But I thought you wanted him to stay here and work on the potions."

"I think we'll need him with us in New Orleans. We have no idea what happened there, and we might need a spell or two to get them out of whatever trouble they're in. Charles can continue his work here."

Monique nodded. "That's probably a good idea. A witch might be just what we need." She paused a moment, before continuing, "My brothers would have used the tunnels to enter the palace. We'll have to assume they're compromised. Abel knows about the tunnels, though I think he only knew about the entrance from the cells, not the ones to my parents' rooms. That's why my father closed off the cell entrance over thirty years ago."

"I get it," Grayson said. "We'd better not follow in John and your brothers' footsteps and land in the same trap. If Abel's men knew that they were coming, they probably knew that they'd use the tunnels and come in invisibly. Let's approach the palace from a different way."

"That's not our only problem," Monique said, concerned with something else.

"What do you mean?"

"We can't assume that everybody at the palace is on Abel's side. There might be some that are only playing along because if they don't, Abel will kill them. We can't simply kill everybody, not knowing whose side they're on."

"There's no way of figuring out who's still loyal to Cain."

"Then we have to find a way. I can't condone killing innocents."

Grayson looked at her as if he wanted to protest, but then he seemed to change his mind. "Okay, then we'll find a way. Now let's get this show on the road."

# 26

The Stealth Guardian portal was hidden in a tunnel in the 16$^{th}$ Street MUNI station, which was closed after midnight. However, the Scanguards staff had a way to disable the underground station's cameras and a key to get in.

Monique was surprised to see Blake wearing a full-body Kevlar suit complete with helmet and gloves.

"It'll protect me from the sun if this takes longer than expected," Blake explained, "and I'm caught outside."

"Where did you get it?" Monique asked as she stepped onto the platform and followed Grayson, who was heading toward the dark tunnel.

"It's the uniform the guards wear at the vampire prison in Grass Valley. Luther consults there, so we got a few uniforms from them."

"We should probably get more made," Grayson suggested. "It'll make life easier for all the full-blooded vampires."

"I'm all for it," Blake said.

"That's a great idea." Monique nodded. If she got to run the new Scanguards branch in New Orleans, she would definitely make this her priority.

"Frankly, I don't know why we don't have more of them already," Wesley said from behind them.

The witch was carrying a large bag slung diagonally across his body. Monique hadn't asked him what was inside it, but she could guess: potions and spells, and most likely a stake, gun, and a silver knife, all weapons that could kill a vampire.

She, Grayson, and Blake were also armed. They had screwed silencers onto the small-caliber weapons which were loaded with silver bullets. But their main weapon would be a stake, because it killed silently. Depending on how many hostiles they encountered and where, they would have to take as many as possible out without alerting anybody.

Inside the train tunnel, Grayson, who was walking ahead of her now, stopped. "We're here."

"Hey guys," a tall man said. "Good to see you, Grayson. Long time."

"Good to see you, too, guys."

Monique peeked past Grayson's shoulder, and Grayson turned sideways, so she could see better.

"This is Hamish, and that's Logan," he said. "Guys, this is Monique, Cain's daughter."

"Hey," Monique said, and the two men, who were armed to the teeth, nodded.

"Let's do this," Hamish said and motioned to the opening in the tunnel wall.

One by one, they entered. Inside the cave, which was about the size of an elevator carrying four people, they stood close together. Grayson put his arm around her, then put his hand on Logan's arm. She saw that the others held on to each other too so everybody had a direct or indirect connection to either Hamish or Logan.

"Don't let go," Hamish advised, "or you'll get lost on the trip."

A moment later, it went pitch black around them, and Monique realized that the opening to the tunnel had closed. They were surrounded by rock walls. Instinctively, Monique tensed and put both arms around Grayson. She felt as if she were tossed in the air and clung to Grayson for dear life.

"It's all good, babe," he murmured softly, his breath ghosting over her face.

Then, his lips were on hers, and he was kissing her. She tilted her head to the side and parted her lips to allow him to sweep his tongue into her mouth. Heat surged through her, and the kiss pushed every thought into the back of her mind. The passion with which he kissed her felt amplified, now that she knew that Grayson loved her. She kissed him back with the same desire, his arm around her waist pulling her closer so her breasts were crushed to his chest. She felt his heartbeat echo her own, and the scent of his arousal drifted to her nostrils and made her want to press him down on the nearest flat surface and ride him.

"Ahem, we're here," Logan said, clearing his throat.

Monique's eyes flew open, and she freed herself from Grayson's arms. She and Grayson were the only ones still inside the portal. The other four had exited and stood in the ruins of an old, burned-out building, which at one time had been a church.

Swallowing hard, Monique exited the portal and avoided looking at her travel companions. What did they think of her? The vampire, Blake, had certainly been aware of the scent of arousal wrapping around her and Grayson, but he had the decency to keep his thoughts to himself. She was grateful for that.

"Okay," she said quickly and rubbed her damp palms on her pants. "By the looks of it, this is St. Tobias Parish church. That means we're about a half hour walk from the palace grounds." She pointed to the left. "That way."

As they walked through the woods, ever vigilant of their surroundings, and thanks to Hamish and Logan, invisible to all others but their own small group, they worked out the details of how to enter the palace and find Zach and David and their friends.

~ ~ ~

"You're sure about that?" Grayson asked as they stood at the edge of the woods from where they could see the palace and the smaller cottages lining the long road leading up to it.

"Yes," Monique said firmly. "I refuse to believe that my uncle was able to turn everybody in the palace against my father."

"Okay, then let's stick to the plan. You all know what to do." Grayson looked at his companions, and everybody nodded.

"Ready when you are," Hamish said.

"Let's go."

All of them were invisible. Grayson walked next to Monique, Hamish on her other side, while Blake, Wesley, and Logan made a wide berth to get behind one of the cottages. The road to the palace was lined with street lights every fifty yards, and from inside the cottages, light shone onto their porches. Two guards stood in the shadow of the first cottage, armed with guns, their eyes roaming, waiting for intruders.

"You know them?" Grayson whispered next to Monique.

"Yes."

The three of them approached the guards, then stopped only a few yards away from them, remaining behind a tree, while Grayson and Hamish walked closer to the two guards. Monique gave Hamish a sign, and a moment later, she turned visible and stepped around the tree. The two guards stared at her in disbelief.

"Princess," one of them said, then grinned.

Monique approached them. "I need your help."

The two vampires exchanged a look, then one of them said, "Perfect."

Both reached for her, gripping her arms to restrain her. "Let go of me! I'm the princess."

"Yeah, and Abel will reward us nicely for bringing you to him," one of them said with a laugh.

It was the last thing he uttered. Grayson slammed his stake into the guy, while Hamish did the same to the other hostile vampire. Both dissolved into dust.

"Guess they weren't innocent," Grayson said dryly.

"Guess not," Monique agreed. She looked at Hamish. "Am I invisible again?"

"Yep." Hamish looked past her. "Logan's group encountered some guards. They're waiting for instructions."

"Let's go."

Grayson took Monique's hand as they continued their approach of the palace. She glanced at him from the side, but didn't withdraw her hand. It looked like she was getting more comfortable with him now that the past was behind them.

From afar, he could now see two vampire guards, both armed, pacing up and down, looking toward the woods.

"I've never seen those two," Monique whispered to him.

"You sure?"

"One hundred percent."

Grayson motioned toward Logan, giving him the agreed sign indicating that the two vampires were hostiles. Logan nodded, then lifted his chin to Blake, who understood. A couple of seconds later, the two vampire guards turned into dust. Their guns and everything else made of metal dropped to the ground, one item hitting a stone, and making a sound that echoed in the night air.

Instinctively, Grayson looked over his shoulder, wondering how far the sound had carried, when he saw a man jumping down from the veranda of one of the cottages.

"Incoming," he whispered to Monique and Hamish.

The vampire ran toward the spot where the two vampires had died only seconds earlier, while looking around frantically, peering into the dark.

Grayson grabbed him from behind, the blade of his silver knife at the man's throat. "One move, and you're dust."

The vampire scoffed. "Go ahead! And give Abel a message from me: nobody hurts the royal family and gets away with it."

Surprised at the words, Grayson looked over his shoulder. "Monique?"

She stepped in front of the man to look at him. "Oh, my God, that's Robert. He'd never hurt my family."

Grayson released him from his hold, and Robert whirled around, a panicked look on his face. "Where are you? Who are you?"

"Hamish, Logan," Grayson ordered. "Make us visible."

A second later, Robert stared right at him and Monique, gasping and taking a step back. "You're real." He shook his head. "I thought I was going crazy, when I saw the two guards turn to dust out of the blue." He pointed to the spot where the two vampires had died.

"Robert, what's going on here?" Monique asked.

"Abel's people have taken over the palace. They killed a lot of the guards. I tried to run, to get help, but I was trapped. I hid in an old root cellar, waiting for an opportunity to escape, but there are just too many of them."

"Have you seen my brothers?"

"No. I'm sorry."

"Are there any others that are still loyal to my father?" Monique asked, her jaw looking tight, her body rigid.

"I think so. But they're too scared that Abel's men will kill their families if they rise up," Robert replied. Suddenly, Robert looked past Grayson, and his eyes widened. "They'll see us! Quickly!"

Grayson looked over his shoulder and saw two guards walk along the road, patrolling.

"They won't," Logan said and looked directly at Robert. "We're all invisible, including you."

Grayson looked at his watch. "We've got two hours left to sunrise. I suggest we eliminate as many guards patrolling the palace grounds as we can, before we attempt to get inside."

"Quickly then," Monique said. "Robert, you're going with Logan, Blake, and Wesley. Point out those vampires who you don't recognize. It's safe to assume they are Abel's men. And if you recognize somebody who's still loyal to us, make sure they don't kill them."

Robert nodded. "Yes, Monique."

They split up, one group heading to the left, the other to the right in search of Abel's forces. For the first time since arriving in Louisiana, Grayson was hopeful that they could defeat Abel's army. As for saving Monique's brothers and his Scanguards colleagues and Stealth Guardian friends, he prayed they were still alive.

# 27

"Why didn't they kill us right away?" David asked.

All seven of them, Zach, David, Virginia, John, Cooper, Enya, and Zoltan were in a large underground cell with stone walls and a heavy iron door. The room was part of the underground prison of the palace, but it hadn't been used in decades.

"They're probably waiting for orders from Abel," Zach mused. "But we're not gonna sit around here and wait for it." He looked at Zoltan. "They might not know that Stealth Guardians can walk through walls."

"My idea exactly." Zoltan took off his jacket.

"What are you doing?" David asked.

Zoltan motioned to the white paint dust sticking to his clothes. He sniffed his jacket. "There's something in this dust that's preventing me from making it invisible. Can you guys smell it?"

The three hybrids and John inhaled deeply, then looked at each other.

"Maybe lead paint?" John asked.

Cooper nodded. "Yeah, I think that's what it is."

"That explains it," Zoltan said and exchanged a look with Enya and Virginia.

"Explains what?" Zach asked impatiently.

"Lead is like kryptonite for Stealth Guardians. Zaps our powers, and we can't walk through it or make it invisible."

That was news to him. Now he understood why Zoltan was taking off his clothes.

"Okay, let's all strip," Zach ordered.

"And don't forget your hair, face, and hands," Zoltan added. "Turn your discarded clothes inside out and use that side to wipe yourself clean."

Everybody began to take off their jackets, pants, and shirts to get to a layer without the white paint dust. While Zach stepped out of his pants, he cast a clandestine look at Enya, the blonde Stealth Guardian. She had to strip down to her bra and panties, and was now busy shaking out her long hair to get rid of the dust.

All of a sudden, his view of her was blocked. Zoltan had stepped in front of him, now only wearing his boxer briefs. "Let me give you some advice," he hissed low and dark. "A wandering eye can get a man killed. I suggest you look in a different direction."

Zach swallowed hard. Judging by the hostile look on Zoltan's face, the man didn't issue empty threats.

"I meant no offense," he said quickly. "You're a very lucky man." He could only imagine what it was like to call a woman like Enya his own.

"Something wrong here?" Enya asked from behind Zoltan.

"Everything's fine, baby," Zoltan said, narrowing his eyes at Zach. "Isn't it, Zach?"

"Yep, just eager to get out of here."

Zoltan turned to his wife. "Let me check your hair to see if it's all out."

To Zach's surprise, Enya made herself invisible, and now he saw it too. There were a few spots of white dust that looked like they were suspended in the air. "Virginia, check the others the same way."

Fascinated, Zach watched as Virginia checked everybody in the same way to make sure no lead particles remained in anybody's hair.

"Everybody clean?" Zoltan asked after a while.

Everybody nodded.

"There are weapons in a cupboard at the end of the corridor," Zach said. "But you'll have to get past the guards to get to it."

"Not a problem." Zoltan looked at Enya and Virginia. "We'll have to take the guards out simultaneously. Let's go."

As the three disappeared in front of his eyes, Zach envied the Stealth Guardians for their powers. At the same time, he listened for sounds from outside the cell. Nobody spoke.

All of a sudden, there was a commotion from outside. A few thuds could be heard, then a woman's cry of pain. Had Virginia or Enya been injured? There was grunting now, then, a gunshot. Zach's gaze met those of his companions. Had one of the guards shot a Stealth Guardian? Because for certain, the three Stealth Guardians wouldn't have used a gun for fear of alerting Abel's men to come to their colleagues' aid. Zach thought he heard the faint sound of footsteps, but his heart was beating so loud, he couldn't be sure of it.

The scraping of metal against metal cut through the silence. Somebody was unlocking the cell door. Had the Stealth Guardians prevailed? Or were their jailors coming to finish them off?

Zach pressed himself against the wall next to the door, ready to attack whoever entered with his bare hands—hands that had turned to claws. He glanced at Cooper, David, and John. Their eyes were glaring red now, their fangs extended, and their fingers had turned into sharp barbs capable of ripping an opponent's throat out.

The rusty hinges of the door creaked as it was jerked open, and light streamed into the cell.

~ ~ ~

"That was a gunshot." Monique's heart pounded.

She, Grayson, and Hamish had just entered the palace through a side entrance meant for deliveries. Only one vampire had guarded this entrance, and Monique had driven a stake through his heart, killing him silently.

"From downstairs?" Grayson asked, his voice but a whisper.

She nodded and motioned him and Hamish to follow her to the stairs. But before they reached them, Grayson jerked her back.

*What?* she mouthed.

Grayson pointed to something on the high ceiling, then to the floor, where a thin layer of dust covered the otherwise pristine wooden floor. She focused her eyes on the ceiling, recognizing something that looked like a fan or a vent. A cable was protruding from it, and she followed it with her eyes, until it reached the floor, where it disappeared under a rug.

She understood immediately. If somebody stepped on the rug, the fan would be triggered, and rain fine ash or dust onto the person below.

*Why?* she mouthed to Grayson and Hamish.

Hamish motioned her and Grayson to step closer to him, then whispered, "If the dust falls on you, your silhouette becomes visible."

"Fuck!" Monique ground out below her breath. "That's how they must have caught the others."

Grayson nodded. "I'll warn Logan to be on the lookout for more of these traps." He pulled out his cell phone and sent a text message. A moment later, Monique saw a reply coming from Logan, though there was no sound. All their phones were set to silent.

"Okay," Grayson said. "Where to now? I think the gunshot came from below."

"To the cells." Monique sidestepped the rug and squeezed past it to reach the stairs leading to the lower levels of the palace.

She felt Grayson behind her, his hand on her lower back, and Hamish followed, when she suddenly heard noise coming from downstairs. Several people were yelling something unintelligible, and there were thuds and the sound of heavy footfalls.

Monique tightened her grip around her stake. At the landing, she turned to the right, the direction the noise was coming from. She bumped into a vampire, and stumbled. Grayson's quick reaction saved her from falling on her ass, and she gasped.

The vampire stared in her general direction, his gaze searching. "Intruders! Invisible intruders!" he screamed from the top of his lungs. A second later, Hamish plunged his stake into the guy's chest, turning him into dust. But the scream had alerted others, and with dread, Monique saw several of them coming from the end of the corridor and rushing toward them.

"We've got this," Grayson murmured next to her. "I'll take the two on the left."

Hamish pressed himself against the wall so the assailants would run past him if he was lucky. "I'll get them from behind."

"I'll take the right," Monique said and braced herself.

The assailants were almost upon them, when the fire alarm suddenly blared. A second later, the sprinkler system came on, and water rained on them. As the water hit them, their silhouettes became visible.

"Fuck!" Grayson charged at the assailants.

Holding her stake in front of her chest with both hands now, Monique collided with a massive vampire, killing him instantly. Yet the collision made her lose her footing on the wet floor and she slipped and hit the wall. She pushed herself off it quickly, and stormed into the melee once more. Hamish and Grayson were both trading punches and kicks with the hostile vampires, but more kept coming, joining the fight.

Monique did her best to fend off her attackers, using her agility to evade blows and kicks, when two vampires suddenly managed to grab her arms and slam her against the wall, knocking the wind out of her for a moment. When they pulled her back, she saw the stake in the hand of a third assailant. It was aimed at her chest.

She tried to free herself from her assailants' hold, and used them for leverage to kick her legs as high as she could to catapult the third assailant backward with such force that he fell on the floor and slid several yards farther on the wet surface.

"Bitch!" one of her attackers cursed. But it was the last thing he said, because he suddenly dissolved into ash. Monique used the other vampire's surprise to wheel toward him and drive her stake into his chest.

She whirled around, completely drenched now. Grayson had saved her. Relieved that he was unharmed, she let out a breath. "Thanks."

Then she looked past him and couldn't believe her eyes. Her brothers were fighting the hostile vampires. They weren't alone: John, Cooper, and the three Stealth Guardians were by their side, killing one vampire after the other. But that wasn't the reason she was stunned. No, the reason was the fact that all seven of them were dressed only in their underwear. In their very wet underwear.

Only three hostile vampires were still fighting, but her brothers and her friends made quick work of them.

"Thank God you're alive," she said and walked toward her brothers.

"Did we miss a party or something?" Grayson asked with a chuckle, pointing at their nearly naked bodies.

"Lead in the paint dust they sprayed on us," Zoltan said with a look at Grayson and Hamish.

Grayson nodded. "How many more are down there?" He gestured to the door at the end of the corridor that led to the floor with the cells.

"None," Zach said. "We took care of them. But I'm sure there are more upstairs."

"Any word from Logan?" Monique asked with a look at Grayson.

He looked at his cell phone and shook his head, then sent another text message. "Let's find them. And can somebody turn off the sprinklers?"

"I'll take care of it," David said. "The controls are in the boiler room."

"Somebody go with him," Monique said.

"I'll go," Cooper offered, and together they walked in the other direction.

The sound of an explosion was suddenly coming from upstairs. Monique exchanged a panicked look with Grayson, and they ran, followed by the others, up the main stairs.

Grayson had his gun drawn, and Monique reached for hers too. The time for killing silently was over. She took two steps at a time, hurrying upstairs. When she reached the landing, Grayson by her side, she saw at least a dozen vampires lying on the floor of the large foyer looking as if they were sleeping.

The only two men standing were Wesley and Logan. Both spun on their heels, guns drawn, pointing them at her and Grayson.

"Don't!" she called out quickly.

Both lowered their guns, and behind Monique, the Stealth Guardians, and the others crowded into the foyer.

"Blake?" Grayson asked, his voice laced with panic.

Wesley made a dismissive hand movement. "He's fine." He pointed to a spot on the floor, and Monique recognized Blake lying on the ground like the other vampires. "I told him not to get too close to the potion when I did the spell... Same with Robert." Wes shrugged. "They'll be fine. Just a bit groggy when they wake up."

"Thank God," Grayson said, the relief evident in his voice.

"Are those all of them?" Monique said with a look at the vampires on the floor.

"We think so, though we haven't had time to check the upper floors yet," Logan said, "but every vampire on this floor is asleep thanks to the spell."

Finally, the sprinklers stopped.

"Let's handcuff them with silver." Monique looked at Grayson and pointed to a door. "In the guards' station—"

"No, let's kill them," Zach interrupted.

"We have to question them," she protested. "One of them might know where Abel is keeping Cain and Samson."

"Unlikely," Zach snapped.

Monique was about to go nose to nose with her brother, when a loud sound came from outside. She looked at the open entrance door, and saw that Wesley was already hurrying toward it.

"Helicopters," Wesley yelled.

"Shit!" Zach cursed. "Get the rifles from the guards' station!"

While Zach raced to the guards' station with Hamish and Virginia following him, Monique noticed John rush to the entrance door and peer out into the dark.

Monique ran to him, her gun drawn. Through the open door, she saw that several helicopters landed in the grassy area around the palace.

Monique aimed at the helicopter closest to her, waiting for somebody to get out. The first person jumped out of the helicopter, gun in hand. Monique aimed, ready to shoot.

"No!" John pushed her hand holding the gun down. "It's Victor. He's come to help."

"The vampire king of Mississippi?" Monique asked, stunned.

John nodded. "I managed to send him a text just before Abel's men captured us."

Monique watched as Victor approached with his clansmen. All had their guns drawn, ready to shoot, their eyes vigilant, their bodies ready for battle.

"Victor," John called out. "We've subdued them."

Victor, a vampire older than Cain, and a strong warrior, approached and looked John up and down. Then his gaze strayed past him to the others who were just as scantily dressed, before he entered the foyer and looked at the vampires lying on the floor.

"Not sure what went on here," Victor said, one side of his lip curling up, "but if you wanted us to come for an orgy, you should have said so, John. I would have dressed accordingly."

Victor's men entered the foyer, their eyes widening when they noticed that several of them were wearing only underwear, and all of them were wet. Monique noticed that Zoltan was shoving Enya behind his broad back, out of view of the other men. She had to smile to herself. Zoltan was clearly protective of his mate, and didn't want any other men to look at her. Would Grayson behave the same way toward her if in the same situation?

"It's good to see you, man," John said and patted Victor on the shoulder. "You could give us a hand with securing these assholes, and sweeping the palace for any others that might have managed to hide."

Victor chuckled. "You should have left us a little something to do. It's just polite."

"Tell you what," John said, "you find any more of Abel's men, you get to kill them. After we question them."

"Abel's men?" Victor looked stunned. "That'll be a very special pleasure."

# 28

Grayson terminated the call and tossed his cell phone on the chair. The sun had risen a few minutes earlier. He was in Monique's room in the palace, updating Scanguards headquarters about the events of the past few hours. Luckily, the top floor where Monique's and her brothers' rooms were located had a separate sprinkler system, which wasn't activated when somebody had pulled the alarm in the basement.

Victor and his forces had helped secure the palace and made sure that all of Abel's men were either dead or locked up. They'd identified a vampire named Oscar who'd led them while Abel was in San Francisco. Attempts at getting anything useful out of him, however, had failed. But Grayson had an ace up his sleeve, and didn't need the thug's cooperation.

Monique entered, a stack of dry clothes in her hands. On top of it lay two bottles of blood. "You can wear these clothes. They are from Zach."

She handed him a bottle, and he unscrewed it. "Thanks, babe." He began gulping down the much- needed nourishment.

"Any news from San Francisco?" she asked, placing the clothes on the bed. Then she took the second bottle of blood and drank it.

"Thomas and Eddie have already tracked down three of the five vans, and they have a good lead on the location of the fourth."

"That's good." She pointed at his wet clothes. "Wanna join me for a shower?"

"That sounds wonderful." He grinned and stripped.

Monique undressed too, before she reached for his hand and ushered him into the ensuite bathroom, where she turned on the shower and stepped inside. When the warm water ran down her beautiful body, Grayson felt arousal charge through him. He joined her in the shower, and Monique put her arms around him, pressing her body to his.

"Thank you for saving my life earlier," she said and kissed him softly.

"I almost had a heart attack." The memory of seeing Monique in the clutches of three vampires about to kill her, had scared the living daylights out of him. And he wasn't scared easily.

"Vampires can't have heart attacks," she murmured.

"Let's just say seeing you in danger does terrible things to me. I don't like that feeling," he confessed. He'd never felt such dread, such horror. The thought of losing Monique had sent an icy chill through his veins.

"I'll make it up to you."

"How?"

"I could think of a thing or two." She slid her hands down to his ass and jerked him to her.

His hard-on rubbed against her stomach, and the contact sent a spear of lust through his body. He put his arms around her, touching the soft skin of her back, caressing her sweet ass, while the warm water ran down their bodies. Grayson brought his lips to hers, and hungrily captured her mouth, while he pressed Monique back against the tiles of the shower so she couldn't escape. He ground his cock against her, while he explored the sweet cavern of her mouth with his tongue, demanding her surrender.

Soft moans issued from Monique's throat, and he could feel her heartbeat match his own. Beating fast and strong, like drums echoing in the night, his rhythm matched hers, and hers his. Everything else vanished, only one thought remained: to make love to the woman he loved. The need to take her became stronger with each second he kissed her, tasted her, explored her. She was everything he'd ever wanted in a woman, even though he'd never consciously realized it before. He wanted a strong woman, a warrior, a fighter. A woman who knew what it meant to crave another's blood. A woman who could hold her own. Monique was all that, and more. She was an alpha. And his equal.

Her passion matched his, her carnal needs equaled his, and the fire inside her, her drive and determination turned him on. It didn't matter that they didn't have much time for this, and couldn't linger in each other's arms for long, he had to make love to her now as if his life depended on it.

He ripped his lips from hers, and felt his fangs descend.

Monique's eyes flew open, and she pinned him, lust blazing from them, while she ground her pelvis against him, demanding more. "Grayson, fuck me!"

He spun her around without a word, and she braced her hands against the tiles, and widened her stance, sticking her ass out in invitation. He centered himself behind her, and led his cock to her pussy. With one thrust, he seated himself in her warm sheath, her juices coating his erection and welcoming him.

"I missed this." He let out a moan, and gripped her hips with both hands.

"Damn, you feel so good," Monique confessed, looking over her shoulder.

She pulled her lower lip between her teeth, her fangs peeking from between her lips. The sight sent a hot spear of lust straight into his balls, making him plunge deeper and harder into her, his tempo accelerating.

"You like that, don't you? You like to be fucked hard."

"Yes!"

He moved his head closer to hers. "Are you ever gonna let another man fuck you like this?"

Monique took a breath, then another one.

"Tell me," he demanded, pounding his cock into her without pause.

"What if I do?" she asked, her voice raspy.

She was challenging him? "Then I'd have to punish you for it."

He pulled his cock out of her and slapped her on her ass. A surprised gasp burst from her lips, but she didn't free herself from his grip. Instead, she looked at him with half-closed eyes, her lips parted, a visible shiver running down her spine.

"Maybe you should punish me with something really hard," she said on a breath and lowered her gaze to indicate his cock. "And long… and thick… That would really teach me not to disobey."

"You mean this?" He thrust his cock back into her with such force that she gasped.

"Oh yes, that's exactly what I need to obey."

Grayson thrust back and forth. "Well, then I'm glad I have what it takes to keep you in line."

"Hmm." She moaned, her breaths uneven. "But…"

"But what?"

"I'm afraid I can only obey for as long as your hard-on is inside me."

"Guess then I'll have to fuck you long and often." Which would be no hardship at all. On the contrary. Besides, he didn't want an obedient partner, but an exciting and challenging one. And Monique was both.

Not wanting to come yet, Grayson pulled back and turned Monique to face him. "On the bench," he demanded and led her out of the shower, before he pressed her down on the white leather bench in the middle of the bathroom. He went onto his knees in front of it and took Monique's legs and put them over his shoulders, so her pussy was fully exposed to him.

"Oh, baby," Monique murmured. "We don't have time for that."

"There's always time for pleasure," he protested and sank his mouth onto her sex.

He licked over her moist cleft, her juices collecting on his tongue. He spread them and licked higher up to her clit. The tiny organ was swollen, and the moment he licked over it, Monique trembled beneath him. Moans echoed in the bathroom as he lavished his attention on her center of pleasure.

Monique shoved her hands into his hair, her fingers caressing him and sending shivers down his spine, while he slipped one finger into her sex and continued licking her clit. Monique writhed underneath him, her body twisting and turning, but he didn't let go of her. He wanted to bring her to the edge of a climax.

"Oh, oh," she cried out. "So close. Please, please."

He lifted his head and quickly stood up, Monique's legs still spread and pointing in the air. He adjusted his position and plunged his cock into her quivering sex, while he used one hand to caress her clit. Monique arched her back off the bench, offering her bouncing breasts like on a silver platter.

Unable to resist the temptation, he dipped his head to one nipple and licked over it, before he drove his fangs into her flesh. A startled gasp burst from Monique's lips, and at the same time, he felt her pussy clench around his cock as she climaxed. While her blood coated his throat, he continued thrusting into her welcoming channel, her muscles spasming again and again, as the waves of her orgasm continued.

He tried to hold on to his control to prolong making love to her, but her interior muscles squeezed him relentlessly, and he couldn't hold back any longer and climaxed. His seed shot into her in hot spurts, filling her, and making her tight sheath even smoother.

When his orgasm ebbed, he retracted his fangs and licked over the puncture wounds and lifted his head. He looked at her face, and found her looking at him, a satisfied smile on her face.

"Mmm," she hummed. "You can do that anytime you want."

"The biting or the licking?"

"Both."

"Glad I don't have to choose, 'cause I don't know what I like more: licking your pussy, or drinking your blood."

~ ~ ~

Monique chuckled. "Join the club."

She would have a hard time choosing too, because she loved the way Grayson lavished pleasure on her and licked her pussy with such devotion, just as much as she loved it when he drank her blood. Both actions aroused her so much that a monumental orgasm was inevitable.

She'd always thought that if she had sex with the same man again and again, the excitement would wane and she'd lose interest in him. After all, that's what had happened with all the men she'd been with. Instead, each time she made love with Grayson, her passion for him grew, and she wanted more of him. She craved his touch, his kisses, the intimacy they shared. Inside her, her feelings for him intensified, and deepened to a point that she hadn't thought was possible.

The words he'd said to her less than twelve hours ago in front of his colleagues, echoed in her mind again.

*I'm in love with you, Monique.*

The words wrapped around her heart like a thick blanket meant to warm her. She felt that warmth now, and it felt good. Could she trust this feeling inside her? Was it the real thing? Was it love?

She pulled Grayson down to her, and brushed her lips over his. "I could get used to this."

"You'd better," he teased. "I have no intention of giving you up." He pulled her up to stand and dragged her back into the shower. "Now it's even more important that I get to run the Scanguards branch in New Orleans, 'cause a long-distance relationship isn't gonna work for us."

Stunned, she froze. How could she have forgotten that he'd told her that he'd applied for a job in New Orleans?

"Something wrong, babe?" he asked, as he took the hair shampoo and began to wash her hair.

"That's the job you were talking about that first night."

"Yes. And once I get it, I'll relocate here." With surprisingly gentle hands, he lathered her hair and massaged her scalp.

For a second, she couldn't think, Grayson's gentle ministrations distracting her. But then she started, "I applied for the same job."

"You? I thought your brothers might be interested... but..."

She raised her eyebrows and looked over her shoulder. "But what? You think I'm not capable?"

"No, no," he said quickly, almost too quickly. "I just didn't think you were interested... I mean, it's not like you were trained to be a bodyguard."

"I don't have to be trained as a bodyguard to be able to run a company." She paused. "Besides, I could kick your ass anytime."

"I know you can." He put his hands on her shoulders. "Let me rinse your hair."

"Changing the subject?"

"No." He reached for the hand-held showerhead and began rinsing her hair. "I guess I should have known that a determined woman like you wants a leadership position." He turned her to face him. "Looks like I've got stiff competition for the job."

"Are you worried that I'll get the job instead of you?"

He hesitated. "There's really no right answer to that question. How about we make a deal?" He pulled her to him, and slid both arms around her.

"What kind of deal?"

"If you get to run the Scanguards branch, you'll hire me as your personal assistant." He grinned shamelessly. "I'm good at a lot of things: washing your hair, making you climax…"

Monique couldn't suppress the smirk that curved her lips upward. "You're not taking this seriously. We're rivals. Doesn't that worry you?"

"Nope. And you know why?"

"Why?"

"Because even if I don't get the job, I'll be sticking to you like white on rice. You're not getting rid of me, babe." He tapped her on the nose. "Now let's get cleaned up and dressed. We need to head back to San Francisco. Gabriel is waiting for us."

"Who's staying here?" she asked, while reaching for the liquid soap, and started to lather her body.

"Your brothers and Victor's army. Wesley, Virginia, and John will head back tonight after sunset. Hamish will take us, Cooper, and Blake back to San Francisco, but the other Stealth Guardians are heading home to their compound until we need them again. We're taking Oscar, Abel's second-in-command, with us to San Francisco."

"Do you think you'll get anything useful out of him in San Francisco? He seemed pretty stubborn when Zach and David worked him over. Doesn't look like torture works on him."

"Trust me, if he knows where Abel is keeping our fathers, we'll find out."

"I hope you're right," she said, then added, "I should talk to my mother to let her know that we're all right. She's probably worried."

"Amaury said he'll update Faye and Delilah." He released Monique from his embrace. "When we're back in San Francisco, we can check in with them."

Monique nodded. "Before I forget it: we need to send the file of all current and former employees of the palace and all clan members to my mother. Now we know why it was never sent. Most likely Mom and Delilah will recognize some of them as the kidnappers."

"I already asked Zach to take care of that," Grayson said.

"You think of everything."

He shrugged and winked at her. "I was born to be a leader."

He would be a good leader, she realized that now.

# 29

"Gabriel is going to do what?" Monique asked, wondering if she'd heard correctly.

She and Grayson stood outside the holding cell on one of the lower levels of the Scanguards headquarters building, where they'd locked up Oscar, the vampire they'd brought back from New Orleans and whom they believed to be one of Abel's lieutenants.

"It's Gabriel's gift," Grayson explained. "He can delve into a person's memories. If Abel told this guy about his plan, and where he's hiding Cain and Samson, Gabriel will find the information."

"That's quite a gift." Monique reached for his hand. "About our discussion earlier…"

"You mean the job in New Orleans?"

"Yeah. I think you'd make a good CEO."

He smiled. "As would you. You're a smart woman, Monique. And strong. Many others would have crumbled already under the stress." He brushed a few strands of hair out of her face. "But you're right in there, in the thick of it, without a break. You must be exhausted."

"Not any more exhausted than you." Though she had to admit, she wouldn't say no to an hour or two of sleep.

Grayson leaned closer. "We'll find them. We won't stop until we do."

"I know. It's just so frustrating that we don't seem to make any progress."

"We defeated Abel's men in New Orleans. I wouldn't call that no progress," Grayson said, his voice kind and soft. "And your brothers will hold the fort there. Now it's up to us to do the rest. We can do it. We're a good team."

"Funny," she said with a smile. "I never really thought that the Grayson Woodford I knew would turn out to be a team player and a leader at the same time."

"We all play different roles and adapt to what's needed in the moment. And I can be more than just a team player or a leader. For you, I want to be much more than that."

His eyes began to shimmer golden, and the sight warmed her heart. "You are," she admitted, but didn't get any further, because Gabriel stepped out of the elevator and marched toward them.

"Hey, guys, glad all went well in New Orleans," Gabriel said without stopping, and swiped his access card over the card reader outside the cell.

A beep sounded, indicating that the door was unlocked. Gabriel pushed it open and entered. Monique and Grayson followed him into the sterile looking room. There was no furniture. Rather, a bed, two chairs and a table were built in. Made of concrete, they couldn't be moved or destroyed, offering the inmate no chance of fashioning a weapon out of them.

The prisoner was chained to the wall by a set of silver chains that burned his skin wherever it wasn't protected by his clothes. The stench of burned hair and skin stung her nostrils, but she felt no pity for the man. He'd tried to kill her and her brothers, and had probably killed countless guards and personnel loyal to the royal family. He deserved more than just a few painful burns.

Oscar glared at them, jerking forward as far as the chains allowed, his fangs extended. He laughed like a madman. "Go ahead, torture me. I won't tell you anything." He spat, but his spittle didn't hit anyone.

"Oh, I'm not gonna waste my precious time with torture, because you, asshole, would probably enjoy it," Gabriel said with a shrug.

Monique watched as Gabriel stood still in front of the prisoner, remaining just outside of the guy's reach, and closed his eyes. She exchanged a look with Grayson, who simply nodded confidently.

The prisoner, however, seemed more perplexed than peeved by Gabriel's behavior. "What the fuck are you doing?"

Nobody answered him, which seemed to annoy him even more. He glared at Grayson. "What is he doing?"

Grayson didn't even acknowledge the question and ignored him.

"Leave me the fuck alone!" the vampire yelled.

A few more minutes passed in the same fashion, until Gabriel turned to her and Grayson. "I've got everything I could find. He's yours now. I'll be outside."

Gabriel left the cell. Grayson reached into the inside pocket of his jacket and pulled out a stake. The prisoner's eyes went wide with fear.

"Hey, what are you doing?" He tried to shrink back, but the chains prevented him from escaping.

"I'm not gonna do anything," Grayson said evenly and handed her the stake.

Monique met his gaze.

"He killed your people. I'll kill him if you want me to, but I figured you'd like to do it yourself."

She appreciated that Grayson gave her a choice. "You assumed correctly." She wrapped her palm tighter around the wooden weapon, before she looked at the prisoner's face. "Look at me, look closely, 'cause I'm the last person you'll ever see. I want you to remember me when you get to hell."

She took aim and plunged the stake into his chest. For a millisecond the prisoner froze in terror, then he dissolved into ash, and the chains swung back and clanged against the wall. It took a few seconds before they stopped moving, and the clanging sound subsided. When silence descended onto the cell, Monique handed the stake back to Grayson.

"Thank you," she murmured. "I needed that."

Outside the cell, Gabriel was waiting for them.

"What did you get from him?" Grayson asked instantly.

"Not much, I'm afraid." He cast them a regretful look. "He basically just confirmed what we already knew. Abel is behind the attack on the palace and the kidnapping. But Abel is too smart to give anybody more information than they need to execute his orders. Oscar didn't know where Abel is hiding Cain and Samson. However, he did know that Abel is still in San Francisco."

"So it's a dead end," Monique said, disappointed.

"I'm afraid so. Oscar might have been Abel's second-in-command in New Orleans, but he's not his right hand. There's somebody else."

"Somebody like Baltimore, his right-hand way back when?" Grayson asked.

"Yes, somebody like him. Though we know that Baltimore is dead."

"Could he have faked his death?" Monique asked.

Gabriel shook his head. "I killed him with my own hands. He turned to dust right in front of me. No chance of faking that. Abel must have found somebody else whom he entrusts with his secrets. It certainly wasn't Oscar."

Gabriel's cell phone suddenly rang, and he answered it. "Yeah?" There was a short pause. "I'm at HQ already. See you in a minute."

Grayson cast him a curious look. "Everything okay?"

Gabriel suddenly grinned, and the scar on his cheek pulsed. "I'm gonna be a grandfather soon. Scarlet just went into labor. Ryder is on his way here with her. Maya is downstairs in the med center, probably taking a quick nap. Neither of us has been home since all this started."

"Go, Gabriel! Take care of your family," Grayson said. "We're good here."

"Thanks!" He turned, then looked back over his shoulder. "You guys should probably go see your mothers. They were asking for you. I think the worry is getting to them."

"Will do," Monique promised. She'd planned to check in with her mother anyway. Hug her. Comfort her. Assure her that they would find Cain and Samson, even if she didn't feel such certainty herself.

Minutes later, she and Grayson were in Grayson's Audi R8, heading toward the Woodford's Nob Hill residence.

"You know what still baffles me?" Grayson said.

"What?"

"How Abel knew that your brothers were coming with the Stealth Guardians." He cast her a sideways look. "They were prepared and had enough time to rig the palace so that they could douse them with dust to render the Stealth Guardians' efforts to keep everybody invisible defunct."

"It bothers me too. How did they know what to expect? What if Abel is watching our every move?"

"That's my concern too."

"Could it be that he's bugging our phones? Or planted bugs?" Monique wondered.

"It's a possibility." Grayson pressed a few buttons on his steering wheel, and an instant later, Monique heard a ringtone.

Monique gave him a curious look. "Who are you calling?"

"Sebastian."

"Hey, Grayson, what's up?" Sebastian asked through the car's loudspeakers.

"Hey, Sebastian. Do me a favor. Have the tech team run a scan of all our phones to see if any of them are bugged. Then call Zach and David in New Orleans and have them do the same on their end. And while those scans are running, drive over to my parents' house and sweep the place for bugs."

"You think somebody is bugging the place?"

"Yeah. Abel knew that the Stealth Guardians were helping Zach and David take back the palace. He couldn't have known that unless he'd overheard our conversations."

"I'll get right on it," Sebastian said and disconnected the call.

Monique sighed. "You know there's another way for Abel to have found out about our plans." She hated to point it out, because she didn't want it to be true.

Grayson met her gaze. "Yes, I know. Somebody is leaking information to him."

"A spy."

Grayson nodded. "I hope we're wrong about that."

# 30

When Grayson entered his parents' home with Monique by his side, Delilah was coming down the stairs. She looked as if she hadn't slept since the kidnapping, and her green eyes had lost the luster he was used to seeing in them. Without a word, he took her into his arms and hugged her tightly.

"We won't give up, Mom," he murmured.

She sniffled, then pulled back a little, looking at him. "I'm so relieved that you didn't get hurt in New Orleans." Then she looked past his shoulder. "Monique."

Monique put her hand on Delilah's arm and squeezed it. "We're all okay. Thanks to your son, and Scanguards and the Stealth Guardians. If they hadn't been there—"

"I just heard you're back," William interrupted, coming out of the dining room. "Monique, what happened in New Orleans? Your brothers? Are they all right?"

Grayson released his mother from his embrace, but kept an arm around her waist.

"They're all alive," Monique said to William.

William released a sigh of relief. "Thank God! We were so worried. Your mother was beside herself when there was no news of your brothers."

"Where is she now?" Monique asked.

He gestured to the wood-paneled hallway. "In the study. She's looking at the database the palace sent over about an hour ago."

"I'll go talk to her." Monique glanced at Grayson, then walked to the study.

"So, is it true?" William asked. "Abel is behind this?"

Grayson nodded. "Yeah. And his men were well prepared. They were expecting Monique's brothers, and got the jump on them."

"How?" William asked, looking stunned.

Grayson shrugged. "We're still trying to figure that out."

"Is there anything I can do? I'm fully healed now."

"For now, you're most useful staying here, protecting Faye. I'm sure she's grateful to have a familiar face around."

"Of course," William said, though he appeared disappointed.

In a way, Grayson understood him. Like Grayson, William didn't like to sit around and wait for something to happen, and take action instead.

Grayson looked at his mother. "Have you and Faye identified any other men from the prison records?"

"No. I closed my eyes for an hour or so, just to doze a little. I was just about to go back and help Faye. She's been at it nonstop. I wish I had her stamina. She doesn't seem to need sleep. Whereas I, I feel so tired…"

"You're human, Mom," Grayson said softly and pressed a kiss to her forehead. "Nobody blames you for taking a nap."

"Mom!" Isabelle said, as she stepped out of the kitchen into the hallway. "What are you doing up?" Isabelle sighed and approached, a stern expression on her face. "I thought we agreed that you would sleep for a few hours."

"I can't sleep not knowing how Samson is, where he is… if he's still…"

She didn't finish the sentence, and she didn't have to. Grayson pulled her to his chest and exchanged a look with Isabelle. He realized that she too was exhausted and that keeping up her spirits to help their mother cope was wearing her down. She needed a break too.

"Have you slept, Isa?" he asked.

Isabelle blew out a breath of air. "Doesn't matter."

"Yet she forces me to sleep," Orlando said, appearing from the door that led up from the garage.

"An order you totally ignored," Isabelle snapped and glared at Orlando. "What were you doing down there? 'Cause last time I checked there were no beds in the garage."

The massive vampire didn't flinch. Instead, he folded his arms across his chest. "I checked the weapons and munition, making sure they are loaded and ready at a moment's notice."

To Isabelle's credit, she didn't look intimidated by Orlando. She opened her mouth, clearly ready for a retort, when the door to the study opened at the end of the corridor.

"I recognized one of the kidnappers on the palace's database," Faye called from there, Monique appearing by her side.

Monique carried a laptop, and together they approached. When Monique and Faye stopped in front of them, Monique turned the laptop for all to see. On the screen was a photo of a bald black vampire with a beard. Next to the photo, information about him was listed.

"He was in the palace's employ before my time," Faye added.

"Let's check him out," Grayson said. Finally, they were making progress. "Have you sent the info to Thomas yet?"

Faye nodded. "A few minutes ago."

"Let's see what he can find." Grayson pulled out his cell phone, and called Thomas, setting it to speaker mode. "Hey, I'm with Mom and Faye. What about the guy Faye just identified?"

"I've got nothing."

"What do you mean by nothing?"

"Alexander Brechtenz doesn't exist," Thomas clarified.

"But I'm looking right at his file from the palace's database," Grayson protested, when Orlando suddenly reached past him and took the laptop from Monique's hands.

"I'm telling you," Thomas continued, "there's nothing on him anywhere—"

"That's because that's not his name," Orlando said firmly.

Everybody stared at Orlando.

"You know him?" Grayson asked.

"Yes." Orlando pointed to the screen. "He calls himself Matt Smith."

"Where can we find him?" Grayson asked.

"You can't. He finds you," Orlando said cryptically. "But I can put out some feelers."

"What do you know about him?"

Orlando shrugged. "Not much. He's an assassin for hire and knows how to stay under the radar. Maybe a tracker might have some luck."

Grayson contemplated his words for a moment. "Thanks, Thomas. We'll be in touch." He disconnected the call. "Orlando, put out some feelers, and I'll see if I can get a tracker on this." And he knew just the guy who could do this. He'd met him only once, and that was more than ten years ago, when Isabelle had been kidnapped. He'd produced results back then, and maybe he would do the same now.

"Will you be all right without me here?" Orlando asked, looking at Isabelle.

She rolled her eyes. "Orlando, we have four other guards, and William is fully healed. I think we can manage."

Orlando grunted something unintelligible, before he turned on his heel and headed for the garage to get to his car without having to be exposed to the lethal rays of the sun. It was still daytime and would be for another eight hours.

"The guy is overbearing," Isabelle said when he was gone.

"He means well," Delilah said and put her hand on Isabelle's arm.

"Uhm, Grayson," William said, motioning to him. "You mentioned a tracker. What kind of tracker?"

"The council employs trackers to apprehend escaped VCONs. I know one of them. I should have thought about him earlier." Grayson took a breath. "Monique, do you wanna stay here with your mom?"

"Where're you going?" Monique asked.

"Gotta speak to Luther to connect me with the tracker. I'm heading back to HQ."

"I'm coming with you." She pulled Faye into a hug. "Hang in there, Mom, we're making progress."

Together they left the house and got back into Grayson's car. He pulled into traffic, then made a phone call.

"Grayson?"

"Hey, Luther. I need a favor. Can you put me in touch with Striker Reed? I need him to track somebody down for me."

"Great minds think alike," Luther said with a chuckle. "I was about to call you. I hired Striker yesterday. His price is exorbitant as always, but he's worth it."

"I don't care what it costs."

"Good. Striker is tracking down some of Rufus's prison buddies. He just figured out the whereabouts of one of them, Cesar Menendez. Striker is on his way there."

Grayson exchanged a look with Monique. "Leave Cesar to me. Send me his location, and Monique and I will talk to him. Striker's time is better used to find somebody else for me. Call Thomas, and ask him to forward you the photo of Alexander Brechtenz. According to Orlando, he goes by the name Matt Smith. Faye recognized him as one of the kidnappers."

"Okay, I'll get right on that. I'm texting you Cesar's location now."

"Thanks, Luther."

"You bet."

The call disconnected, and a chiming sound indicated that Luther had sent the text message. Grayson looked at the address and made a U-turn.

"I should have thought of getting a tracker on this much earlier," Grayson said, disappointed in himself.

"Don't second-guess yourself," Monique said and put a hand on his. "We're all stressed out and sometimes it just takes a while for all possibilities to become clear. That's why you're not working alone."

"But a real leader would have known what to do right away."

Shaking her head lightly, she said, "A real leader takes input and inspiration from others to make the best decisions. He doesn't have to know it all. He just needs to surround himself with the brightest people in their field and draw on their expertise."

"Then I'm very lucky." He smiled at her. "'Cause you're by my side."

"And you by mine."

At the next red light, he leaned over to her and kissed her.

The ringing of a cell phone interrupted them.

"Mine," Monique said and looked at the display, before tapping on it to accept the call. "Delphine?" Her eyes lit up. "Thanks so much for calling me back."

Grayson concentrated on the traffic, while listening in on Monique's conversation. He realized instantly that she was talking to the voodoo practitioner she'd contacted for a location spell.

"Do you think you can try that?" Monique asked, her voice sounding hopeful. There was a brief pause, then she added, "Yes, the witch I mentioned is actually at the palace right now. If you can go there, I'll tell him to expect you, and then the two of you can work on this together."

Monique nodded to herself, while listening to Delphine's answer. "I don't know how to thank you. Yes, I'll call Wesley right now. He'll be expecting you. Thank you, Delphine."

She disconnected the call and looked at him. "What's Wesley's number?"

"I'll call him for you." Grayson clicked on Wesley's number on his cell phone. It rang once, then Wesley picked up.

"Hey, Grayson, miss me?" His voice came through the car's speakers.

"It's Monique," she said. "Wes, I just spoke to the voodoo practitioner I was telling you about. She's on her way to the palace to meet with you. Can you please work with her and see if you can get a location spell working?"

"I'll definitely give it a try. Just don't expect too much," Wesley cautioned. "As I said, certain magic doesn't work when it comes to vampires."

"I know. But it's worth a try."

"I'll give it my best shot," Wesley promised and disconnected the call.

Grayson reached for Monique's hand. "We have a few irons in the fire now. Something will pan out."

It had to.

# 31

"Cesar Menendez?" Grayson asked into the intercom of the small, dilapidated apartment building in the Outer Mission neighborhood.

Monique let her gaze wander. The neighborhood was busy and colorful. There were several shops on the same block as the apartment building. Outside one grocery store, boxes of fruits and vegetables were stacked on the sidewalk, and shoppers were perusing the wares.

"Who wants to know?"

The man sounded scratchy and annoyed. It appeared that the doorbell had awakened him.

"I doubt my name will mean anything to you. Let's just say a friend from Grass Valley sent me. I have a mutually beneficial proposition for you."

There was a brief pause, then the buzzer sounded. Grayson opened the door and ushered her inside.

"I'm surprised he let us in," Monique said.

Grayson smirked. "He's probably curious about my proposition."

"Which is?"

"I'll let him live if he answers my questions."

They walked up to the third floor, where one of the apartment doors was open a few inches. A vampire peered out into the windowless hallway. She noticed how he ran his eyes over her, the lecherous glint in them giving her the creeps.

"May we come in?" Grayson asked. "I'd rather not discuss our business out here."

Slowly, Cesar nodded and opened the door wider. "Mi casa es su casa."

Monique followed Grayson into the flat, and Cesar closed the door behind them. She glanced around. It was a one-bedroom flat with old furniture and dark curtains in front of the windows. The lights were on in the tiny hallway and the living room, where Grayson now turned around and looked at Cesar.

"So, who in Grass Valley sent you?"

"It's not so much that somebody from Grass Valley sent us," Grayson started. "Rather, we'd like to talk to you about a friend of yours there, Rufus."

Cesar narrowed his eyes and scoffed. "He's no friend of mine."

"That's not what I heard. Apparently, you two were pretty chummy when you were in prison. And you were released about the same time."

"That doesn't make us friends." He pointed to the door. "Get out."

Monique noticed the resentment emanating from Cesar, and made an educated guess as to what had caused this hostility. "I guess Rufus didn't keep his promises to you, did he? Did he owe you a favor and didn't deliver? Is that why you can't stand him now?"

Cesar grunted something indecipherable. "You've got that right! First, he promised to let me crash at his place, and then he just tossed me out. Now beat it, both of you. And tell that bastard I'm not his lackey. So whatever proposition you have, I'm not interested."

Monique didn't move, neither did Grayson.

"We'd be happy to tell him that, but we don't know where he is," Grayson said.

"Who do you think I am? His babysitter? Go to his flat."

"Yeah, tried that," Grayson said with a shake of his head. "But somebody torched the place."

To Monique's surprise, Cesar suddenly smirked. "Don't you just love it when bad things happen to bad people? That's what I call karma."

"So he had it coming, didn't he?" Grayson probed.

"You think I burned his place down?" He huffed. "Do I look suicidal?"

"Not particularly," Grayson said dryly.

Monique glanced at Grayson. "I'm getting impatient with this guy." She pulled a stake from her jacket and lunged at Cesar, slamming him to the wall and pinning him there. "Now tell me where to find Rufus."

Cesar stared at her with wide eyes, clearly not having expected her to get physical. He glanced past her to Grayson. "So she's your attack dog? You don't wanna do your own dirty work?"

"I believe women should have equal rights and all, don't you?" Grayson said with a chuckle. "Besides, she's really good at this. Cutting guys down to size. It's a beauty, really."

Monique suppressed a smirk. She'd never seen this side of Grayson, and she liked it. "Now talk, before I lose my patience."

"Fine!" Cesar grunted. "When I was released from prison, I needed a place to stay, and Rufus owed me a few favors. So I called him and he let me crash at his place. All was fine, until some asshole shows up. Next thing I know, Rufus tosses me out on my ass. I haven't seen him since."

Grayson approached from behind her. "Did that asshole look like this?"

From the corner of her eye, Monique saw Grayson hold up his cell phone to show Cesar a photo. She turned her head to see it better, and recognized it immediately. It was Abel. From an early age, her parents had drilled into her that if she or her brothers ever saw this man, to kill him or to run.

"Yeah," Cesar said, "that's him."

"And that was the last time you saw him?" Monique asked.

"I swear. And I have no idea where he is now."

She sighed and looked at Grayson. He shoved his phone back into his pocket, when she suddenly realized something. "Cesar, you said you called Rufus. You have his number?"

Cesar nodded. "Yeah, it's in my phone."

Monique exchanged a look with Grayson. "We can trace it."

Grayson looked at Cesar. "Where's the phone?"

Cesar tilted his head toward the bedroom. "On my bedside table."

Grayson left the room and went to the bedroom. Moments later, he was back with Cesar's phone. "Passcode?"

"1-2-3-4."

Grayson raised an eyebrow, then unlocked the phone. A few moments later, he typed something on his own phone, and tossed Cesar's cell phone on the coffee table. "Got it."

Monique released Cesar and pocketed the stake. "Thanks for your cooperation."

Cesar grimaced derisively. "Yeah, sure, pleasure."

Outside, Grayson took Monique's hand. "Thomas will be able to ping Rufus's phone."

"If he's still using the same number," she added.

"He has no reason not to." Grayson made a few key strokes on his phone. "I've just sent it to Thomas, so he can get started on it."

"Good. We need a win." She cast him a hopeful smile. "Where did you get Abel's picture from?"

"I had Zach text it to me when we were in New Orleans. I've already sent it to Thomas to distribute to everybody at Scanguards so they know who to look out for. Just in case."

"Good thinking. Mom and Dad made us memorize his photo since we were kids. I guess they were worried that one day he'd be back and try to hurt us."

"Not for much longer," Grayson said confidently, putting his arm around her as they walked to where he'd parked the car.

She loved the affection he showed toward her, the warmth of his regard, the encouraging tone in his voice. With every hour they spent together, her feelings for him became clearer to her. She knew what was growing between them, trust and love. And a deep appreciation for their individual strengths. They complemented each other, trading leadership almost instinctively depending on what the situation demanded.

"Thanks for letting me deal with him my way," Monique said.

"You kidding?" He chuckled. "You going all Rambo on him was such a turn-on. I almost envied the guy."

She gave a soft laugh. "You got turned on by me manhandling a guy?"

"Totally." Arriving at the car, he pressed her against it and leaned in. "You can do that to me anytime."

"Threatening your life with a stake?"

"As long as you don't plunge it into my heart, and rub your hot body all over me instead."

"How about tying you up?" she suggested, enjoying teasing him. She craved a few hours alone with him, away from their problems, but she knew there was no time for that right now. A few teasing words would have to tide her over.

"Tied up or not, you'll never get rid of me," he promised, his eyes suddenly shimmering golden.

A shudder went through her, and it was evident that he noticed it. His mouth turned into a satisfied grin, before he dipped his head to hers and pressed his lips to hers, kissing her deeply. She sighed contentedly and kissed him back. But too soon, he severed the kiss.

"Let's get back to HQ," he said, "before I do something I shouldn't be doing in broad daylight and in view of way too many witnesses."

# 32

On the executive floor of Scanguards headquarters, they ran into Sebastian.

"Hey, Sebastian. Any news about the phones?" Grayson asked.

"Just got done with it. We ran a scan on all Scanguards registered landlines and cell phones. Nothing. And your parents' house is clean of bugs too."

"So nobody is tapping our phones?" Grayson asked, his forehead furrowing.

"No," Sebastian replied, "definitely not. Not that I expected to find anything. The security we have in place makes it virtually impossible to bug us without alarm bells going off everywhere."

"Thanks, Sebastian."

Grayson exchanged a look with Monique. "Then we have a leak somewhere."

"But where?"

"I wish I knew. The bodyguards who're protecting my parents' house are absolutely trustworthy. They've been with us forever," Grayson assured her. He would put his life in their hands without hesitation.

"You're not saying that somebody on my side is the leak?" Monique shook her head. "William is the second-in-command of the Kings' guard, and he's been with us for two decades. He practically raised me and my brothers. He's one hundred percent loyal. Besides, he nearly died saving my mother's life during the attack. And the other two guards were killed. Both our mothers confirmed that. Nobody else came to San Francisco with us."

"I know, and I'm not saying it's William. But the entire palace was compromised. We don't know who else Abel has in his pocket. Maybe somebody is leaking information without even knowing it."

"Hmm. Are you sure about the bodyguards at your parents' house? Have they all been with Scanguards for a long time? Can you trust them?"

"Yes, Conrad and Robbie have been with us for eight or nine years, as have all the human guards. And Orlando is—" He stopped himself. Orlando was a wild card. Nobody knew much about him. And he was relatively new.

"What about Orlando?"

Grayson hesitated, and took a breath, before answering. "Dad hired him over a year ago."

"So he's new." Monique looked at him, her forehead furrowing. "He insisted on staying at your parents' house. He didn't want to be relieved for a break. Don't you think that's odd?"

"He's very dedicated," Grayson protested. "My father trusts him one hundred percent."

"Yeah, but nobody knows anything about him," Sebastian interjected, making him realize that the young vampire hybrid hadn't left.

When Grayson cast him a look, Sebastian shrugged and added, "You know as well as I do that that's the truth. He's strange, doesn't talk much, and who knows what he does in his spare time. He's never once gone out with any of us. You know, letting off steam."

"That doesn't mean he's not trustworthy," Grayson said, his voice firm. "Not trusting Orlando means not trusting my father's judgment. And no matter the differences Dad and I might have had, his judgment is sound."

He suddenly felt Monique's hand on his arm. "Nobody is saying that about Samson, but don't you think we should explore all possibilities?"

Monique was right, even if he didn't want to admit it outright. It was true that Orlando had been one of the first to arrive at the rental house in Russian Hill after the kidnapping, even though others lived much closer than him. If he'd gone home after the Scanguards party, he would have had to drive all the way from Glen Park to Russian Hill, which wasn't exactly a short drive. Orlando had left the party prematurely, which was also suspicious. And something else he remembered now too. Orlando had said he'd been *in the area*. What had he been doing in Russian Hill?

"Fine, let's check him out," he finally conceded. "But we should also check out William. After all, he might know Abel from a long time ago."

Monique looked like she wanted to protest, but then she conceded, "Fine, if that makes you feel better."

Grayson nodded. "I have an idea how to go about it so they won't know what we're doing. Let's talk to Thomas and Eddie."

Moments later, Grayson knocked on Thomas and Eddie's office, before opening the door and entering with Monique following him. Only Eddie sat behind the desk.

"Hey, Eddie, where's Thomas?"

Eddie sighed. "Finally taking a nap in Blake's office. He hasn't slept a minute since all this started. I had to force him to take a break."

"Good. I texted him a number earlier. Did—"

"I got it." Eddie put his hand on a cell phone on his desk. "I just got started on it. Program's running. By the way, good news: we found the fourth van from the kidnappers."

Grayson felt excited. "Excellent! Where? Monique and I can check it out."

"Not necessary. Your brother and Benjamin are already en route. They'll check it out. We've provided them with photos of Abel, Rufus, and that Matt guy. I'm sure they'll report back soon."

There was a pinging sound coming from Eddie's computer. He looked at the screen again, then back at him and Monique. "Okay, we have good news and bad news."

"Give me the good news first," Grayson demanded.

"Rufus's cell phone pinged off several cell towers in the last few days, all within city limits. And one of those pings coincides with the location where the fourth van is parked."

Monique's chest rose, as she pulled in a breath. "That's the area where they're probably holding my father and Samson, right?"

"Possibly," Eddie hedged. "But here's the bad news. Rufus's cell phone is currently switched off."

"So we don't know where he is right now," Grayson said, contemplating their next action.

"Nope, but it's very likely that he's somewhere close to where his cell phone was last traced to. The fourth van is our best bet right now."

"Show me where," Grayson said and walked around Eddie's desk so he could look into the screen.

Eddie pointed to a location on the map, while Monique sidled up to him. "He was somewhere along this area, between Bayview and Silver Terrace."

"With the freeway close by. Good place to make a quick getaway," Grayson commented.

"What are these buildings here?" Monique asked.

Eddie zoomed in. "That's an old post office, but it was shut down long ago. Asbestos issues and who knows what else. The city is waiting for the federal government to pay for the abatement, but they're dragging their heels."

"So it's empty," Monique concluded.

Grayson met her gaze. "Good place to hide."

"I'll let Patrick and Benjamin know to not get too close to it. Don't wanna spook Abel's people if they're really in there." Eddie swiveled in his chair. "Maybe Wesley and Charles can confirm that this is the right location before we do anything else."

"Wesley is back?" Grayson asked.

"Got back half an hour ago. He's probably already down in his lab."

"Let's check on him," Grayson suggested and looked at Monique.

She nodded.

"Oh, and one other thing, Eddie," Grayson started.

"Yes?"

"Do me a favor and cross-check Orlando's cell phone with Rufus's. I wanna know if they ever called or texted each other. And compare Orlando's GPS locations to the areas where Rufus's cell phone pinged off the towers."

Eddie raised a surprised eyebrow. "Orlando? Our Orlando?"

"Yes."

"What's this about?"

"Somebody is leaking information to Abel, and since he's not bugging our phones or my parents' house..." Grayson shrugged.

"Okay, if you say so."

"And, not a word about this to anybody."

"Understood."

"And there's a second person I want you to check out. William. He's one of the King's guards who came to San Francisco with the royal family. Monique, you have his phone number?" Grayson asked.

"I do." She pulled out her cell phone and navigated to William's contact information and handed it to Eddie, who copied it.

"Got it. I'll check where he's been and whom he called," Eddie confirmed.

"Thanks, Eddie, and have Patrick call me once they've checked out the van," Grayson added, before he and Monique left Eddie's office.

As they walked to the elevator, Monique slipped her hand into his. "I hope Delphine was able to explain to Wesley how the spell works."

"Don't worry about Wesley. He's a very accomplished witch. He'll make it work." As long as a voodoo spell worked on a vampire. If not, even Wesley would be out of luck. But he didn't want to crush Monique's hope.

On the ride down to one of the subterranean floors, where both the medical center and Wesley and Charles's lab were located, Monique leaned her head against his shoulder, breathing evenly. Neither of them said anything. They didn't need to speak. He put his arms around her, and simply held her. If somebody had told him three days earlier that he would develop such a deep emotional bond with Monique Montague after two days and two nights together, he would have laughed the person out of the room.

# 33

Monique enjoyed the feel of Grayson's arms around her, comforting her. So much had happened in such a short time, and she was still processing everything. She fought off the exhaustion that sat deep in her bones. There was no time for rest right now.

When the elevator doors parted, Grayson took her hand and led her into the hallway. It wasn't busy here, though she could hear sounds coming from behind a set of double doors. The sign next to it identified it as the medical center. Grayson ushered her in the opposite direction.

Before they reached the end of the corridor, the loud boom of an explosion made the ground beneath her feet shake. The door at the end of the hallway was blown off its hinges and crashed to the floor, the wood splintering. A cloud of white and red smoke, mixed with debris, shot out of the room.

"Fuck!" Grayson cursed.

Instead of running in the other direction, he ran toward the room where the explosion had taken place. Monique had no choice but to follow him. Whatever had happened, she couldn't let him deal with it on his own.

Inside the room, the smoke already started dissipating. She let her eyes roam, quickly assessing the situation. The room was large with lots of cabinets holding glass containers—some of them broken—with odd-looking ingredients, a wall with books looking older than Methuselah, and chairs and tables, as well as a large caldron over a firepit in a corner.

Wesley lay on his back on the floor, his face covered in red dust, his dark hair standing up as if he'd gotten an electrical shock. He coughed and sat up.

"Fuck, Wes!" another man groused.

Monique looked at him and recognized him as a witch. He too was on the floor, trying to get up.

"Charles, Wes? You guys okay?" Grayson asked, holding out his hand to help Wesley up.

"Yeah, we're fine," Wes said with a dismissive hand movement.

"What happened here?" Monique asked.

Charles got up too, and shook his head in Wesley's direction. "This idiot here didn't measure the ingredients of the spell correctly. That's what happened."

"Hey, could have happened to anybody," Wes said, shrugging.

"Sure, but it keeps happening to you," Charles retorted.

"Was that the voodoo spell from Delphine?" Grayson asked.

Wes nodded. "Yeah. Let's see if it worked."

He walked to a workbench. It looked like a tornado had touched down there. Monique approached, as did Grayson and Charles.

"Hey, I'm Charles; you must be Monique." He extended his hand to her, and she shook it.

"Nice to meet you, Charles." She looked a little closer at him and pointed to his face. "I think your eyebrows are singed."

He grunted, then narrowed his eyes at Wesley. "I swear, one of these days, I'm gonna wring your neck."

The warning rolled off Wesley as if he were made of Teflon. "Don't worry, they'll grow back."

Monique couldn't help but smile at the exchange. Two witches working together in one lab couldn't be easy. She caught Grayson's eyes, and he too grinned. Apparently, the two witches arguing wasn't new.

"So, did the spell work?" Grayson asked eagerly.

Wesley reached for a small piece of paper with charred edges. It looked like a part of a map. He turned to Charles. "Charles, the map please."

Charles opened a drawer and pulled out a map, then unfolded it on the workbench. Wesley bent over it and compared the charred piece with the map, until he finally laid it on the intact map and looked up.

"Looks like they're being kept somewhere between the Bayview and Silver Terrace. Sorry that it's not any more precise, but I guess it's a start," Wesley announced.

Monique's heart leapt. This was good news.

"Not just a start," Grayson said. "This is in line with Rufus's cell phone's last known position, and where the fourth van has been found."

"Glad we could help," Wes said. "Now, maybe you could put in a good word with Amaury to approve some minor renovations for the lab." He motioned to the busted door and the charred walls and broken furniture.

Grayson smirked. "That can be arranged. But I suggest you don't start with repairing anything until you're done with mixing potions for the rescue mission."

"Don't you trust my abilities?"

"Oh, I do," Grayson said, winking at Charles, before looking back at Wesley. "Just not your execution."

"Finally," Charles said, "somebody recognizes what I'm dealing with on a daily basis. Maybe I should get my own lab."

Wesley turned to him. "You *had* your own lab. And see how that turned out."

"Hmm."

"What happened?" Monique asked curiously.

Grayson grinned. "His mate, Roxanne, put the kibosh on him working out of the basement of their home. Apparently, she was sick of the explosions rocking the foundation of the house."

Charles lifted his hand in protest. "Hey, it wasn't that bad. Besides, it was my choice to move my operation to headquarters. I mean, who would keep Wes in check if I weren't here?"

"I don't need to be kept in check," Wes protested.

"Do too."

"Thanks guys," Grayson said quickly, and took Monique's arm. "We'd better leave."

They left the lab, while Wesley and Charles continued arguing, and walked back toward the elevators, when Monique suddenly heard what sounded like babies crying. But she had to be wrong.

She glanced at Grayson. "Do you hear that?"

# 34

Grayson pushed the double doors to the medical center open, and entered, Monique by his side. The large room looked like any emergency room in a midsize hospital. In the middle was a nurses' station, and around it, along the walls were several treatment berths with curtains separating them for patient privacy. On one end of the room were several private patient rooms as well as Maya's office.

"Wow," Monique said, looking around. "And Maya runs this place?"

Grayson nodded. "Yes. This is her domain."

"It's impressive," Monique said.

Grayson motioned to the people crowding around the entrance to one of the private patient rooms. Gabriel stood there with Brandon King, while Maya stood near the bed, and Ryder sat on the edge of it, a newborn in his arms, while Scarlet held the other twin.

When they walked closer, Gabriel looked over his shoulder.

"Hey," he said, "what was that commotion earlier?"

"Little explosion," Grayson said casually and peered into the room.

"Wesley?" Gabriel asked.

"Yep. At least the spell worked. We've got a pretty good idea where Cain and Samson are being held."

"Guess that means I don't get to hold my grandsons right now," Gabriel said.

"Take a few minutes," Grayson said. "I'll call everybody in, so we can work on a rescue plan."

When Brandon approached the bed, Scarlet put her son into his arms. Grayson stood there for a moment, just watching the scene. Monique leaned closer to him, and he put his arm around her waist.

"Oh my God, he doesn't weigh more than a feather," Brandon said with a look at his daughter. "I don't remember you being so small when you were born."

"Congratulations, Scarlet, Ryder," Grayson said, and both of them lifted their heads and looked at him.

"Thanks, bro," Ryder said. He looked at his two sons, then at Scarlet, and pressed a soft kiss to his mate's lips. "I love you, baby. You did great." When he looked up again, his eyes were shimmering golden.

Grayson cast a sideways look at Monique, feeling the urge to kiss her rise up inside him. "We should…"

She nodded. "Yeah." Then she addressed Scarlet and Ryder, "Congratulations to you both. The babies are adorable."

Ryder grinned. "Thanks, Monique. I'm sure they'll be running roughshod over us soon enough."

Scarlet chuckled. "How much trouble can two little boys really be? Look at them, they look like little angels."

"That's what they said about my brothers and me too," Monique said with a smirk.

"The three of you were adorable as babies, but you're right, you guys were a handful," Maya said with a smile at Monique, her gaze zeroing in on Grayson's arm around Monique's waist. Her eyebrows lifted in surprise, but she didn't comment on what she saw.

"We'd better get going," Grayson said, then nodded at Gabriel. "Meeting room in thirty minutes?"

Gabriel nodded, and Brandon turned to him. "I'll join you guys too."

"Thanks, Brandon, appreciate it."

Brandon wasn't a Scanguards employee. Rather, he was a partner and investor who'd joined them after Gabriel had turned him into a vampire in order to save his life. A very successful entrepreneur as a human, Brandon King had adapted to life as a vampire very quickly. The fact that his daughter had blood-bonded with Ryder, a vampire-satyr hybrid, had certainly helped make the transition smooth. And now, he was a grandfather of two vampire-satyr hybrids, though he didn't look old enough for that, and could easily pass for a man in his late forties.

When the elevator arrived, Grayson was glad to see that it was empty. He pulled Monique inside, and punched the button for the top floor, before drawing her against his body, his arms imprisoning her.

"Damn, babe, right now I wish I could toss you on the nearest flat surface, and—"

"—and bury your cock inside me?" she interrupted and whirled him around so his back was against the wall, and she was pressing her lush curves to his hard body. "I didn't realize that seeing newborn babies can make a guy horny."

"It's not the babies." Though the sight had stirred his heart unexpectedly. "It's knowing that Ryder drinks Scarlet's blood when he makes love to her. And she drinks his."

Monique's lips parted, and a breath rushed from her throat. Her eyes began to shimmer golden, and when he took his next breath, he could smell the aroma of her arousal as it wrapped around him like velvet ropes trying to shackle him. He welcomed those shackles, in fact, he yearned for them.

Monique lifted her lips to his, offering them, and he captured them, kissing her passionately. When the elevator beeped, Grayson reluctantly severed the kiss, but held Monique for a moment longer, his forehead resting against hers. "I wish we—"

She put a finger to his lips. "I know."

His cell phone rang, and he pulled it from his pocket. "It's Patrick." He accepted the call, while he and Monique exited the elevator. "Hey, what did you find?"

"Hey. There was blood in the van, and both Benjamin and I are pretty sure that it's vampire blood. It's dried, so it's hard to tell if it was Dad's, but I'm assuming it was."

"Did you spot any of the vampires you had pictures for?"

"No, no sighting of Abel, Matt, or Rufus, but that doesn't mean they're not here. There are definitely a few possible locations where Abel could hide Dad and Cain. We'd need to check them out, but we didn't wanna be too obvious and tip them off."

"Good work. Good news is that the location spell that Wesley did, points us to the same area as Rufus's cell phone. At least his last known location. It's currently switched off."

"So, what now? You're gonna send a few teams out to help us check out all the empty buildings?"

"No. Let's go with drones and infrared cameras. It's safer."

"All right, you're the boss, bro."

"Thanks, Patrick. Come back to HQ. We're meeting to work out a rescue plan."

"Be there soon," Patrick promised and disconnected the call.

Grayson put his cell phone back into his pocket, before casting Monique an encouraging look. "Let's go see Quinn. He can organize the drones."

Quinn, a blond vampire who looked barely a day over twenty-five, even though he was over two hundred years old, was in his office on the executive floor.

"Hey, what do you need?" he asked after greeting him and Monique.

"We've got a possible location where Abel might be keeping Cain and Samson. We need to send in drones with infrared cameras. Can you get that organized?"

"Sure, show me the general location on the map," Quinn said and pulled up a map on his computer screen.

Grayson walked around the desk to look at the screen, when Monique's phone rang.

She pulled it out and looked at the display. "It's Mom, I'll take it outside."

"Sure, babe."

She stepped out into the hallway and pulled the door shut behind her.

"Babe, huh?" Quinn asked with a smirk.

Grayson shrugged. "Guess our fathers weren't completely wrong after all."

"Well, they have been around for a while and know a thing or two."

"And hopefully they'll be around for a lot longer." Grayson pointed to the screen. "This is where all our leads point to. Apparently, there's an old decommissioned post office that's been condemned because of asbestos. That's where I would lock up hostages. I'd start there."

"I'll get right on it," Quinn promised and reached for the phone. "We should know more in the next half hour."

"Thanks, buddy. And can you please send a message to all hybrids who're not on assignment as well as the top brass for a meeting in half an hour?"

"Will do."

Grayson left the office. In the hallway, Monique was still talking to her mother, giving her encouraging news. He exchanged a quick glance with her and pointed to Thomas and Eddie's office to make her understand, where she could find him.

He knocked on the office door, then entered. Eddie was still on his own, and looked up from the computer.

"The voodoo spell worked," Grayson said.

"Oh, was that the boom I heard earlier?" Eddie shook his head and rolled his eyes. "What did he destroy this time?"

"Blew out the door."

"Is that all?"

"Hmm. The spell confirmed the same location as the one you found for the van and Rufus's last cell phone location. So I asked Quinn to send in drones to check out that old postal facility."

"Good." Eddie pointed to the screen. "About Orlando…"

When he hesitated, Grayson felt his heart pound faster. "What did you find?"

"No phone calls or text messages between him and Rufus, so that's a good thing. But the night before New Year's Eve, Orlando's and Rufus's cell phones were in the same area at the same time. Now, that's not definite proof that they met, particularly since it happened in the Castro. There's one bar after the other, so they might have been in different bars, but since we only have Orlando's exact GPS location because we own his phone, but not Rufus's, I can't say with a hundred percent certainty that he and Rufus met."

"Hmm." But what if they had? "What would Orlando do in the Castro? It's mostly gay bars. And I'm pretty sure he's straight."

"He is," Eddie confirmed. "But he might have just been there to find somebody to feed from. It's a very lively area, crawling with humans in various states of inebriation. Easy prey."

Eddie had a point. But until he could rule out Orlando as the leak, it was best to take precautions. "If Orlando calls you for any reason and asks you how the rescue mission is going, tell him we've got nothing new."

"Do you think that's really necessary?"

"Yes. What did you find on William?"

"I had to hack into his cell phone provider's records, since we don't own his phone. He had no contact with Rufus, and he didn't cross paths with him in San Francisco either, at least not according to the cell phone data."

"Okay, so he's probably clean."

"Looks like it."

"Thanks, Eddie. I'll talk to Isabelle to make sure Mom and Faye don't let anything slip in Orlando's presence."

If necessary, Isabelle would have to distract him. He'd make sure of that.

Grayson pulled his cell phone from his pocket and scrolled to Isabelle's number.

# 35

Monique let her gaze roam. The large conference room on the top floor of Scanguards' HQ was bustling. Grayson had pointed out those people she hadn't met before and told her their names. Now, he stood in the front of the room, ready to address the assembled. Almost a dozen hybrids were in attendance and a similar number of vampires.

John wasn't back from New Orleans yet, but Virginia had traveled back there after she'd brought Wesley back to San Francisco, and both would be returning within the hour. John wanted to be part of the showdown with Abel.

"Everybody, let's get started," Grayson said, and the conversations in the room died down. "Thanks to everybody's relentless efforts, we finally have the location where Abel is keeping Samson and Cain locked up. Quinn, you sent the drones in. Let's have your report."

Quinn nodded and stood. He clicked a remote, and the screen on the wall flickered. An arial video began to play. "What you're seeing here is an old postal facility in Silver Terrace, just where it borders on the Bayview. The building was decommissioned over ten years ago. It's boarded up, and supposed to be empty, but"—he pointed to the monitor, where heat signatures inside the building were now visible—"there are lots of people inside. We have to assume that those are Abel's men. After examining the drone footage, we're estimating that more than two dozen people are inside. And most likely they're heavily armed. Eddie?"

Eddie stood and took over from Quinn. He used a laser pointer, which he directed at the screen. "The building has cameras at every egress point. We'd assumed that they were inoperable, since the facility is shut down, but after scanning the building for any electrical activity, we're pretty sure that Abel and his men reactivated the existing cameras to keep an eye on who's approaching the building. They will see us coming."

Grayson took the remote from Eddie. "Thanks, Eddie." Then he looked at the assembled. "That's where the Stealth Guardians come in. They'll be our eyes, and will enter the facility invisibly and get us a read on the situation inside. If necessary, they'll cut the kidnappers off from the hostages, so that they can't harm them once they realize that we're attacking."

"Can't the Stealth Guardians just kill Abel's men while they're in there?" Nicholas asked.

"They could kill a few, sure," Grayson replied, "but that would alert the rest of them and considering how many hostiles we believe are in the building, they'd be heavily outnumbered. Besides, it's not their fight, it's ours. They'll assist, but we'll be doing the heavy lifting. They'll do their best to locate Samson and Cain and keep them safe, until we can extract them."

He clicked the remote, and three pictures appeared on the monitor. "Make yourself familiar with these faces. This is Abel, the mastermind behind the kidnapping. This is Rufus. And this guy,"—he pointed to a bald black guy with a beard—"is Matt Smith. He, together with Rufus, was part of the kidnapping team that attacked the rental house in Russian Hill where Cain and his family were staying. I don't care who kills them or any of the other hostile vampires. But if you can get Abel alive, do it. I'm sure Cain will want to kill him himself."

Zane cleared his throat. "Just to be clear. I shoot to kill."

Grayson met Zane's stare, then gave a light shake of his head. "Everybody but Zane, if you're able to safely capture Abel alive, do it."

"When are we going in?" Ethan asked.

"After sundown tonight."

"What?" Ethan's forehead furrowed. "It's much easier during the daytime. Abel and his men won't be able to escape, because the sun will get them."

"That's not gonna work," Grayson insisted.

Ethan glanced around. "But we've got at least ten hybrids, and we have several Kevlar suits for the full-blooded vampires. That should be enough."

"And what about Samson and Cain?" Grayson asked. "We have no idea in what state they are. And how quickly we have to get them out. If the sun is up, it limits us. We can't risk exposing Samson and Cain to the sun. And we don't have enough Kevlar suits to suit them up. We need those for the fighters if we go in during the day."

"Grayson's got a point," Gabriel said to Ethan. "I hate waiting as much as the next guy, but we have to consider Samson and Cain's safety first and foremost."

Ethan shrugged in a gesture of surrender. "Got it."

"Let's talk logistics," Grayson said.

Monique couldn't help but admire Grayson. He was a born leader without being a dictator. He had sound reasons behind his arguments, and was comfortable in his role. It was evident that he thrived under pressure, and what greater pressure could there be than the fear of losing one's father? He couldn't afford to make a mistake, nobody could. The more she heard Grayson talking about his plan of how to free their fathers, and took suggestions and comments from his colleagues, the more she realized that he would be perfect for leading the new Scanguards branch in New Orleans. He would be a leader everybody could respect. A man with a strong sense of right and wrong, a man who did everything in his power to save the people he loved.

She didn't just respect Grayson and trust in his knowledge and training. Her feelings ran much deeper, and she was wondering now why she hadn't realized much earlier what was happening between them. Grayson had already professed his love for her, in public no less. Yet, she'd held back, scared that he would hurt her again, like he'd hurt her when she was a child. But it was stupid to think that way. They'd both changed. They'd both grown. She was an adult now, and being an adult came with risks. And rewards. She was ready for both. And she wasn't going to wait any longer to take her future into her own hands and take what she wanted. Her father's kidnapping had taught her one thing she would never forget: there was no time like the present. Tomorrow wasn't certain. But the present was here, and she wouldn't allow it to run through her fingers. She would grip it firmly, and never let go.

"You okay?"

Grayson suddenly stood in front of her, and she realized that the meeting was concluded, and everybody was leaving to get a few hours of rest at home until they would execute the rescue plan.

"I'm all right."

"Good. Let's go back to my place, and get a little rest."

She nodded, but knew that it wasn't rest she wanted. It was Grayson, the man she'd fallen in love with over the last few days without realizing how it had happened.

# 36

"You can't come with us to rescue Cain and Samson," Grayson said.

He and Monique were back at his loft. He'd shrugged off his jacket and kicked off his shoes. They had a few hours until he would lead his colleagues to rescue Cain and Samson, and he wanted to make the most of it.

Monique stopped in front of him. "I figured you'd say that."

"And I won't budge this time, and there's nothing you can say to change my mind. You don't have the training that's required for a mission like this. I know you want to help, but if—"

She put her index finger over his lips. "I'm not trying to change your mind. I know that you and your colleagues are trained for this, and I'm not."

Surprised that she didn't oppose him, he stared at her. He'd been prepared to list a whole lot of reasons why she couldn't come with him and would have to stay with Faye and Delilah at the Woodford residence.

"But there's something you need to know…" she said, hesitating.

"What is it?" He snaked his arm around her waist, pulling her to him.

"I realized something today," she started, and a small breath rushed from her lungs. "The thought that you'll be putting yourself in danger tonight to save our fathers does something to me that I wasn't expecting." She took his hand and pressed it to her breast.

He waited with bated breath, eager to hear what she wanted to tell him, and worried that any interruption by him would make her stop.

"The thought that you could get hurt, or worse, killed, is hurting in here." She lifted her lids and pinned him with her eyes. "Because I realized today that I love you."

Grayson's heart stopped, and Monique's words echoed in his mind, repeating as if on a loop. Was he hallucinating? Had he fallen asleep and was dreaming?

"Would you pinch me please?" he choked out, his throat as dry as sandpaper.

"I can do better than that," she murmured and pressed her lips to his.

Her kiss confirmed that what was happening was real, not a dream or a hallucination. Monique had really confessed that she loved him. He brought his hands to her face, framing it as he kissed her, before he interrupted the kiss and looked into her eyes.

"I love you, Monique." He inhaled deeply, his heart feeling lighter than it ever had. "You can't imagine how happy you make me." For a moment, all his worries disappeared into the background.

"Grayson, you probably think it's stupid, but I'm worried about you going into the lion's den tonight…"

He stroked over her hair. "But you know I have to go. I have to get our fathers back."

"I know that, and I'm not saying you shouldn't go… uhm, I… I want to be able to know you're all right… if anything goes wrong… I need to be able to reach you… to know what's happening to you…"

He noticed that she was babbling nervously and pulled back a little. "What are you trying to say?"

Monique sighed. "Are you really gonna make me say it? Do you need me to go down on my knees?"

"On your knees? Why would you—" He stopped himself, realization finally dawning. His chin dropped.

Monique suddenly pulled back. She dropped her gaze, turning halfway. "Sorry, like I said, it's stupid. Clearly, you don't want—"

He pulled her back to him and put his finger on her lips, stopping her from finishing her sentence. "Babe, are you saying you want to blood-bond with me so we can communicate telepathically when I'm going on the rescue mission?"

"Forget it, as I said it's a stupid idea."

"No, it's not," he said firmly, and put his fingers under her chin to tip her face up so she had to look at him. "But I don't want to blood-bond with you just for the telepathic bond." He shook his head.

Her lips quivered as if she was going to burst into tears any moment.

"I want to blood-bond with you," Grayson continued, "because I love you and can't imagine my life without you."

Her face lit up. "You do? You want this?"

He grinned. "Yes, though I had hoped that I'd be the one to propose." He shrugged. "Guess there's nothing conventional about our relationship."

"You'd get bored if we had a conventional relationship," Monique said with a smile.

"No chance of that happening with you." He lifted her up and started walking toward the bedroom. "I hate to rush this, but I'm afraid we don't have much time."

"Then let's not waste it with idle chit-chat."

"A woman after my own heart."

He laid her on the bed and began undressing her.

He couldn't believe his luck. Monique would be his. And the thought of her being the only woman he'd make love to from now on didn't frighten him in the least. He'd always thought that giving up his freedom, his bachelor lifestyle would scare him, but no such feeling took hold of him now. Instead, excitement filled every cell of his body. He understood now why Damian and Ryder had blood-bonded with Naomi and Scarlet so quickly, despite barely knowing them. The heart knew what the heart wanted. And his heart wanted Monique. There was no need to wait any longer. They were meant for each other. Instinctively, he'd known it since the moment he'd laid eyes on her twenty years earlier.

And now, Monique lay in front of him in the nude, while he shed his last items of clothing, her eyes roaming over him. In her gaze, he recognized something he'd never liked in any woman before: possessiveness. Yet in Monique, he welcomed it, in fact, he craved it. He would be hers just as much as she would be his.

When he pulled down his boxer briefs, his cock jutted out, hard and heavy. Monique dropped her gaze to it, and her eyes began to shimmer golden. She sat up and scooted to the edge of the bed, while he still stood there. He knew what she wanted, and he didn't protest as she put her hand around the root of his cock and sucked his erection into her mouth.

"Fuck, babe!"

Her mouth was pure heaven, her tongue silky soft, her breath warm. He placed his hands on her cheeks, holding her head gently so he could withdraw if the sensation became too intense. He loved the way she worshipped him with her mouth, while she moved her hand around the base of his cock up and down. When she used her other hand to cradle his balls, he jerked back so his erection slipped from her mouth.

"Enough!" He couldn't take more of this sensual pleasure, or he would come in her mouth. "Lie down."

With a sinful smile, she lay back. "I enjoyed that," she murmured, looking at him from under her dark lashes.

"So did I," he confessed and lowered himself over her. "But we don't have the luxury of time right now."

Monique spread her legs wider, and he adjusted himself at her center. Warmth and wetness greeted him there. With one thrust, he plunged into her, seating himself to the hilt, his balls slapping against her flesh, his breath rushing from his lungs.

Monique moaned and arched her back. "Baby, you're bigger today. It feels so good."

"'Cause you feel tighter."

He began to move inside her, withdrawing a bit, before thrusting back inside. A breath tore from her throat, and her eyelashes fluttered. He loved seeing her react to him like this. Loved the way she gave into her feelings and surrendered herself to him.

"I love you," he murmured and captured her lips with his.

~ ~ ~

Monique placed one hand on Grayson's nape to intensify the kiss, while she crossed her legs behind his butt, wanting him as close as possible. She loved it, how he drove into her over and over again, his tempo increasing with each thrust, while he licked his tongue over her canines, driving her crazy with lust. Her fangs extended to their full length. When he swept his tongue over them again, her entire body exploded with pleasure, her sex spasming around his pistoning cock.

Grayson growled without releasing her lips, and the possessive sound seeped into every cell of her being. He was staking his claim, making her understand that he would never let her go. Just as she would never let him go. No other woman would ever get to touch him again. She would be the only one he'd find pleasure with, the only one who understood him. She would be the keeper of his heart.

Using her vampire strength, she rolled them, so he was on his back, and she was the rider now.

He severed the kiss and grinned. "I see, my future mate wants to have the upper hand. Show me who's boss, huh?" He gripped her hips firmly and thrust his cock upward.

Monique gasped at the forcefulness of his movement. "Oh!"

"Yeah, babe, doesn't matter what position I'm in. I'll take you any which way I can." He slapped her on the ass.

At the unexpected touch, a spear of excitement shot through her core.

"Now ride me!"

"Is that an order?"

"It is." His fangs descended, and his eyes were glowing golden.

A shiver ran down her spine. She'd never been so turned on. "Then I have to do what my master commands."

She bent over him, and began to ride him, moving her hips up and down, while he kept his hands on her hips to set the tempo. Their bodies moved in synch, while their heartbeats echoed each other. She could feel Grayson holding on to his control by only a thread, his jaw clenching, his eyes boring into her. She felt her clit respond to him, and sensed the approach of her orgasm.

"Now," she demanded breathlessly and brought her mouth to his neck, where she felt his vein pulsing against her lips.

"Yes," he whispered into her ear, before she felt his fangs brush over the spot where her shoulder connected with her neck.

Monique drove her fangs into Grayson's neck and sucked on his plump vein, the rich blood filling her mouth. Greedily, she swallowed. In the same instant, she felt his fangs pierce her skin and lodge deep in her flesh. When he began to suck, waves of bliss crashed over her, drowning her in a sea of pleasure. Their bodies now moved as if steered by an invisible force, their love guiding them from one peak to another. Monique put her hand on the back of Grayson's head, wanting to make sure that he kept drinking her blood, while she gorged herself on his.

*You're mine now*, she heard in her mind. It was Grayson's voice, though he hadn't spoken. It was the telepathic bond blood-bonded couples shared.

The implications of what they were doing finally sank deep into her, permeating her heart and her soul. *Grayson, I love you, always, and forever.*

Again, his voice echoed in her mind. *And I'll always love you. You're my forever now, no matter what happens.*

She couldn't describe the feeling of closeness, of intimacy that the telepathic bond was giving her. She'd always thought it was merely a way to communicate, but it was so much more. It was a look into her mate's heart and soul. And what she saw in Grayson's was more beautiful than she'd expected. Pure white light shone back at her, filling her with the knowledge that the man she loved was true and good, and that his love for her was endless.

When she withdrew her fangs from him, and felt him release her too and lick over the puncture wounds, she sighed contentedly, and nestled her head in the crook of his neck.

Grayson hummed and caressed her back, his erection still inside her, still hard, but resting, for now. "I can't even put into words how happy you make me, accepting me with all my faults."

"I saw your heart," she murmured. "It was pure. And I saw your love for me."

"Just like I saw yours."

She lifted her head and kissed him, then looked into his eyes, where she saw the same love she'd seen in his heart. In that moment she knew that everything would turn out all right, because they had each other and a love that would last an eternity.

# 37

Grayson stopped the car in front of the garage to his parents' house and switched off the engine. Monique sat on the passenger seat, and he leaned over to her, still on a high from their blood-bond. Her blood was coursing through his body, permeating every cell. The knowledge that Monique was his now, and he hers, made him feel as if he was floating on air. He'd never thought that a blood-bond could do that to a vampire. He understood so much now. And he could feel his mother's fear and pain now, and understood how crucial it was to rescue Samson. Because without him, she would die of a broken heart.

He put his hand on Monique's cheek and gazed into her eyes. "Don't mention to anybody yet that we're blood-bonded. It will only make it harder for your mother and mine to know that their mates are still in danger."

Monique nodded. "I know. They must be in so much pain already. I never understood before…"

He touched his lips to hers and kissed her tenderly. Monique put her hand onto his nape, caressing him there, while she kissed him back. Her taste was drugging, and he deepened the kiss, dueling with her tongue, both hands framing her face now, not wanting this moment to end. Heat surged inside him, and his heartbeat accelerated.

*I love you, babe.*

*Oh, Grayson, you're everything to me.*

A knocking sound suddenly penetrated his bliss, and he let go of Monique's lips, and glanced past her. Isabelle stood on the sidewalk, knocking on the car's passenger side window.

Grayson opened the car door and exited. He walked around the car to Isabelle, while Monique was getting out of the car.

"Hey, Isa."

Isabelle looked at him and then at Monique, then made a gesture. "So, you two are dating, huh?"

Grayson couldn't help but smirk. Dating wasn't quite the truth, but he wasn't going to go into the details right now. "Yep." He took Monique's hand and squeezed it briefly. "We'd like to keep it under wraps for now."

Isabelle shrugged. "No problem."

"Thanks, Isabelle," Monique said with a smile. "We appreciate it."

"Thanks for meeting us out here," Grayson said. "Did anybody mention to Orlando that we've found the location where they're holding Cain and Dad?"

"Orlando hasn't come back yet."

Grayson's eyebrows pulled together. "He left hours ago to find Matt Smith."

"Exactly." Isabelle shook her head. "First he makes a big fuss about wanting to stay at the house and doesn't even leave to sleep, and then he's gone for hours on end? Something is up."

"Do you think he's warning Abel?" Monique asked.

"It's possible," Isabelle said, though she didn't sound very convincing. "But then why would he even tell us the name Matt Smith now uses? It doesn't make sense. He could have just kept his mouth shut, and we wouldn't be the wiser."

"Unless he wanted us to chase a ghost," Grayson said.

"You mean by sending the tracker on a wild-goose chase?" Monique asked.

Grayson nodded. "So he can't chase a more promising lead. And to give himself a convenient excuse to leave the house."

"I don't know," Isabelle started. "Orlando may be a big brute, but I don't see him betraying Dad's trust."

"Better safe than sorry," Grayson said and pulled out his cell phone. "I'll give Striker Reed a heads-up." He navigated to the cell phone number for the council tracker that Luther had sent him earlier and tapped on it. It rang several times, before it went to a recording.

*"Leave a message, or don't,"* the gruff recorded voice said.

"Striker, there's a chance that Orlando is playing us, and that Matt Smith isn't the name of the suspect after all. Be careful. You could be walking into a trap."

Grayson terminated the call and looked back at Isabelle and Monique.

"I need to get going," he said. "The sun will be down in a few minutes."

"Wait," Isabelle said. "I forgot the blood."

"What blood?"

"Mom's." Isabelle motioned to the entry of the house. "I drew her blood so that you can give it to Dad the moment you find him. We have no idea what shape he's in." She already hurried up the few steps to the house, passing by the two human guards flanking the entrance.

When Isabelle disappeared in the house, Monique turned to him. "Promise me you won't get yourself killed."

He pulled her into his arms. "You're not getting rid of me, remember?" He kissed her, then let go of her lips. "But you have to promise me something too."

"What's that?"

"Stay in the house with your mom, my family, and the guards. Don't under any circumstances believe anybody telling you that I might be in danger, and I asked you to come save me. That's a ruse." Years earlier somebody had tricked Blake's now-mate with such a lie, and she'd almost gotten killed. He didn't want that to happen to Monique.

She nodded. "I know that. Oldest trick in the book. I'm not gonna fall for it."

"Good." He smiled.

Isabelle came out of the house again, a small thermos in her hand.

Grayson reached for it. "Thanks, Isa. I'll make sure Dad drinks it the moment we free him." It would lend him instant strength, and hopefully heal whatever injuries Abel had inflicted on him. Grayson assumed that for Samson not to be able to communicate with his mate, he had to be in bad shape. Very bad shape. But he didn't voice his assumption, knowing that Isabelle was assuming the same. That's why she'd thought ahead and drawn the blood.

With a quick reassuring smile, he turned his back and walked to the driver's side of his car. He got in and started the engine. He glanced back at Isabelle and Monique, and saw that Isabelle had put her arm around Monique's shoulder. Knowing that Monique was safe with his family, Grayson kicked the gas pedal down and headed for headquarters where he'd join his colleagues to take several vans to the abandoned postal facility in Silver Terrace.

# 38

Two blocks away from the postal facility, and out of sight of any cameras, several of Scanguards' blackout vans were parked on the street. Both vampires and vampire hybrids were waiting in the vans. The two witches, Wesley and Charles, were in Grayson's van, together with three Stealth Guardians, Hamish, Zoltan, and Enya. They were tasked with giving them an inside view of the building by invisibly walking through the exterior walls into the facility. Their mission was strictly a scouting mission. The battle would start once the hybrids and vampires entered the building.

Everybody was equipped with an earpiece and a mic in order to communicate during the rescue mission. And everybody was armed to the teeth, both with weapons that killed silently like stakes, and weapons that killed from a distance like the small-caliber handguns that many of the Scanguards' staff preferred. Nobody had bothered with silencers, because once it was time to employ guns, the kidnappers would already be aware of them.

Grayson nodded at the Stealth Guardians. They were adjusting their headbands which were equipped with tiny cameras that transmitted in real time what the Stealth Guardians were seeing. Thomas sat in the van with them, making sure the three cameras fed into the monitor correctly. Should anything go wrong with the feed, he would be able to fix it on the spot. Eddie had stayed back at headquarters to manage any other technical issues remotely.

"Okay," Thomas said. "Feed looks good."

Grayson looked over his shoulder into the monitor. The screen was split into several windows. The three video feeds were labeled with the names of the three Stealth Guardians.

"You know what to do," Grayson said to them. "Get in, show us the position of the hostiles and the hostages, and get out as quickly as you can."

Hamish nodded, as did his two colleagues. "Got it. Wes, you've got the spray so they can't smell us coming?"

Wes pulled a spray bottle from his bag. "Let's do this outside."

"Thanks for doing this, guys," Grayson said.

"Of course," Hamish answered and left the van.

The others followed him, while Thomas watched the monitor.

"You worried?" Thomas asked.

"I'd be lying if I said I wasn't," Grayson admitted. A few days ago, he would have never admitted that. His father's kidnapping had made him grow up in a hurry. He understood so much now about leadership, about strength, and about responsibility. This mission was his responsibility, and if anything went wrong, it was on him. The buck stopped with him. "Any number of things can go wrong."

"We're all worried," Thomas said. "But everybody is giving it a hundred-and-ten percent. And with the Stealth Guardians scoping the place out, we have the advantage."

Charles slapped his hand on Grayson's shoulder. "And don't forget the witches. We have an ace or two up our sleeves."

Despite the stress he felt, Grayson smirked. "Yeah, like blowing up labs?"

"Not my fault. That was Wesley's screw-up." He shrugged. "At least now we know how to blow doors off their hinges when we don't have explosives on hand."

Thomas rolled his eyes, and continued watching the screen, when the cameras started to move.

Wesley entered the van. "Okay, they just made themselves invisible and are off."

Grayson turned so he could see the monitor better. The Stealth Guardians were moving at a fast clip. A few seconds later, they were already on the same block as the postal facility. They walked half a block farther then turned to walk straight toward the exterior wall of the building. The white of the wall came closer and was suddenly filling all three feeds. In a second they would be inside and giving the Scanguards team valuable intel.

"Fuck!"

Several more curses came over the earpiece, all coming from the Stealth Guardians, and their feeds shook. The video still showed the white color of the exterior walls, rather than the interior.

"What's going on?" Grayson asked over the microphone, while he exchanged a concerned look with Thomas and the witches.

"We can't get in," Zoltan reported.

"What the—"

Hamish interrupted Grayson. "There's something in the walls. We can't get through it. My guess is lead."

"Fuck!" Grayson cursed.

"Yeah, probably lead paint," Enya added. "It's an old building."

Grayson ran a hand through his hair. What now? It was up to him to make a decision about how to proceed. "How about the doors?" He turned to Thomas. "Blueprints?"

Thomas instantly switched the window and pulled up the building's blueprint.

Grayson quickly looked at it. "There are only two accessible doors. Doors are probably made of steel, which means there shouldn't be any issue with getting through them. The closest ones are on the East side of the building and on the street side."

"Let's try them," Zoltan agreed. "Hamish, take the door on the East side; Enya and I will try the one on this block."

Anxious, Grayson watched as the camera feeds showed the Stealth Guardians move in different directions. He hadn't expected the building to have lead paint, a material they couldn't penetrate. He'd seen the lead cells that the Stealth Guardians used when they had to incarcerate one of their own. A normal cell couldn't contain a Stealth Guardian prisoner, because he could simply walk through the walls.

Knowing that the postal facility was condemned because of asbestos, he knew he should have assumed that it also had lead paint on the walls. It was a failure of leadership, and normally he would beat himself up about it and wallow in his mistakes, but he couldn't afford those kinds of thoughts. He had to roll with the punches and improvise.

Moments later, his gaze was drawn back to the monitor and he focused his eyes.

"Fuck! Unbelievable," Hamish cursed. "I'm bouncing back from the door too. Zoltan, Enya?"

"Same," Zoltan said. "I can only assume that they painted the doors with lead paint on the inside."

Grayson cursed silently.

"Just like they used the lead paint dust in New Orleans," Enya said.

"They were expecting us," Hamish said.

"And prepared accordingly," Grayson ground out. "Come back to the vans. We'll regroup."

While the Stealth Guardians made their way back to the vans, Grayson was already going through all the remaining options in his head. Surprising Abel's men wasn't an option anymore. They were expecting an ambush.

"Okay," Grayson started, speaking into the mic for every member of his team to hear. "Here's how it's gonna go. Eddie, you'll need to take out the postal facility's cameras on my command. I also need the power out in this grid. We don't need any nosy neighbors calling the cops."

"Not a problem. I prepared for that already," Eddie announced. "I'll need about five minutes for the power grid though."

"Good!" Grayson was relieved to hear that Eddie had been anticipating hiccups and planned accordingly. "I need the best lockpicks to open the doors for us. We're going in on the street side and the East side. Cooper, pick the lock on the East side."

"Sure thing," Cooper said through the earpiece.

"I'll take the street side," Sebastian volunteered.

"You've got it, Sebastian." Grayson took a breath. "Eddie, how far away is the drone with the infrared cameras?"

"About three minutes out," Eddie replied.

Grayson looked at Thomas. "Can you steer the drone from here?"

Thomas nodded. "Yep. I'll take care of that." He started tapping away on the laptop. "I can send it to everybody's cell phone, and alert you via the comms when I see movement of people inside."

"Do that," Grayson ordered, feeling more confident with every moment. He had a team of experts at his disposal, the best in their fields. They would succeed. They had to.

Several tense minutes passed, until everything was finally in place.

"The power grid is going down in five, four, three, two, one," Eddie said, counting down.

Grayson looked outside through the windshield. It was pitch-black in the neighborhood. "Okay, it's a go." Grayson jumped out of the van, and saw his colleagues do the same. Thomas stayed in the van to give updates on the heat signatures the drone was delivering. "Eddie, cut the cameras."

"They're blind now," Eddie confirmed.

Cutting the cameras was necessary, even though the electricity was already out, because there was a chance that Abel had anticipated this too and was using battery power to operate the cameras on the outside of the building, so his men were alerted when the Scanguards team approached.

Grayson and his colleagues approached the building, walking swiftly but silently. One group made their way toward the street entrance, the other toward the East entrance. He reached the East entrance at the same time as Cooper, who was already reaching for his lockpick.

Grayson pulled his gun and let his eyes roam, while listening to any sounds from inside. There were none.

"East side door is open," Cooper murmured.

"How about street side?" Grayson asked via the mic.

"Street side door is open too," Sebastian replied.

"Okay. On my command." Grayson took a deep breath, then motioned for Cooper to press the door handle down. "Three, two, open!"

Cooper ripped the door open, and Grayson rushed inside, gun drawn, his colleagues on his heels.

# 39

"I ran you a hot bath, Mom," Monique said and looked at Faye.

Despite the fact that she was a vampire, she looked fragile. The worry for her blood-bonded mate was getting to her.

"I can't. I have to wait for news from them," Faye protested.

"I promise you I'll come running the moment we get word from the rescue team." She shooed her mother toward the ensuite bathroom. "I laid out some fresh clothes for you. Just do it for me. There's nothing you can do right now but wait. And you might as well do that in the bathtub."

Faye looked at her, pinching her eyebrows. "You promise you'll let me know immediately when you get any news, no matter if it's good or bad?"

"I will. And it'll be good news. Grayson and his team are trained for this."

Finally, Faye nodded and turned to the bathroom. Monique let out a sigh of relief and left the large guest room Isabelle had prepared for her mother. It was quiet on the second floor of the old Victorian mansion, and for a moment, Monique just stood there in silence, alone with her thoughts. She was worried too, even though she believed in Grayson's abilities, and in that of his colleagues. But no matter how well they'd planned the operation, anything could go wrong at any time.

When she walked down the stairs, she encountered Isabelle walking upstairs.

"Hey," Monique said.

"How's Faye?"

"She's finally taking a bath. I hope it helps her relax a bit. She's so tense."

"Yeah, my mom too. But it'll be all right. I know it." Isabelle smiled softly. "Though my gut feeling isn't as sharp as I thought."

"What do you mean?"

"I'd never thought Orlando would betray us. He's gruff, and a pain in the butt. But I thought he was a hundred percent loyal to us, to Dad." Isabelle shook her head and sighed.

"We don't know for sure that he's been feeding Abel information," Monique said.

"But it sure looks like it." She shrugged. "I'm just gonna take a quick shower too, and get changed. You okay? You can use one of the guest rooms if you need to."

Monique shook her head. "I showered at Grayson's. I'm good. But I'll help myself to some blood."

"There should be plenty in the fridge," Isabelle said.

"Thanks." Monique continued descending the stairs while Isabelle went upstairs.

A few seconds later she heard a door opening then closing. Monique walked into the kitchen, and found William there. He was closing the refrigerator door, before looking at her.

"Monique," he said with a nod. "Do you need anything?"

She motioned to the fridge and approached. "Just need a bottle of blood. I'm exhausted."

He remained standing in front of the refrigerator. "One of the guards just took the last bottle. There's more down in the garage. Turn left at the end of the stairs."

It didn't look like William had any intention of going down into the garage himself. She wasn't surprised. He wasn't a servant, and he'd never gone out of his way to do her any favors. Maybe the fact that she'd always acted like a spoiled princess had something to do with that.

"I'll bring a few bottles up," she offered. "You'll probably want some too."

"Great," he said.

Monique left the kitchen and headed for the door that led down to the garage. As she approached, she looked out through the window next to the entrance door and saw the silhouette of one of the two vampire guards stationed outside the house. When she'd been in the guestroom to draw a bath for her mother, she'd heard footfalls above her on the third floor.

Two more guards were stationed there to look out over the backyard and the street in the front should Abel's men attempt an attack on the house.

She opened the door and flipped the light switch, but nothing happened. Perhaps the lightbulb had burned out, and nobody had had a chance to replace it. It didn't matter. Her vampire vision helped her navigate the stairs safely. In the large garage, several cars were parked. Monique turned to her left and opened the door there. She flipped the switch next to it, but the light wasn't working there either. Frowning, she sighed, when she heard footsteps on the stairs.

"The lights aren't working," she called out.

William came into view. "Let me see what's wrong." He sidled up her and tried the light switch next to the door.

"I just did that. It's not working."

"Hmm." He grunted. "Oh, it's working." He turned to her and lifted his arm. He held something in his hand she couldn't immediately identify.

He grabbed her and jabbed something into her neck. She felt a sharp hypodermic needle piercing her skin. The liquid with which he was injecting her stung painfully.

She tried to free herself from his grip, but he didn't let go. "What the fuck! Let me go."

"Shut up, bitch! You've had it coming for a long time," he sneered.

Monique tried to scream so the other guards or Isabelle would come to her aid, but her throat tightened, and she was unable to get anything coherent over her lips. "What…"

"Personally, I would kill you right here, but Abel wants you alive."

Fuck! William was the traitor, not Orlando. He'd played his role well. Because he'd been injured in the attack on Samson and Cain, nobody had suspected him. He'd probably had one of the attackers injure him only superficially, yet in a place where he'd bleed profusely, so it would look real.

Fuck! She felt dizzy, her knees suddenly buckling under her.

*Grayson!*

She tried to use the telepathic bond she shared with Grayson, but couldn't concentrate, couldn't muster enough strength to send a message to him.

"Spoiled brat! Looking down on the rest of us. Now you're gonna suffer for it."

She could barely feel her own body now, but noticed that William was dragging her toward one of the cars. He opened the trunk.

"And don't worry, you'll be awake for what he'll do to you."

Again, she tried to scream, but the searing pain that spread through her veins made it impossible. William tossed her into the trunk of the car, and everything around her blurred. She tried to keep her eyes open, tried to fight the encroaching darkness, but it was to no avail. Whatever William had injected her with acted fast. A few more seconds, and pain engulfed her and rendered her unconscious.

# 40

Grayson was the first to enter the abandoned postal facility, his colleagues hot on his heels. It was dark inside, but he had no trouble seeing that the place wasn't empty. Several men were taking cover amidst overturned furniture, shelves, and storage containers, using them as barricades to shoot at the entering Scanguards team.

"Take cover!" Grayson yelled, and dove behind a stack of pallets, while aiming at the hostile vampire closest to him.

A painful scream came from the vampire's direction, indicating that Grayson's bullet had hit him, but not killed him. For a vampire to die from a silver bullet immediately, only a head shot or a shot into the heart would do, though if the wounded vampire couldn't get the silver bullet out of him quickly, he would die a slow and agonizing death, the silver poisoning him from inside.

Grayson saw his friends fan out and take positions from where to attack without making themselves into prime targets. Gunshots echoed in the huge building, and screams and grunts now mingled with them.

Over his earpiece and mic, Grayson issued his commands. "Cooper, you're with me looking for Samson and Cain. The rest of you: give 'em hell."

Cooper sidled up to him, and nodded, indicating he was ready.

"Grayson, wait," Hamish said through the communication device. "I'll come with you, and make the two of you invisible."

He hadn't expected the Stealth Guardians to join the fight, but he was grateful for it. "You sure, Hamish? What about the lead paint on the walls?"

"Once I'm inside, it's not enough lead to impede my powers to make us invisible."

"Okay, then, thank you."

Moments later, he felt a hand on his shoulder. He turned his head and saw Hamish. "Ready?"

Grayson and Cooper nodded. Grayson pointed to his left. "This way."

The three of them walked along the outer walls of the building. To one side were several doors, most likely offices of the managers of the postal facility. They weren't locked. Grayson pushed the first one open and peeked inside. Except for an old desk it was empty. Hamish was already at the next door and opened it, while Cooper covered him.

"Oh crap," Hamish cursed, keeping his voice low.

Grayson looked past him into the room. Three men in dirty clothes, smelling of urine and feces, were huddled in a corner, their eyes hollow, blood on their necks and clothing. Abel's men had used homeless men as food while holed up in this building.

"We'll take care of them later," Grayson murmured to Hamish, then gestured for him to close the door.

He tapped on his earpiece, activating the microphone. "Everybody, watch out for mortals. We found three homeless men Abel's men used to feed on. There might be more."

There was no reply from anybody, but Grayson didn't expect one. From the loud noises, the thuds and gunshots, it was clear that everybody was too busy fighting their opponents.

Grayson led Cooper and Hamish farther along the outer edges of the building, searching for other rooms where his father and Cain could be locked up, when he saw a movement from the corner of his eye. He whipped his head toward it, and saw a metal bin hurtling toward him. He jumped out of the way, and the bin hit the wall behind him.

He exchanged a quick look with Hamish. "Aren't we invisible?" he whispered to the Stealth Guardian.

"We are." Hamish motioned in the direction from where the bucket had come.

Grayson saw Zane fighting with a hostile vampire, who was quickly running out of options and had started to toss anything he could get his hands on at Zane. Not worried about his colleague, Grayson continued his search for Samson and Cain.

"There," Cooper suddenly whispered and pointed to a door just beyond a partition.

In front of it, somebody had fashioned a barricade with parts of a desk and a turned-over shelving unit. From behind it, a vampire peeked out, gun at the ready. He wasn't joining Abel's men in the fight, instead he was guarding the door.

Grayson exchanged a look with Hamish and Cooper, and gave them a sign to stay close, while he approached. As he cleared another partition, he noticed a second vampire. The man was rushing toward the guard at the door.

"We're outnumbered," the hostile vampire said. "Go to plan B."

Then the vampire abruptly turned in Grayson's direction, and stopped only inches from Grayson. The man's nostrils flared.

Fuck! Wesley's spray to disguise a vampire's scent was wearing off.

The vampire's eyes flashed red, and his fangs descended. His hand holding a stake jerked upwards. Not wasting any time, Grayson lifted his hand holding the gun and aimed for the guy's heart. He pulled the trigger.

The vampire swayed toward Grayson, and would have collided with him, had he not dissolved into ash a second later. Gray ash rained over Grayson, and he coughed involuntarily. Alarmed by the vampire's death, the hostile guarding the door aimed his gun in Grayson's direction and pulled the trigger.

A push from the side made Grayson stumble out of the line of fire. As he tried to regain his footing, he saw Cooper charge past him toward the gunman. He slammed his stake into the guy's chest, before his opponent knew what was happening.

"Another one bites the dust," Cooper said and brushed his opponent's remains off his clothing.

Grayson nodded. "Thanks, Coop." He pointed to the door. "Locked?"

Cooper tried the door knob. "Yep."

Grayson let his eyes roam where a thin layer of dust covered the floor. There was a cell phone, and a key. He picked up both, pocketed the cell phone, then tried the key. The lock clicked.

He took a deep breath, then looked at Cooper and Hamish. "Cover me."

Grayson pushed the door open. It was even darker in this room than in the rest of the building, but he didn't need light to confirm that he'd found the right place. He inhaled deeply, and Samson's scent drifted to him. There was another scent too, but he wasn't as familiar with it. But he knew it had to be Cain's.

"Dad! Cain!" He rushed into the room, his eyes slowly adjusting to the darkness. "Cooper, Hamish! It's them." He tapped on his earpiece. "We have the hostages. Southwest corner of the building."

"Understood," Thomas reported from the van. "There are still moving heat signatures in the Southeast quadrant of the building."

"Nicholas and I have them in sight," Zane reported. "We'll take care of them."

Grayson tuned out the voices coming through his earpiece and crouched down next to his father. "Dad, it's Grayson, I'm here now." He looked at his father's face, shocked at the pain that contorted his handsome features. "Cooper, feed Cain the blood." From the corner of his eye, he saw that Cooper kneeled down next to Cain, while pulling a bottle of human blood from his small backpack.

Grayson retrieved the small thermos of his mother's blood and propped his father up, holding him. "Dad, you have to drink."

Samson's body coiled in agony, and he pushed the bottle away.

"It's Mom's blood," Grayson assured him. "Delilah's blood."

A pained sound issued from his throat and Grayson set the bottle to his lips. "Drink it, Dad, please. Delilah loves you. She needs you. I need you."

Finally, Samson took his first sip. Relief washed over Grayson, and he urged him on to drink more.

"That's it, Dad. Drink it all, so I can take you back home. I love you, Dad."

Samson's eyelids lifted only for a brief moment, and their gazes connected, before he closed his eyes again, the effort too great in his weakened state.

"Mom can't wait to see you," Grayson said gently. "Now, drink up. And when we get home, you'll drink from her. You'll drink from Delilah."

Now more greedily, Samson swallowed the liquid, the only blood that could heal and sustain him, until there was nothing left in the bottle. Grayson put the empty bottle aside, then looked to Cooper, who was feeding Cain bottles of human blood. Hamish stood at the entrance to the door, making sure that nobody would attack them in this vulnerable position.

"Grayson," Samson said, his voice hoarse and barely audible.

Grayson pulled him closer and lowered his head. "I'm here, Dad. Everything will be all right now."

Samson's lips quivered as if he was trying to smile, but was too weak. "Son, I'm so proud of you."

At his father's praise, tears welled up in Grayson's eyes, and he sniffled. "I love you so much, Dad."

Grayson wasn't sure that Samson had heard him, because his head rolled back. He was still weak, and his body needed time to heal, and sleep would help him.

He tapped his earpiece again. "Thomas, we need two stretchers to take Samson and Cain out to the vans."

"Understood. I'll send them in once all hostiles are dead or tied up. Situation update please," Thomas replied.

A moment later, some crackling came through the earpiece. Then a voice. "Everybody's dead. Except for the homeless men," Zane reported.

"Did you kill Abel?" Grayson asked. "I said to leave him alive."

"I would have, if I'd seen him," Zane replied. "But I didn't lay eyes on him, or the other two we identified, Rufus and Matt."

"Anybody see Abel? Or Rufus and Matt?" Grayson asked.

One by one his team members came back with a negative.

"They weren't here," Wesley concluded. "And Charles and I placed a magical warding along the building once you were all inside. They wouldn't have been able to break through it."

"Fuck!" Grayson cursed. "Why weren't they here?"

"Rats and sinking ships, you know," Wes said. "They must have known we were coming and decided to split."

"We have to find them. As long as Abel is out there, our families won't be safe. He'll try again." He knew enough about Abel to know that he'd only be satisfied if he got his revenge. "Collect the cell phones of all the dead vampires. Maybe we can find something on them to tell us where Abel would run to hide. Sebastian, you, Ryder, and Yvette will remain here to heal the homeless men, and to wipe their memories and remove anything incriminating from this building."

"Got it," Sebastian replied, and Ryder and Yvette issued the same answer.

"Zane, you, Patrick, Cooper and I will take Samson and Cain back to our house. The rest of you, return to HQ and extract any information you can from the collected cell phones. Eddie, go through the traffic cams to see if you can catch when Abel, Rufus, and Matt left this building."

"If they were ever in it," Eddie added.

"Yeah, it's possible Abel stayed away, knowing we'd find the place eventually."

"He was here…" The faint voice came from behind him. Grayson looked over his shoulder and saw Cooper helping Cain sit up. He looked like death warmed over. "Abel… he was here… spoke to me…"

"When?"

Cain shook his head. "Don't know… I was unconscious… in and out…" He lowered his eyelids.

"Don't worry," Grayson assured him. "It helps. At least we know he was here. We'll figure out when he left and where he went."

"Dad!" Patrick appeared in the door and rushed past Hamish.

"He'll be all right."

Patrick kneeled down next to Samson and put his arms around him. Then he looked at Grayson. "Did he drink Mom's blood?"

Grayson nodded. "The entire bottle. Let's get him home. He'll need more. The blood they forced him to drink really did a number on him."

Patrick looked over to Cain. "And what did they give Cain?"

Cain opened his eyes a sliver. "Dead man's blood…" He swallowed, his voice breaking. "More painful than silver."

But less lethal: silver would eventually kill a vampire, but dead man's blood would inflict excruciating pain, without ever killing its victim. It was the perfect means for prolonged torture.

Abel was more vindictive than anybody he'd ever known.

# 41

Isabelle heard the sound of the front door being opened. They were back! Her heart pounding into her throat, she charged out of the kitchen into the hallway. Robbie, one of the vampire guards stationed outside the house and a vampire she didn't know were dragging Orlando into the foyer. His clothing was torn and drenched in blood, his face swollen and bloodied. She ran toward them.

"Oh my God! Orlando! What happened to you?"

Orlando lifted his head. His lips moved, but only a pained groan came from him.

"He got ambushed," the stranger said.

"Get him into the living room," she ordered, and watched them place Orlando on the large sofa. Isabelle addressed the stranger, "Who are you?"

"Striker Reed."

"I'm Isabelle."

He nodded. "I know."

Of course, he did. And she knew about him, even though she'd never met him in person. He'd been instrumental in finding her kidnapper and rescuing her over ten years ago. He'd been a tracker for the vampire council, though back then he'd already left the council and started working freelance. He was one of the best trackers the council had ever had, but he'd never disclosed why he'd left the council, and why they'd let him leave, which added to the mystery around him.

"Robbie, get me the first aid cart. And bottled blood. In the pantry," she directed the vampire guard.

Robbie complied and left the living room. Isabelle crouched down to Orlando and inspected his injuries. He had a deep knife wound across his abdomen, and more angry-looking gashes on his arms, all inflicted by a silver blade, which made the wounds look as if burned with acid. She peeled some of the shredded fabric away from the stomach wound, and

Orlando groaned in pain. She shot him a look and noticed that his fangs had descended, and his eyes were wide open and glared red. The cords in his neck bulged, attesting to the fact that he was holding on to his control so as not to lash out.

His injuries were severe, and they confirmed one thing immediately: Orlando wasn't the traitor her brother had assumed him to be. He was innocent. In fact, he'd risked his life to help their family.

Wanting to assure Orlando that she wouldn't hurt him, Isabelle gently stroked her hand over his dark hair. He flinched as if he hated being touched, and she quickly withdrew her hand.

"I'm not gonna hurt you, Orlando, but you'll have to let me help you," she said calmly.

Finally, Robbie rolled the first aid cart into the room, and Isabelle reached for a bottle of human blood and twisted off the cap. Orlando ripped it from her hand and gulped it down greedily.

Isabelle reached for the pair of scissors on the cart. "Thanks, Robbie. You can go back to your post."

Robbie glanced at Striker. "You're sure?"

"Yes," Isabelle replied. "I can handle these two."

Robbie nodded dutifully and went back outside to guard the house.

She looked back at Orlando. He'd emptied the bottle, and she took it from his hand. "What happened, Orlando?"

With the scissors, she cut through the front of his T-shirt. Gently, she peeled the fabric away from the wound and laid his chest bare. She'd always assumed that Orlando was ripped. It was evident under the clothing he wore, but she hadn't expected his skin to be so smooth and his muscles so defined. An odd flutter settled in her stomach. She'd seen plenty of handsome men half-naked or naked, but there was something about seeing Orlando laid bare like this.

To distract herself from his perfect chest, she asked, "Who did this to you?"

"Matt Smith," Orlando pressed out, still in obvious pain. "He knew I was coming. Somebody warned him."

Isabelle used a surgical cloth and started cleaning Orlando's stomach wound. He winced.

"Only a few people knew you were going after him," she said. She lifted her head and looked into his eyes, and for a moment neither said a word.

Her family and Monique's family would have never warned Abel's man. Which left only one person who'd known about Orlando's plan.

"William," they said in unison.

She looked over her shoulder, and called out, "Mom?" She listened for sounds from upstairs. "Striker, take one of the guards from outside and check on my mother, and on Faye and Monique too. Be careful. William is somewhere in the house."

"Don't worry, I don't get ambushed easily." Striker cast a sideways glance at Orlando. "Not like this guy here."

Orlando grunted at the direct jab. "I didn't need your help. I could have gotten him on my own."

"Yeah, I saw that." Sarcasm was practically dripping from Striker's voice. "If I hadn't found you in time, you would be dust now."

Orlando growled. "Instead, you killed Matt Smith before I could interrogate him."

"You're welcome," Striker said and left the living room.

Isabelle turned back to Orlando. "So Striker saved your life?"

"Hmm. I would have managed."

Isabelle raised an eyebrow, but decided not to pursue this subject. Apparently, Orlando was a proud man who didn't like to admit that he needed help on occasion.

"Now let me clean this wound."

"I'm fine."

He made an attempt at sitting up, but Isabelle had no trouble pushing him down. It confirmed what she already knew: Orlando was badly injured, but too hardheaded to admit it.

"We have to stem the bleeding."

She took a fresh sheet of gauze and laid it over the deep gash on his abdomen, while she reached for another bottle of blood. She twisted it open and handed it to him.

"Here, drink this."

He grunted something incoherent, before he set the bottle to his lips. She pressed her hand on the stomach wound, and Orlando jerked back in pain.

Not wanting to alarm him as to the severity of his injuries, she said, "Don't be such a baby."

"I'm not a—"

She pulled the soaked gauze away from the wound, and Orlando cried out in pain, even though she could tell he was trying to suppress it. Thanks to the human blood he was drinking, his stomach wound didn't bleed as badly anymore. But it was still not closing, and he was still losing blood.

"Keep drinking the blood," she ordered, before she lowered her head to his stomach.

"What are you doing?"

Clearly alarmed, Orlando tried to scoot back, but she placed her hands on his hips to stop him from moving.

"What does it look like? You're losing too much blood. I'm gonna close the wound."

"Don't!"

But she ignored his protest, and licked over the large gash on his stomach. A hybrid's saliva had the same healing properties as that of a vampire. It could seal lacerations and cuts, closing a wound to prevent further blood loss. While Orlando would heal eventually by consuming sufficient human blood, the revelation that William was the traitor made it necessary that Orlando get back on his feet swiftly. She was doing this for the good of her family, because in the fight against Abel, every man counted, and an injured member of the team could become a liability.

The fact that she was tempted by Orlando's blood, wasn't a factor in her calculations at all. Nevertheless, she couldn't deny that she liked the taste of his blood as she lapped it up and swallowed it. There was something forbidden about this. The big brutish bodyguard who'd come out of nowhere a little over a year earlier and started working for Scanguards was an enigma. He never talked about himself, never spoke much at all, never seemed to do anything for fun.

Beneath her lips and tongue, she felt the shape of the wound change. Her saliva was starting to close the cut, stemming the blood loss. Less and less blood was seeping from it, but she continued to lap it up, and swallowed it. The blood did something to her, as did the fact that she was licking his skin. His masculine scent awakened everything female in her.

"Stop," Orlando ground out, his voice gruff.

Did he hate being touched? Reluctantly, Isabelle lifted her head and met his gaze. She had expected his eyes to glare red to match the displeasure in his voice. Instead, they shimmered golden.

"Isabelle?"

At the sound of her mother's voice, Isabelle spun around and stood up as if caught doing something she shouldn't be doing.

"Oh my God, what happened to Orlando?" Delilah asked and rushed into the living room.

Orlando groaned as he sat up on the couch. "I'm fine. I'm healing."

When he tried to stand up, Isabelle put her hand on his shoulder and pressed him back down on the couch. "Rest!"

Then she looked at her mother. "He got ambushed. Somebody warned Matt Smith that he was coming. We think it was William. Have you seen him?"

Delilah shook her head. "No, not in a little while."

Striker suddenly appeared in the door to the living room, Faye behind him.

"No sign of William," Striker reported.

Isabelle approached him, craning her neck to look past him, when the entrance door was opened. Faye and Delilah turned toward it.

"Oh, thank God," Delilah gasped in relief. "Samson."

# 42

Together with Patrick, Grayson helped their father over the threshold. Samson was still weak and in pain, but he was getting better with every minute. Behind them, Cooper and Zane were helping Cain into the house.

Delilah was the first to reach them. "Oh, Samson, my love!" She wrapped her arms around him and pressed herself to him, while Grayson and Patrick continued supporting his weight.

"Sweetness," Samson murmured.

Teary-eyed, Delilah looked at Grayson, then at Patrick. "Thank you for bringing him back to me." She gestured to the living room. "Bring him in here."

While they helped Samson onto the loveseat in the living room, Grayson's gaze fell onto the other couch, where Orlando sat, his clothing ripped and bloody, his face mangled at the hands of a vicious assailant.

Isabelle put her hand on Grayson's arm. "Orlando wasn't the traitor. He got ambushed by Matt Smith."

"Fuck!" Grayson cursed.

"Traitor?" Orlando repeated and rose, though he looked unsteady on his feet. "You thought I was the traitor feeding Abel information?" He glared at him and Isabelle.

Grayson lifted his hand. "I'm sorry, Orlando, but there was circumstantial evidence that pointed to you."

"What fucking circumstantial evidence?" he growled.

"Your cell phone location. It coincided with that of Rufus's a couple of days before the kidnapping. And you were the first to show up at the Russian Hill house, even though you live the farthest away."

Orlando stared at him, stunned. He gripped the high armrest of the couch for support. "You checked up on me? What I do in my private time is my business. Fuck you, Grayson! I would never betray your father."

"Orlando…" The voice was Samson's.

Grayson looked over his shoulder, and saw his father cast a pleading look at Orlando. "He doesn't know you the way I do. Please, forgive him. He was only trying to save me and Cain."

Orlando nodded. "I'm happy to see that you're back."

He stomped out of the room, and Grayson's gaze was drawn to Cain. Faye was embracing him, while Zane and Cooper were watching them to make sure Cain didn't collapse.

Grayson let his eyes roam, surprised that Monique wasn't greeting her father. "Monique?" he called out, then looked at Isabelle. "Where's Monique?"

Robbie entered from the hallway. "Striker and I searched the whole house." Only now, Grayson noticed Striker Reed lurking in the hallway. "Monique is gone. And so is William."

Grayson's heart stopped. Everything around him seemed to turn as if he stood on a carousel, desperately trying to jump off. Panic paralyzed every cell of his body, and fear settled around his heart like a vice that became tighter with every passing second.

"No, not Monique, no!" he cried out, his eyes focusing again.

Only now, he realized that everybody was staring at him. He noticed pink tears run down Faye's cheeks. Cain's mouth set into a thin line, trying to hold back the pain.

Faye sobbed. "My baby. He has my baby."

"Not for long," Grayson promised. "I'll get her back." He inhaled a deep breath. "Monique is mine." Stunned looks landed on him. He turned to face his father. "Monique and I blood-bonded a few hours ago."

Several people gasped, but Grayson looked only at his father.

Samson's mouth formed into a gentle smile. "You get her back, son. You'll find her. Trust yourself. You can do it."

Grayson nodded, before he closed his eyes to concentrate on the psychic bond he shared with his blood-bonded mate.

*Monique! Monique! Babe, where are you? Please, I need to find you. Monique!*

~ ~ ~

Monique felt the numbness in her extremities wane. It was replaced by a burning pain as if her veins were filled with acid. An odd sound had awoken her. She felt something soft beneath her, a bed or a thick blanket. Her eyelids were heavy. She lifted them nevertheless. For a short moment, she couldn't remember what had happened. But then, it all came flooding back.

William had knocked her out by injecting something into her neck. He'd tossed her into the trunk of a car where she'd lost consciousness. She let her gaze roam. It was dark in the room, but it wasn't musty-smelling or damp, which told her that she wasn't in a basement. There was a large window covered with heavy curtains. She had no idea how long she'd been out. Was it still night?

She lay on a bed, fully dressed. She made an attempt to sit up, and she would have succeeded, if she hadn't been chained to the bed's headboard. She pulled on the chains in an attempt to free herself, but her skin sizzled, and she cried out in pain. The scent of burnt skin and hair rose to her nostrils and made her gag. Her chains were made of silver, a metal that burned a vampire, and one that she couldn't break despite her preternatural strength.

She heard footsteps just outside the door to the room. Panic slithered down her spine like a snake.

*Grayson! Grayson! Help me!*

Could he hear her? Was her telepathic message reaching him?

The door suddenly opened, and light shone into the room from outside. She turned her head toward the door and saw the man she'd been warned about all her life: Abel. There was a self-satisfied grin on his face as he entered the room.

"Finally, you're awake."

He approached the bed, and Monique instinctively withdrew as far as the chains allowed her.

"I guess William injected you with a little too much dead man's blood, or you wouldn't have been unconscious for so long."

"What do you want?" she spat.

Abel sat down on the edge of the bed and leaned in. "Well, isn't that obvious?" He let out a sinister chuckle. "You look a lot like your mother."

He reached for her and twirled a lock of her long hair around his index finger.

"Don't touch me!" The very thought made her nauseous.

"I'll do much more than that."

Abel put his hand on her leg, and she tried to shake it off, kicking her legs toward him. But she didn't hit her target.

"A veritable wildcat, just like your mother. I'm gonna enjoy taming you." He looked toward the door. "I would have already fucked you, but what's the fun in it when you're not conscious for it?"

Disgust rose inside her. He was going to rape her, while she was chained and helpless.

"Besides, I'd like for my men to watch so they can learn how to punish their enemies." He leaned in. "And maybe I'll let them take turns."

She spit in his face. "Over my dead body!"

"Yeah," he said, drawing out the word, "about that. I'm not planning on killing you, but the dead man's blood will keep you weak and subdued. Worked on your father. I wouldn't want you to die while I'm torturing you. That would be too easy."

"You're a sick bastard!" Evil through and through. She couldn't believe that he and Cain were brothers. They were nothing alike. Abel possessed nothing of Cain's compassion.

"Frankly, I don't care what you think of me. All that matters is that Cain and Faye will suffer knowing what I'll be doing to you." He pulled a cell phone from his pocket and showed it to her. "Really nifty, these things. My men will video us so I can let your parents know that you're still alive."

Monique shuddered, but tried not to show it outwardly. She had no intention of letting Abel know that she was truly scared now. The thought of her parents and Grayson seeing her being raped by Abel and his men… no, she couldn't let that happen. It would break Grayson's heart to know that he couldn't save his blood-bonded mate. She had to stop Abel.

"Please," she begged now. "I won't put up a fight, as long as you don't film it."

"Well, look at that. Nice to know how to push your buttons." He looked toward the open door. "Rufus!"

A moment later, Rufus, whom she recognized from his photo, appeared in the door.

"Is Matt back?"

Rufus shook his head. "No. I have a feeling that he got in trouble."

"Hmm." Abel contemplated something for a moment. "Who's guarding the house?"

"Jimmy, Elvis, and Craig," Rufus replied.

"Okay, I need to speak to William." He got up from the bed. "In the meantime, get her ready. Cut the clothes off her if necessary."

Abel stalked out of the room, leaving the door open, while Rufus approached the bed.

Monique held her breath, apprehension paralyzing her. From the hallway, a sound drifted to her.

*Cuckoo, cuckoo…*

A cuckoo clock. What were the odds of more than one house in San Francisco having a cuckoo clock?

"Well, let's get these things off you," Rufus said with a grin, clearly eager to please his boss.

"Fuck you!" Monique cursed.

When he started by taking off her shoes then proceeding to her pants, she didn't fight him. Instead, she used all her energy to send a message to Grayson.

*Grayson, William kidnapped me. I know where Abel is keeping me. Grayson, can you hear me?*

With bated breath she waited, while Rufus stripped her of her pants. His lascivious look didn't escape her attention, but she couldn't waste her energy on that now. She needed to get through to Grayson.

*Grayson?*

*Monique! Monique, babe!*

Relief at hearing her blood-bonded mate's message reverberating in her mind, she closed her eyes.

*Abel is keeping me chained in the Russian Hill house my parents rented. Please, hurry! He's planning to rape me. Grayson, please hurry.*

# 43

Grayson stared at his and Monique's family, who were all assembled in the living room of his parents' house. Monique's telepathic message made him feel relieved and petrified in equal parts. Relieved, because he knew where she was, and petrified, because of what would happen to her if he didn't get to her in time.

"Abel has Monique locked up at the Russian Hill rental property."

"Where we stayed?" Faye asked, her eyes wide.

"That's the last place I would have guessed," Isabelle said.

"That's probably why. We have to hurry." Grayson motioned to Patrick. "Patrick, send a text to all vampires and hybrids at Scanguards, and have them assemble a block away from the property."

He was already hurrying toward the door.

"Grayson, you can't just charge in there without a plan," Isabelle cautioned him.

He looked over his shoulder. "There's no time for a plan. Abel is going to rape her."

Shocked gasps echoed in the room.

"I'm coming with you," Isabelle said and rushed to the door to the garage. "I'll get the weapons."

"I'm coming too," Striker said from the hallway.

Grayson nodded. "Appreciate it, Striker."

Zane and Cooper already checked their weapons, and nodded, indicating that they were ready to fight.

Patrick typed away on his cell phone. "Message is sent. Let's go."

Before Grayson reached the door, Orlando called out to him. "I'll help too."

Grayson didn't get a chance to protest, because Isabelle was entering the foyer from the door to the garage.

"Out of the question, Orlando," she snapped, strapping a gun to her hip, and tucking a stake into her pocket. "You're not even half healed."

"I can fight," he ground out, casting her a petulant look.

"I prefer you stay here with my parents, and protect them. We're taking Robbie and Conrad with us." Without waiting for a reply, Isabelle headed to the door.

Grayson was the first one to leave. Outside, he ordered the two guards, "You're coming with us. We have a hostage situation. Let's go."

"I'll drive," Zane said with a voice that brooked no refusal.

Grayson nodded, then looked at Isabelle. "Isa, take Robbie, Conrad, and Cooper in the SUV. You know the way. The rest will go with Zane and me in the blackout van." He tossed Zane the keys.

Once in the van, Zane kicked down the gas pedal, and raced toward Russian Hill. "We need to know how many hostiles we're dealing with."

Grayson nodded. "Okay. Let me concentrate."

He took a few deep breaths, calming himself, then focused on Monique to connect with her.

*Monique, we're on our way.*

"ETA?" he asked Zane.

"Nine minutes."

Again, he concentrated on Monique.

*We're nine minutes out. Tell me how many men Abel has.*

There was a pause, and Grayson's heart beat out of control. Had they already hurt her?

*He can't have many. William and Rufus are here. And three other vampires are apparently guarding the house.*

"At least six hostiles, including Abel," Grayson reported to his colleagues.

*Where in the house are you?*

*I don't know. But I heard that cuckoo clock, so I'm either on the first floor or the second. You can't hear that clock well enough farther up.*

*Are you in a bedroom?*

*Yes. Small. Not as fancy as the ones my parents and I stayed in.*

Grayson nodded to himself.

*Got it. Are the chains silver?*

*Yes.*

*Okay, babe. We're almost there. I love you.*

*Hurry.*

"They're keeping her in a bedroom. It might be the staff quarters on the first floor, just off the kitchen." He looked over his shoulder to Patrick. "She's chained with silver. Get the bolt cutter."

Patrick got up from his seat and, hunched over, walked to a metal box in the back of the van, which held various tools. "Got it."

"Are there any gloves in there?" Grayson asked. They would need them to protect themselves from the silver chains Abel was using on Monique.

"Yep."

Patrick pulled out several pairs of gloves and distributed them to everybody in the van.

"Got my own," Striker said.

Grayson acknowledged his words with a nod. He was glad that two of the meanest vampires he knew where helping with Monique's rescue. Zane was a lean, mean fighting machine. And Striker was rumored to be lethal and cold-blooded. The only one of that caliber missing was Orlando, but Grayson agreed with Isabelle that Orlando wasn't in top shape. Hell, he would take another day to heal properly. Grayson knew he had to apologize to the guy for suspecting him to be the traitor, but that could wait. Monique couldn't.

Grayson slipped the gloves on and noticed that his hands were shaking. Fuck! He couldn't lose his nerve now. His future depended on this. Without Monique, he was nothing. She'd turned him into the man he'd always wanted to be: strong, decisive, complete. If he lost her, he would lose everything, even himself. He needed Monique like he needed blood to survive. To save her he would do anything he could. Even if it meant to give his life for hers. That revelation hit him in the gut, making him realize just how much he loved her.

*I love you, Monique. Hold on just a little while longer. I'm almost there.*

~ ~ ~

Monique kicked her foot into Rufus's stomach, catapulting him back. But still being chained to the bed didn't give her a lot of leverage. Besides, barefoot, she couldn't do much damage anyway. Not that it mattered. All she was trying to do was to buy herself some time until the cavalry arrived.

Rufus grabbed her left arm to jerk her toward him and punched her in the face. Her head whipped sideways, but he'd have to do a lot more to cause her any significant pain.

"Bitch!" Rufus cursed and reached for her bra again.

This time, he used his claws to cut the garment in half. The cups peeled away from her breasts, freeing them, but the straps remained on her shoulders, and with the way she was chained—hands over her head—it was impossible to remove the garment completely unless Rufus decided to cut the straps too. Not that it mattered. She was exposed, and the satisfied grin on the asshole's face proved that he enjoyed her humiliation.

"Go ahead, look your fill while you can. But you won't enjoy the sight for long," she promised. Because once Grayson was here and had freed her, she would turn the bastard to dust.

Now all she still wore were her panties. When Rufus's gaze landed there, her fangs lengthened, and her hands turned to claws. She reared up from the bed as far as the chains allowed, ignoring the searing pain the silver inflicted. Her wrists would heal. But she had no intention of making it easy for Abel and his men. Especially not now that she knew that help was only moments away.

"Get the hell away from me!" she yelled, not because she thought it would do any good to keep Rufus's hands off her, but because she had to make sure that Grayson could hear her and find her quickly, once he was in the house.

Rufus gripped her ankles with both hands, preventing her from kicking him again. "Oh, I'm gonna so enjoy fucking you when Abel is done with you."

She reared up again. "Sloppy seconds? Guess you have no self-respect left."

Angered by her words, Rufus let go of her legs and punched her in the face, this time harder. Monique inhaled and sucked in her own blood. The blood was coming from her nose, but she didn't care. How long had it been since Grayson had sent her the last message? Had nine minutes not passed yet? Was time crawling at a snail's pace?

"You'll pay for that!" she yelled.

"What the fuck is going on here?" Abel appeared in the doorframe. "Are you letting this little bitch goad you?"

Rufus turned his head to his boss. "She's—"

Abel cut him off with a movement of his hand. "Get her panties off her, now! It's time." He looked over his shoulder. "William, get the fucking lights in here so we can film this."

Rufus grabbed her again. And this time she couldn't shake him off. He pulled on her panties and ripped them to shreds. Panic suffused every cell in her body.

*Grayson! Help me!*

There was no reply.

"Damn it, William, I said I need the lights," Abel yelled toward the open door, while he stepped closer to the bed now.

Abel let his gaze roam over her naked body, his mouth twisting into an evil grin. "Oh yeah, this'll be fun." He swept his eyes up to meet hers. "Not for you, of course, but that's how I like it."

"Sick bastard!"

Abel put his hands to his belt, and began to undo it.

Suddenly, a bright light streamed into the room from the open door.

"About time. You got the camera? I'm ready," Abel announced and pushed his pants down to mid-thigh.

Nobody answered.

"William?"

Monique twisted her head to look at the door. She saw a silhouette behind the standing lamp. The lampshade had been tilted back so the bulbs beneath it served as a makeshift spotlight aimed at the bed. The silhouette was too tall for William, too tall and too slim.

"Yeah, not William."

It was Grayson's voice. He'd come.

A gunshot echoed in the small room, and Rufus dissolved into dust. Abel frantically tried to pull his pants up, but Grayson was faster. He lunged for Abel and tackled him to the ground. Behind Grayson several more people charged into the room, but Monique only had eyes for Grayson who was trading kicks and blows with Abel.

Abel was at a severe disadvantage. His pants were down to his knees, and he couldn't reach his weapon, which only left him with defending himself with his claws. Grayson delivered blow after blow to Abel's face and chest. Seconds ticked by and turned into minutes. But Grayson kept punching him until his face was unrecognizable. She knew he could have killed Abel easily by slamming a stake into his chest, but he didn't. She knew why: he needed to hurt him, and a quick death would have been too merciful..

"Monique." It was Isabelle who bent over the bed now, placing a blanket over her naked body.

"Thank you," Monique said.

"Patrick, the bolt cutter," Isabelle ordered, and a moment later, Patrick handed her the tool. It took only another few seconds, until Monique was free of the silver chains.

She rubbed her wrists and looked at Isabelle. "Thank you." Her gaze went back to Grayson, who was still delivering blow after blow. Abel wasn't fighting back anymore. Only pained moans came from Abel's body.

"Grayson…"

He turned his head to her, his face covered in blood—not his, but his opponents. She stretched out one hand, and with a nod at Patrick and Cooper, Grayson rose.

"Watch him."

Then he walked to the bed, and she sat up and pulled him into her arms. "You came. You saved me."

He hugged her tightly to his body, and a sob tore from his chest. Monique stroked her hand over his hair.

"It's all over now," she murmured and kissed him.

Hungrily, he kissed her back, and she could feel his heart settle into a more normal rhythm. He severed the kiss and looked into her eyes. "I was so scared thinking I would lose you. I love you, Monique. More than life itself."

"Always," she said. She loosened her hold on Grayson and looked past him at Isabelle. "Isabelle, do you think you could find me something to wear? I'm afraid Rufus shredded my clothes with his claws."

"Of course," Isabelle said with a smile and left the room.

Grayson turned to Cooper and Patrick. "Get him out of here. Watch him. We're not done with him. And have the others do a sweep of the property in case Abel had more men than the five we got."

Monique watched as the two hybrids dragged Abel out of the room. "Is William dead?"

"Yes," Grayson said. "We couldn't risk him making a sound. Striker staked him. The other three vampires on Abel's payroll are dead too."

"Good. They all deserved it."

Grayson pressed a kiss to her forehead. "I think it was fate that we blood-bonded. Or I would have never been able to find you so quickly."

Before Monique could agree with him, Isabelle appeared in the doorframe, a few items of clothing hanging over her forearm. "I found these in the laundry room. Somebody must have forgotten them in the dryer."

"Thank you, Isabelle." Monique took the clothes that were far too large for her.

Isabelle left the room, and Grayson helped her get dressed and handed her the shoes she'd been wearing earlier. When she stood up, he pulled her into his arms, squeezing her tightly.

"You want to finish him yourself?" Grayson asked.

"I have to. I need this nightmare to end."

Grayson took her hand, and together they left the room. Zane and Striker came down from the stairs.

"Nobody else here," Zane said.

"Thanks, Zane, Striker," Grayson replied.

In the living room, Cooper and Patrick were keeping Abel restrained. Robbie and Conrad, the guards she recognized from the Woodford household, joined them.

"Perimeter is clear," Robbie said.

"Garage too," Conrad added.

"Thanks, guys," Grayson said.

Monique approached Abel. His face was a bloody mangled mess, every bone in it broken, every blood vessel ruptured.

"Finally, you look as evil on the outside as you're on the inside," she said, tipping her chin up toward him.

Abel grunted. "If you'd been there that night…" His voice broke, and he coughed, before he continued, "I would have had you already." He lashed her with a defiant glare.

She walked closer and stopped only a foot away from him. Cooper and Patrick were holding him up.

"Careful," Grayson warned.

Monique looked over her shoulder. "He can't hurt me anymore."

"So how did he do it?" Abel asked, his voice hard to understand. He glanced past her. "How did you find her?"

"The same way Faye would have found Cain," Grayson said, "if you hadn't continued to pump him full of dead man's blood."

Something lit up in Abel's eyes, and he pinned her with them. "A telepathic bond." Abel shook his head in disbelief, though the movement was slow and barely perceivable, the pain this action cost him evident. "William should have told me. Useless bastard."

Monique moved her head from side to side. "Still blaming everybody else for your failures. Yeah, you're really not worth my time." She looked at Isabelle and pointed to her belt. "May I, Isabelle?"

Isabelle handed her the stake, and Monique gripped it firmly.

Abel's eyes widened as much as they could given the injuries to his face. "You wouldn't—"

She slammed the stake into his heart. "Yeah, I would."

Before her eyes, Abel dissolved into dust. A cell phone and a ring clattered to the floor, together with his belt buckle. Abel was no more.

She felt Grayson's hand on hers, taking the stake from her. He handed it back to Isabelle.

"I've already called home to let them know that you're okay, Monique," Isabelle said.

Monique gave Isabelle a grateful smile. "Thank you." Then she looked at the other vampires and hybrids in the room. "Thank you, all of you."

"Let's go home," Grayson said softly.

She turned to him and locked eyes with him. The nightmare was over.

# 44

After returning to the Woodford residence with her rescuers, Monique and her parents had shed tears of joy, and she'd never hugged her parents so tightly. But there was still something on her chest that she had to take care of.

"Dad, can we talk?" she asked him. "Just you and I?"

Cain nodded, and she motioned to the stairs and ushered him to the guestroom the Woodfords had prepared for Faye. Once inside, she pulled the door shut behind them. He turned around to her, and she noticed that he wasn't quite himself yet. The effects of the dead man's blood he'd been injected with multiple times over the last few days had not completely waned.

He smiled at her. "So you and Grayson…"

"Yeah. You were right all along. We are made for each other." She hesitated. "But there's something…"

Monique tried to find the right words, and Cain waited patiently. She appreciated it.

"Oh, Dad, I'm so sorry for all the terrible things I said to you." The words suddenly burst out of her. "It was out of line. I should have never spoken to you like that. I don't hate you, Dad. I don't. I love you, and when you were gone, and I was scared that I would never see you again, I felt so ashamed. And I wished I could turn back time. I hurt you, Dad, and I'm so sorry for that. It's all my fault. If I hadn't run out like that, if I'd come to the party with you and Mom, then maybe Abel wouldn't have—"

"Stop, Monique," Cain said softly and took her hand. "It's not your fault. It was good that you weren't there, or Abel would have gotten you too. And you know what would have happened then? He would have touched you…" Cain shook his head, a painful expression on his face. "It was fate that you and Grayson had to work together to rescue me and

Samson. And it was fate that Grayson and you blood-bonded. Otherwise, he wouldn't have been able to rescue you."

Cain pulled her into his arms and stroked his hand over her hair.

"I love you, Dad."

"I love you too, sweetheart."

She sniffled and lifted her head. "There's something else. About the new Scanguards branch in New Orleans."

"Yes?"

"I don't want the job anymore."

"I thought you wanted to lead the branch. What changed?"

"I realized that I'm too emotional to lead. Give the job to Grayson. He deserves it much more than I. He's a good leader. He's strong. He's decisive. He doesn't crack under pressure."

Cain smiled. "That wouldn't have anything to do with you wanting Grayson to move to New Orleans?"

She shook her head. "Grayson and I will be together no matter where we have to go. If he stays here, I'll stay here. You know that. And we'll be happy no matter what. But he's the right man to run Scanguards in New Orleans."

Cain nodded. "I understand." He pointed to the door. "Come, let's join the others."

~ ~ ~

Grayson looked at his father. They were alone in the den on the first floor of the Woodford residence. When he and his siblings were kids, this had been their playroom.

"What was it that you wanted to talk about?" Samson asked.

He looked better now. Grayson knew that he'd fed from Delilah, and her blood had healed the damage the foreign human blood had done to his body.

"I need to apologize to you, Dad. What I said to you at the New Year's Eve party… I should have never said such hurtful things. If I could take those words back, I would. But I can't. But believe me, I've regretted every single word I said that night. And it haunts me. Nobody should treat their father like that. I'm ashamed, Dad. I've been such a disappointment to you. I know that. And I want to be better. I know I *can* be better. I *will* be better."

Samson shook his head lightly. "Son, you're not a disappointment. I'm proud of you."

"But I never do anything right in your eyes. I'm not like you. I'm not perfect."

"Grayson, nobody's perfect. Least of all I." He blew out a breath. "All I wanted for you was to become the best man you can be. That's why I pushed you harder than anybody else. Because you have the potential." Samson smiled. "And now I can see that you *are* the man I knew you could be."

"Oh, Dad." Grayson tried to suppress the tears that were welling up in his eyes. "I love you, Dad. I'm so sorry for all the hurt I've caused you."

Samson pulled him into his arms. "I love you too, son."

Grayson sniffled. "Thank you, Dad."

Samson released him from his embrace. "Now, let's go join the rest of the family. Everybody wants to celebrate your blood-bond with Monique."

"You were right about her, too," Grayson admitted. "She's perfect for me. She's so much stronger than I could ever be."

"You deserve a strong mate."

Grayson nodded. "Monique is strong, and she's incredible. That's why I have a favor to ask."

"A favor?"

"I'm withdrawing my application for the CEO job in New Orleans."

Samson lifted his eyebrows in surprise.

"Give it to Monique. She's the leader the company needs. Without her, I doubt we would have been able to save you and Cain, and to take the palace in New Orleans back. She's a natural leader."

"I'm stunned to hear this," he said slowly. "But, Grayson, the decision of who will lead the branch in New Orleans has already been made. Cain and I are in agreement."

"But, Dad," Grayson said.

Samson lifted his hand. "Come. I think you will be pleased with our decision." He walked to the door and opened it.

Grayson followed him back to the living room, disappointed that he couldn't sway his father to consider giving the position to Monique.

Only family was now left in the living room. All Scanguards staff had left. Striker had disappeared too. The only ones missing were Monique's brothers, but they had been notified that everybody was safe, and were expecting their parents to return home soon.

Grayson's gaze fell on Monique who was hugging her mother. He walked to her, and Faye released her from her embrace.

"Grayson," Faye said. "I'm so happy for you two." She embraced him.

"I love Monique. And I'm so lucky that she loves me too." He peeled himself out of her embrace and reached for Monique. She put her arm around his waist, and he pulled her close. "Hey, babe."

There was a faint golden shimmer in her eyes, and he pressed a soft kiss to her lips.

"Cain and I have an announcement to make," Samson said.

All conversations died down, and silence descended on the room. Cain stepped next to Samson, and the two exchanged a conspiratorial look.

"We've made a decision as to who will run the new branch in New Orleans," Cain said and nodded at Samson.

"Grayson," Samson said.

"And Monique," Cain added.

"They'll be joint CEOs of Scanguards in New Orleans," Samson said.

Stunned, Grayson stared at Samson and Cain, who both grinned now.

"Congratulations," Samson said.

Monique threw herself into her father's arms. "Thank you!" She turned her face to Samson. "Thank you both!"

All their family members started clapping.

Grayson approached Cain and Samson and put his arms around Monique, pulling her into a hug. He looked at Cain and Samson. "It's perfect." He squeezed Monique and gazed into her green eyes. "I can't imagine anything better than spending every day and night with you."

Monique smiled at him, her eyes beaming with delight. "And I with you."

*I love you, babe.*

*I love you more.*

# 45

*New Orleans – one month later*

Pulling her silk robe tightly around her, Monique stood on the miniscule balcony and looked down onto the streets of the French Quarter. The sun had just set, and tourists milled about, hopping from one bar to the next.

"I can't wait until our house is move-in ready," Grayson said from behind her, and put his arms around her, pulling her against his body.

Monique molded her back to his chest and leaned her head back. "The house *was* move-in ready when we bought it."

He chuckled at her ear. "Yeah, but not fit for my princess."

She turned in his arms, smiling, and put her arms around him. He wore only boxer-briefs, and his dark hair was ruffled. She loved this look on him: the look of a man who'd just gotten out of bed and wanted to go back to it.

"You don't need to spoil me," she murmured softly. "I would live in a hovel with you if I had to. As long as you make love to me every day."

"That can be arranged. The *making love*, I mean." His green eyes sparkled, and his hands slid down to her butt, while he pulled her back into the bedroom. She kicked the French doors shut.

"I thought you wanted to sleep in since we don't have to go to the office today," Monique said, already caressing his back and slipping her hands underneath his boxer briefs.

He shook his head, grinning. "Mrs. Woodford, I believe what I said was that I wanted to spend the night in bed. I didn't mention anything about sleep."

He loosened the belt of her robe and pushed the fabric off her shoulders, until it fell to the floor and pooled around her feet.

"My bad, Mr. Woodford." She gazed into his eyes, noticing how they started to shimmer golden. "Maybe you want to punish me for not listening when my master speaks?"

His breath hitched, and with satisfaction Monique noticed that the thought aroused him. She felt the evidence of it press against her stomach now. She tightened her grip on his ass, and rubbed herself against his groin.

"Are you making fun of your man?"

"I wouldn't dare." She didn't even attempt to suppress her smile. She loved playing with him, teasing him, testing the limits of his control and his stamina.

"Of course not," he said with a smirk. "'Cause you're an obedient wife."

She was, when it suited her. And Grayson knew it. He accepted the fact that she didn't roll over easily when they had different opinions on how to run the New Orleans Scanguards branch. They were a good team, complementing each other. She'd had doubts that two headstrong individuals could work together day-in and day-out without killing each other. But they were making it work. And their sex life was benefiting from this partnership too. Whenever they argued at work, she could be sure that the sex once they got home was even hotter than before.

"Now get on your hands and knees," Grayson ordered with a glance at the bed.

She took a step toward the bed, while Grayson took off his boxer briefs. She looked at his groin, where his cock stood fully erect. The thick shaft was almost purple, and a drop of precum was glistening on its tip. She licked her lips.

Instead of getting on her hands and knees on the bed, she sat down and beckoned Grayson to approach.

"You're not gonna obey, are you?" he asked.

"We'll see."

Monique gripped his hips and brought her face closer. She wrapped her hand around his root, and guided the tip to her lips.

"Fuck, babe!" he cursed. "I don't think I'll ever get used to you doing this."

Monique lifted her eyes to look up at him. "Guess then I'm doing it right."

~ ~ ~

Grayson palmed her cheek. "Better than right. Perfect." He nudged the tip of his cock against her lips. "Now open your pretty lips, and suck me."

She obeyed his command, and took his cock into her mouth. Grayson moaned, letting out a shuddering breath. Fuck! Whenever she sucked him, he felt like it was the first time again, even though she'd done this dozens of times since they'd moved to New Orleans.

There wasn't a place in this apartment where she hadn't gone on her knees in front of him to suck him. Nor one where he hadn't pressed her against the wall or bent her over a piece of furniture to make love to her. He was insatiable when it came to Monique, just as insatiable as her.

Looking down at her now, his cock in her mouth, while she was sitting on the bed in the nude, was a sight that never failed to arouse him. Monique was beautiful and sensual, and she was his. Her soft moans bounced against his cock, making him shudder with pleasure. But he didn't allow himself to come yet. He wanted to enjoy her tender ministrations a little while longer.

"Fuck, babe, that's so good!"

He put both hands on her cheeks so he could pull out whenever it got too much. His balls pulled up tightly, and the little minx cradled them now, squeezing them to send a spear of pleasure through his body.

"Fuck!" He stepped back, and his cock slipped from her mouth. "Enough!" He felt his fangs lengthen and his hands turn into claws. The vampire inside him was now controlling him.

Monique met his gaze with a sultry look. "Yes, that's what I was looking for." She bit her lower lip.

"Now you've done it," he said.

Monique lay down on the bed, her legs slightly parted, her breasts topped with hard nipples. "Yes, now I've done it." There was no regret in her words.

Unable to wait a second longer, he joined her on the bed and plunged deep into her warm sex, seating himself to the hilt.

"Yes!" Monique cried out.

He rode her hard and fast. The room filled with sounds of pleasure and the aroma of their arousal. It was always like this between them, playful at first, until they couldn't hold back their desire and passion for each other.

He didn't know why he'd ever been afraid of bonding with a woman, of making love to only one woman for the rest of his life. He wasn't afraid anymore. He was happy, because making love to Monique for eternity was all he wanted and needed.

"Oh, babe," he murmured and drove his fangs into her neck.

Her sweet blood filled his mouth, and he swallowed it greedily. A moment later, he felt Monique's fangs in his shoulder as she drank from him.

*I love you so much.* Monique's words filled his heart with joy and bliss. He climaxed without warning.

*You're all I ever wanted. Forever. My princess.*

~ ~ ~

# Reading Order Scanguards Vampires & Stealth Guardians

## Scanguards Vampires

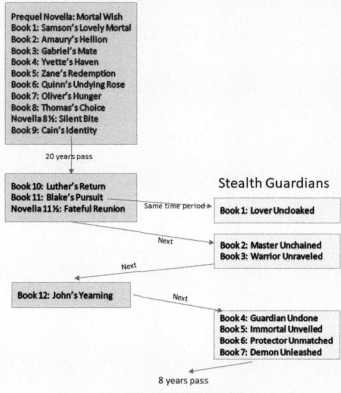

Prequel Novella: Mortal Wish
Book 1: Samson's Lovely Mortal
Book 2: Amaury's Hellion
Book 3: Gabriel's Mate
Book 4: Yvette's Haven
Book 5: Zane's Redemption
Book 6: Quinn's Undying Rose
Book 7: Oliver's Hunger
Book 8: Thomas's Choice
Novella 8½: Silent Bite
Book 9: Cain's Identity

20 years pass

Book 10: Luther's Return
Book 11: Blake's Pursuit
Novella 11½: Fateful Reunion

Same time period →

## Stealth Guardians

Book 1: Lover Uncloaked

Next

Book 2: Master Unchained
Book 3: Warrior Unraveled

Next

Book 12: John's Yearning

Next

Book 4: Guardian Undone
Book 5: Immortal Unveiled
Book 6: Protector Unmatched
Book 7: Demon Unleashed

8 years pass

## Scanguards Hybrids

The Scanguards Hybrids will also be numbered within the Scanguards
Vampires series (SV 13 = SH 1) to preserve continuity.

Book 1 (SV 13): Ryder's Storm
Book 2 (SV 14): Damian's Conquest
Book 3 (SV 15): Grayson's Challenge
Book 4 (SV 16): Isabelle's Forbidden Love (2023)
Book 5 (SV 17): Cooper's Passion (2023)

# ABOUT THE AUTHOR

Tina Folsom was born in Germany and has been living in English speaking countries for over 30 years, since 2001 in California, where she married an American.

Tina has always been a bit of a globe trotter. She lived in Munich (Germany), Lausanne (Switzerland), London (England), New York City, Los Angeles, San Francisco, and Sacramento. She has now made a beach town in Southern California her permanent home with her husband and her dog.

She's written 50 romance novels in English most of which are translated into German, French, and Spanish. Under her pen name T.R. Folsom, she also writes thrillers.

For more about Tina Folsom:
http://www.tinawritesromance.com
http://trfolsom.com
http://www.instagram.com/authortinafolsom
http://www.facebook.com/TinaFolsomFans
https://www.youtube.com/c/TinaFolsomAuthor
tina@tinawritesromance.com

Printed in Great Britain
by Amazon

23560624R00148